PRAISE FOR
THE EMANCIPATION OF EVAN WALLS

—**Mary Batten**, author of *Aliens from Earth*

"Jeffrey Blount has written a timely novel of enormous power. Evan Walls shows the kind of courage we wish weren't needed, but still is today--the courage to defy convention, step beyond boundaries and risk everything to live the life you desire. *The Emancipation of Evan Walls* is a page turner and more, an important addition to today's crucial conversations about race and privilege."

—**Masha Hamilton**, author of *31 Hours*

"I found this story shocking and thought-provoking. There is so much inherent drama to Evan's story. His world is well-drawn from the get-go. There is a great feel for the place and time and the dialogue is superb."

—**Christina Kovac**, author of *The Cutaway*

"Jeffrey Blount has crafted an engrossing novel that pries open an often-overlooked dimension of racism in America today. To achieve his dreams, an eleven-year old Evan Walls discovers he must not only do battle with white prejudice in his rural Southern community, he must also struggle against the diminished expectations of his own people. Blount conveys powerfully the loneliness of an intellectually gifted child caught between these two worlds and the real costs of freedom. *The Emancipation of Evan Walls* is one of the most sensitively told, yet brutally honest reflections on race and identity in recent history."

—**Jonathan Odell**, author of *Miss Hazel and the Rosa Parks League*

"With his new novel, Jeffrey Blount gives us a poignant and profound witness to the complexities and dynamics of racism, identity, and courage. As young Evan Walls navigates his deep need for community and his burning desire to learn, he discovers hidden strength to overcome obstacles. He broke my heart, but then gave it back to me, along with an invitation to hope. I applaud Mr. Blount for his extraordinary work."

—**Rebecca Dwight Bruff**, author of *Trouble The Water*

"Every so often a book comes along that you believe everyone should read. For me, *The Emancipation of Evan Walls* by Jeffrey Blount is that book . . . This incredible story might shock you, or at the very least will move you to tears. Either way, you won't forget it any time soon, if ever."

—**Viga Boland**, author of *Learning to Love Myself*

"*The Emancipation of Evan Walls* is a gut-wrenching read, delivered by a brilliant, award-winning author and television director, Jeffrey Blount. He is a master of telling a story, revealing characters and their motivations primarily through dialogue. This style of writing

recommend it highly enough."

—Readers' Favorite Reviews

The Emancipation of Evan Walls
by Jeffrey Blount

ISBN 978-1-63393-810-6

Published by

 köehlerbooks™

210 60th Street
Virginia Beach, VA 23451
800−435−4811
www.koehlerbooks.com

THE EMANCIPATION OF
EVAN WALLS

JEFFREY BLOUNT

VIRGINIA BEACH
CAPE CHARLES

For my wife, Jeanne Meserve

In the morning, as always, her eyes will meet mine
and she will smile. She'll say, "Jeffrey, I love you."
And I will close the front door behind me, knowing that
I can move mountains.

"Don't take it to heart,

don't let 'em break you baby child,

and pity the mouths

as they try to unmake you . . ."

"Hometown Hero,"
Megan Jean and the KFB

1993

HOBOKEN, NEW JERSEY

Through the rivers of my youth swam many moccasins. In the fields of golden corn and swaying wheat, copperheads lay in wait.

Although I spent much of my time watching my step, I was often bitten. I wandered blindly in circles, in a daze, unsure of who I was, of where I'd come from, and to where I was going. To say that I did not like my childhood would be a monstrous understatement. For that portion of my life, I was a cornered and wounded animal fighting for survival. And even though I endured, I cannot look back on those days without feeling a deep-seated ache throughout my bones.

From the late 1960s through the '70s, my war raged on in a small industrial and farming town in southeastern Virginia. A town, like most Southern towns, split by a plague of overt and clandestine hatred.

The veiled hatred belonged to the "Negroes," as we called ourselves then, although it wasn't really concealed. Whites in the town knew they were hated, but they also knew blacks would shut up before they stood up. And so, as far as the whites were concerned, emotion not shown was emotion that didn't exist.

Blacks spoke of their hatred only in the company of other blacks. We could be a fiery bunch in the safe haven of our collective misery, but we all knew how impotent we were in the face of our adversary. If we tried to forget, all it took to remind us was the sight of other blacks walking down Main Street, their eyes directed toward the sidewalk so there would be no chance of meeting the eyes of an oncoming white person. It seems to me that most blacks never looked up and faced life head on. They had been beaten into an overbearing and worrisome fit of submission. Who among them had the strength to look up? Who among them had the desire?

Life was always the two or three feet in front, whether it was the two or three feet of weeds being chopped out of somebody's field, the two or three feet of hog being gutted on a line in the meatpacking plant, or the two or three feet of parquet floors being waxed in a white family's home.

Life fatigue and fear smothered ambition, even after Martin Luther King Jr. marched and the civil rights bill passed. Maybe the assassination of Dr. King reaffirmed the certainty of who was in charge and the reason to not get uppity. In a way, King was fortunate, wasn't he? He just got shot. Others—neighbors of my parents and other friends they had known—suffered much grislier deaths.

But in the thick of all of this, I got lucky. Or did I? I suppose it's a matter of perception.

At the budding of my youth, my eyes were opened like those of Saul on the road to Damascus. I was preemptively frightened, warned off from the trap lying in ambush for young black men—a quicksand called "the status quo."

While I did escape, traveling the long road through and beyond my hometown was not a pleasant journey. I was in one crash after another, and the trip, which isn't even done yet, has left me emotionally damaged.

• • •

Two days ago, my daughter Jennie was born. My eyes grew wide with fear when they first asked me to leave her side. Sensing my discomfort, the nurses allowed me to return and sit by Jennie, watching protectively as they checked her temperature and changed

talk. They beckoned, but I couldn't leave her. Izzy met them in the corridor and told them that I was overwhelmed. Our friends thought that was cute, and it satisfied them, but not Izzy. There had been a dead spot in our relationship.

When we approached the subject of my past, whether it was just us or with friends, I would grow silent. It was particularly painful when we were with friends. Izzy was always on edge, afraid I would someday burst out and tell them something that she'd never heard. Maybe she was afraid that she wouldn't be able to handle it and would lose her composure in front of them.

When we were alone, she tried not to ask too much. I'm sure she hoped that whatever I found too painful to tell her wasn't something that would reflect badly on me. I'm sure she hoped it wouldn't have changed her mind about marrying me.

How could I explain to Izzy that I was not worried for Jennie because of the threat of nuclear war, cancer, or AIDS? How could I explain the depth of my fear for the breaking of the fragile hope of a child? How could I explain to her that I didn't want Jennie to have to come home from school bullied, dejected and friendless. And what about the most important point, the most painful for me? The near paralyzing fear that Jennie would suffer not because of anything she did or said, but because she has my genes, which means she would never be hip enough, or in tune enough, to recognize the warning signs.

• • •

I was sitting in the hospital room, holding one of Jennie's toes as Izzy playfully cooed at her.

"I'm afraid," I said, "that, like me, she will always want the right things at the wrong time and not understand why people react to her as they will. That she'll be like me as a child—a misfit, a snowball. Confused and ungrateful."

I looked up at Izzy, who was smiling. I could tell she wanted to help me, but I had given her no clues.

"Evan," she said. "End this craziness. Why don't you get the monkey off your back? Just blurt it all out. Just tell me the whole story. It'll be cathartic."

"I'm afraid you won't see the significance," I told her. "It might be impossible for you to understand."

"Why? Because I'm white?"

"Yes."

Izzy put her hand on my cheek, and she smiled tenderly.

"I can't promise you it will have the same significance for me. After all, I didn't live through whatever you did. But if it hurt you so much, it will be important to me. Try to explain it to me for our sake, and Jennie's. I can't help her avoid something if I don't know what it is."

"You're right," I said. "Maybe it's time."

Izzy's expression changed to a mix of happiness and fear. Happy that the suspense might almost be over, but afraid that, with her new baby in her arms, she might find out something about her husband that she couldn't live with.

I held onto my daughter's toe, looking into my wife's beautiful brown eyes. For too long I had forced her to display her superhuman patience. For too long I hadn't been true to myself. I took a deep breath. I let go of Jennie and took Izzy's hand.

"I am a refugee," I said. "On the run and still looking for some kind of asylum. I escaped from a very different kind of race war. And you know, it blew me away. Because before I got caught up in it, I thought all the cruelty inflicted on blacks was done by whites, but I

1968

CANAAN, VIRGINIA

I was on the back porch, preparing to pull the wings off a fly. It struggled vigorously as I held it between my left index finger and thumb. I yanked the wings off quickly and placed the fly on the screen near Mantis. Then, under the fading light of the setting June sun, I sat back to watch the kill. It was like having *Mutual of Omaha's Wild Kingdom* on my own porch.

Mantis was the nickname my older brother, Mark, gave our pet praying mantis. In early May, he'd opened the screen door on his way inside, and this scrawny, green bug flew in behind him. Daddy told us that if we left him on the porch, we wouldn't have much trouble with mosquitoes all summer. His prophecy had been correct. In fact, we'd started feeding flies to Mantis because the mosquitoes had become so scarce.

It didn't take Mantis long to catch the fly and begin his dinner. Satisfied with having taken care of his hunger, I lay back on the wicker lounge and stared out over the backyard. A slow drizzle had just ended, the last remnant of a thunderstorm that passed an hour before. I sat there thinking about how much I liked thunderstorms. Most people I knew hated them. There were folks who hid in closets and others who ran around unplugging every electrical device. One of my cousins even slept with her sneakers on during thunderstorms, feeling that as long as she had rubber on her feet, lightning couldn't harm her.

Storms created no such anxieties in me. They relaxed me. I would stand at the big window in the living room and listen to the rhythm of cracking thunder breaking against the clouds like ocean waves against a shore. I would watch the rain come down in sheets, my head jerking from side to side, trying to catch the bolts of lightning. I'd hope that the lightning would hit the electric lines and short out the transformer high on its pole, leaving our house in darkness. When Mark was younger, he and I would run to our parents' bedroom, where they usually spent their nights reading the papers and talking. Daddy would reach into the drawer of his nightstand and pull out a flashlight.

"Grab ahold, boys," he would say.

Mark and I would each grab a pant leg and hold on for dear life as Daddy turned on the flashlight and led us ever so slowly through the house. Of course, we could find our way with our eyes closed and not bump into a thing, but there was something different about the darkness brought on by thunderstorms. Something mysterious. Daddy knew that, and he helped us enjoy it.

All of a sudden, we'd be on safari, trudging carefully through a hazardous jungle. I swear I heard the roar of big Bengal tigers, the squawks of parrots, and the heavy steps of elephants bearing down upon us. Daddy pretended he heard them, too. He would stop suddenly at times and shout, "Hide!" Mark and I would quickly fall to the floor or pin ourselves to a wall while Daddy inched around a corner or poked a flashlight into a room and then declared it safe for passage. We'd attach ourselves to him again, and the adventure would continue.

Mark became too old for this after a few years. I kept it up for a while until Daddy lost interest in it—and everything else. I understood because I knew he was in pain. For a long time now, thunderstorms had gone unnoticed in the Walls' home.

"Evan! Where are you, son?"

"I'm out here, Mama."

hadn't noticed a good storm any more than Daddy had. The way she stood behind me taking in the fragrant odors and staring at the twilight startled me and made me happy. The situation reminded me of one of my favorite memories. Across the road in front of our house, a row of dogwood trees had grown close together. Years when they bloomed thickly, they looked like a puffy white blanket. Mama would be so moved by the sight that she would sit and look at them for hours.

One day, I joined her, and she held me close. As she rocked us, she whispered over and over, "Sweet springtime snow." She had never been more beautiful to me.

Mama was long and lean at just under six feet tall. Her imposing height and brash personality made her at times seem harsh and unsympathetic. She easily frightened us into good behavior. But those characteristics were generally softened by the single braid of hair ending midway down her back. Her beautiful smile and, at that moment, an aura of peacefulness made me want to stay in her arms forever.

But those days were long gone. Mama and Daddy shared the pain that had ruined so many of our family traditions. Mark and I felt it, and a lot of other people in Canaan felt it too. That was why everyone gathered on our porch once a week. In a way, it was a support group—a collection of people who came together with the common goal of helping each other endure the next week.

Mama took her hands off my shoulders. "Come on inside, and help your dear old mother make the Kool-Aid."

"Yes, ma'am," I said and followed. While I stirred the big pitcher of orange-flavored drink, I thought about the meetings, which ran from May to October of each year. They had been going on for as long as I had been alive and always took place at our house. I could remember back as far as 1964, when I was six years old.

At that age not much held my attention. But on this particular night, they were talking about John F. Kennedy. At the mention of his name, I sat up and listened. Here was a white man my parents had never spoken of, at least not to me. Then all of a sudden, that past November, he was killed, and my mother was crying like she had lost a son. I wanted to know why. When I asked her after his funeral on television, she just shook her head.

"Every time Moses come along, he gotta die before the job gets done. We ain't never gone catch a break."

I wanted to ask her what that meant, but she looked so broken, I let the moment pass.

The following May, as I served Kool-Aid to the folks on our porch, I perked up when I heard somebody mention JFK.

"Was the shot heard 'round the world," Nate Applegate said proudly, as if he'd coined the phrase.

"It was more than just one shot," Ethel Brown noted.

"I know that," Nate replied. "Who don't? But it was the first one that got him."

"So you say! Next you gonna be telling us you was there," Mama said to him.

"Now come on, Treeny," Cora Applegate said. "Cut my old man some slack."

They all laughed and then continued to discuss their various trials and tribulations which, according to them, were the direct result of Kennedy's death.

Now, four years later, Mama caught me daydreaming while

stirring and slapped me gently on the bottom with a wooden spoon.

"Wake up, mister."

"I'm sorry, Mama."

"That's all right. Just put the Kool-Aid in the refrigerator. Then

that night in 1964. The ritual had continued. The same people, save for the Applegates, were still coming around. Two years ago, the Applegates had proclaimed to the whole town that they were off to join the civil rights movement. There was a *March Against Fear* from Memphis, Tennessee, to Jackson, Mississippi. But they never made it.

"They talked too much and let the wrong folks hear," Mama had said after Nate and Cora were found dead in a cornfield.

Even still, when eight o'clock rolled around, when the red-hot sun had retired and it was cooler out, the rest came around to our back porch. And they came because our family was one of the most prominent black families in Canaan. For many years, we were one of only three black families to run their own farm. This fact and the large four-bedroom, nineteenth-century farmhouse we lived in gave us an aura of wealth that we didn't deserve. Our 100 acres of land and our home had been a gift to my great-great-grandfather from his master after the Civil War. His master had respected him as much as a slave could be respected.

Information about the "gift" had not been passed along to the other black families of Canaan. My parents, Augustus and Treeny Walls, were not about to tell anyone. They wanted to perpetuate the idea that their benefactor was an ancestral black man with the strength of a giant who had wrestled away what he needed to survive from the white man. The land was taken—not given—the myth went.

My maternal great-grandmother, Mama Jennie, was the oldest Negro in town—loved and respected by all. She once explained to me why my parents shied away from telling how they came to own the farm.

"Negroes," she said, "has got to feel like they got something in this life. Augustus and Treeny the closest thang around to colored folk who got something. They got they own farm and they be they own bosses, or as much they own bosses as Negroes can be. If they has to tell folks the truth that they ain't earned it, then they got to admit they ain't much more than anybody else. That they just lucky. Colored folk get tired of going through life feeling like anythang they got is cause they lucky. That's why all them folks come to your house every week. They want to be near someone what got something because they worked hard and conned Mr. Charlie."

Mama used to love to show off what the Walls family had supposedly earned. If we had guests for dinner and Mama put out a loaf of bread, she would always take the heel. That proved she was a big enough person to let the less fortunate have the good stuff for a change. That was why the porch sessions were held at our house; we were letting the less fortunate get close to the good stuff.

But somewhere between 1964 and 1968, the good stuff went dreadfully sour. Daddy lost the ability to work our farm. The civil rights movement had upset the status quo.

The whites of Canaan became afraid and felt they needed to put Negroes back in their place. Daddy was put in his place through economic sanctions.

Dusty and tired from a hard summer's work in the field and damn proud of it, Daddy drove into town. He backed our big grain-hauling truck up to the Farmer's Market silo and went in as usual to sell his corn. But this time, he was told that his "colored, nigra-type crops" were worth only a fourth of "white" crops. He had no choice but to sell it to them at a vastly reduced price. The next year, Daddy couldn't afford to plant and was forced to rent the land to a white farmer, who hired my father and paid him slave wages to work on his own property.

This nearly shattered our life in Canaan. From that point on, we kept up our daily routines, but we never really enjoyed living. Daddy never again noticed thunderstorms, and Mama never m~~~~~~

~~pp~~ ~~~~ ~~~~~, ~~~~ they were happy to do so, I think. Mama Jennie said they knew that sharing the load would make plain the fact that the Walls had lost control of their lives. If that was true, then the rest of them had no hope at all.

• • •

I filled the bucket with chopped ice and hauled it up to the kitchen. I put some ice in the glasses and then went back out onto the porch. Mantis was resting in a corner after his meal. Daddy drove up in the pickup with Mark and Bullet, our cocker spaniel, who ran off into the cornfield. I sat, preparing for my weekly fix of adult conversation, which was sometimes so boisterous that it used up all the space and air on our porch. And that was saying something because it was pretty big. Mark was fond of saying that it was as wide as the house and as deep as half a living room. Full of eclectic furniture, from wicker chairs and lounges to metal slides and wooden rocking chairs, it was our church away from church.

I thought of the people who would be coming. Most nights, Ethel and Jim Brown were first to arrive. They were first wherever they went. Townsfolk believed it was because they couldn't stand to be alone with each other. Jim was a drunk and Ethel a nag.

"Nagging and drinking mix about as well as a Negro and the Klan," Chauncey Mae Jones would say.

Chauncey Mae was a widow. She was tall, and so thin she seemed unhealthy. She had high cheekbones, big lips, and eyes that looked like they would pop out if she leaned over too far. Daddy liked to say she had "uglied" her husband to death. I never really cared what she looked like. I would just remember her as the mother of Rosetta and as a nosy woman who Mama said would pretend to be sweeping her front porch at three in the morning in order to see what was happening at parties across the street. Parties she claimed she was too much of a Christian to attend.

Then there was my aunt Mary, my father's sister, and her ex-husband, Bojack. She was short, light-complexioned, and "painfully buxom," my mother used to say. And like my mother, she had a fiery personality. Bojack was her opposite. He was a tall, lean, dark-complexioned man who seemed incredibly sad. He always wore reflector sunglasses and sat quietly behind them.

Back in 1964, they came as a couple. In fact, they had been newly wed that year, even though my grandmother tried to stop the marriage by throwing a knife at Bojack during the wedding ceremony. She claimed he lacked responsibility and was the black sheep of his family. She swore that the marriage wouldn't last more than a few years. Time proved her correct. But Aunt Mary and Bojack still came to the sessions, albeit separately.

Finally, there was Cozy Pitts and her daughter, Eugenia. Cozy was a very sad woman who, like Bojack, said very little. I always figured she came just to feel like she was a part of something that wasn't painful. At her home, she was always in pain, agony dealt by her huge and usually drunken husband, Arthur. One winter night, Mark and I were leaving Days Neck, which was the section of Canaan where the other members of the session lived. We passed behind the Pittses' home, trudging through three inches of snow. We stopped in our tracks when we saw Arthur Pitts drag Cozy out into the snow. She was in her nightgown and crying hysterically. Eugenia, who was my age, stood on the back steps crying just as wildly.

Arthur Pitts ripped off his wife's nightgown and threw her heavyset, naked body into the snow. He stood over her, yelling about some chore she hadn't done, but I knew that the reason for this exhibition went way beyond any housework left und... not see Cozy's f...

...ng to light off the belt. As she started to get up, her wig fell off. It looked like a lost shrub in the snow. She tried to run, but all she could do was hop a step at a time as Arthur whipped her. Then Eugenia's older brother, Taliferro, who was big for a boy of twelve, ran out of the house and grabbed his naked mother. He shielded her, taking the sting of his father's belt. Arthur just continued to whip them both until he was exhausted and collapsed into the snow.

The next week, out of the blue, Mark asked Taliferro about the incident. The three of us had been walking and shooting the breeze. We wandered over the Morgart's Lake bridge, and then up the hill through the tall pines and maples until we found a good place to sit. We could watch the cars cross the bridge to our left and to our right we looked down over the lake. Below us, a little ways down the hill, was my aunt's ex-husband, Bojack. He was reducing a block of wood to splinters with his .22 rifle.

At first, Taliferro seemed embarrassed. I guess I would have been, too, if he'd seen my mama naked being whipped by my daddy. Next, he seemed mad at Mark for having the nerve to bring it up. I was too, but Mark was like that—nosey and direct. He had to know about everything.

Taliferro was quiet for a while, and tears welled. I knew that men and boys weren't supposed to cry. In Canaan, they either were tough enough to put aside all feelings, or else they got drunk. Watching

Taliferro on the verge of breaking down made me nervous. I looked down at Bojack, who was reloading his rifle. Then he shot again. The piece of wood jumped, and so did Taliferro. The shot brought him out of his trance.

"I hate anythang white," Taliferro said.

Mark and I simply stared at him, not knowing what he meant.

"White people," he continued. "That why my daddy beat my mama. White people done made him thank he ain't shit. He don't like feeling like shit. It makes him mad. But he can't hit the peoples that make him mad, 'cause they got more power than he do. They white. So he need to feel like he a man about something. Like he can control something. So he beat us and Mama."

Taliferro displayed an understanding beyond his years. Mama Jennie had already talked to me about racism's effect on black children: "Little colored chillen know who they is earlier. They grows up faster. Oh, they plays and all, but the minute they finds out about racism, they suddenly takes on a burden that makes 'em grow up fast. It's a heavy one, too. Heavier than most folks of different persuasions carry all they lives."

Taliferro looked out over the lake so we couldn't see his tears. "You know why my mama be wearing that five-dollar wig?" he asked.

"Nope," Mark said. "Why?"

"'Cause Daddy set her hair afire, and it done scorched her head so bad, her hair don't grow back."

I looked at Mark, and he looked at me. We both felt helpless.

"I really hate white people," Taliferro said. "I truly do."

• • •

Before long, everyone was present and accounted for except Chauncey Mae and Rosetta. We all sat, saying as little as possible, not willing to spill any gossip until every ear was present. Mama wouldn't even serve the Kool-Aid.

"When are they coming? I'm thirsty," Mark said.

"Me too," I said.

"Be quiet! The both of you," Mama said. "You'll get it soon enough."

No sooner had she spoken than Chauncey Mae, sucking on a toothpick as usual, and Rosetta came across the yard

"Chauncey M⸱⸱ ⸱

⸱⸱⸱ ⸱⸱⸱⸱ spoke to me.

"Hey."

"Hey," I said back.

"I just seen T. Wall. He say to say hello to you."

"Thanks, Rosetta."

Rosetta went off to play with Eugenia, who was trying to feed Mantis another fly.

"Sit down and rest yourself, child," Mama said to Chauncey Mae.

Chauncey Mae eased into her seat. "What's rest? Something you eat?"

"You ought to be glad it ain't, cause if it was, all us be dead and gone," Jim Brown said.

"He ain't told no lie yet," Aunt Mary added.

Everybody laughed.

"Well," Chauncey Mae continued. "If John Fitzgerald Kennedy was still alive, we'd be resting better and prob'ly eating better, too."

"Tell the truth, child. Tell the truth!" Cozy Pitts shouted. Everyone became quiet for a second—no doubt, like me, thinking of the cruelty Cozy had escaped at home that would make her speak out so.

Mama got up, went inside, and came back with a tray of glasses filled with Kool-Aid. She told Mark to go in and get the potato chips off the kitchen table. When he got back, Ethel Brown had just seconded

Chauncey Mae's speech about how we'd all be better off if Kennedy were still alive. A rash of "amens" and nodding heads followed.

Bullet came out of the cornfield, barking at us. I let him on the porch. I started brushing his golden hair, talking quietly to him, and drifting in and out of the conversation. That is, until I caught sight of Bojack behind his sunglasses, squeezing the glass in his hand so hard I thought he'd break it. His whole body was tense. I stopped rubbing Bullet and paid closer attention to the conversation. They were talking about their problems, which never really changed from week to week. As always, they blamed them on the death of Kennedy.

Above Bojack's sunglasses, I saw a crease running up the middle of his tight forehead. His eyebrows were pushed together. I tried to figure him out, but I didn't know enough about the man to know what could upset him so. Since his and Aunt Mary's divorce, he had become a loner. I, along with most of the others, never spoke to him much. He usually stuck to himself.

On Saturdays, he went down to Morgart's Lake or to his backyard to shoot his .22. From the back steps of his house, he would shoot cherries off a cherry tree, forty feet away. Or he'd sit on the hill over the lake, shooting at a piece of wood he'd tossed in. On Sundays in the fall, after all the football games on television, we would see him out in the fields. He would punt to imaginary people, throwing passes and tackling them, refining the art of football.

I continued to stare at him. He just sat there behind his glasses, thinking. Mama said that he hadn't always been quiet at the sessions. He acted that way lately, she said, because he couldn't stand to be near Aunt Mary, but he didn't want to miss the gossip, either. So, he came, he listened, and he thought. But on this night, I knew there was more.

Bojack had been looking down into his Kool-Aid. I watched him look up. He glanced at each person as the conversation continued. When he could stand it no more, he shot up out of his chair. His quickness jolted me, as it did the rest of the group. Mark, who had been sitting next to me, rubbing Bullet's stomach, sat back quickly in his seat. Rosetta and Eugenia turned so abruptly that they scared Mantis, who flew over our heads to the other side of the porch. Cozy Pitts put her hand to her heart as Bojack began to shout.

"It's been five damn years since that man was shot. Since th

...mean, knocking John F. Kennedy? Don't he know what the man did for us? Don't he realize the way things have been going since Kennedy died?

Lyndon Johnson wasn't doing anything with any oomph to it. He wasn't sending federal troops to help the situation in the South like Kennedy had done. He was just in the White House signing pieces of paper that the white Southerners couldn't care less about. They needed to be forced into things, and Kennedy had been the man for the job. What kind of nonsense was Bojack talking?

Bojack didn't understand what Mama Jennie would explain to me later. "Folks," she would say, "have got to have something to keep them from looking at life the way it really is. We Negroes is in a bad situation. If you takes away our faith in thangs like supposing how life would be if John Fitzgerald Kennedy was alive, then peoples would be forced to look at they real situation. Most folk hurts a lot if they really, really has to look at theyselves. When some folk finally see the light, it hurt so much it kills 'em."

Bojack continued with his assault. "I don't see what y'all thank one white man can or would do for us poor black folk in this redneck town anyway."

Everybody simply stared. Bojack took his seat and the session fell silent. I figured that they had come to the painful conclusion that Bojack might be right. But he was trying to kick their only significant crutch out from under them, and they were not about to take that lying down.

Their silence didn't last long.

"Where you coming from with that nonsense, man?" Daddy asked Bojack.

"It ain't no nonsense in it, Augustus," Bojack replied.

"You just don't know what you talking about," Ethel Brown said. "I don't know what's done got under your skin, but you ain't got to try and ruin our night with it."

"Boy, ever since that divorce, you been one fool nigger," Chauncey Mae added.

"He ain't getting none," Aunt Mary said. "That's his problem."

"Shit!" Bojack yelled. "I been having that problem since before I was divorced."

Aunt Mary and Bojack continued arguing and it took nearly five minutes to break it up. Aunt Mary eventually quieted down, but Bojack was not to be denied. He stretched out his arms, pleading.

"Y'all got to stop fooling yourselves. You know what's going on. You read the papers, don't you?"

"Ain't no need to go and be making fun of nobody now," Ethel said. "You know I can't read much."

"I ain't making fun of you, Ethel. Sorry if you taken it that way. Hell, I don't read too good neither. But what I *can* read is 'Nigger Die,' and 'Colored Only.' And I sho' as shit can spell *L-Y-N-C-H*! I'm sorry I brought up the papers. I don't thank we need no paper to know what our situation is in this town."

Canaan was a beautiful place southeast of Richmond and charmingly nestled along the James River. We lived inland and on the outskirts of town, where the fields seemed to roll on forever. At any time of day, a person could look out over those fields of green, brown, and gold, and feel the beauty of nature. The days were filled with the chirping of birds and the nights with the cries of whippoorwills and crickets. In the country, Mother Nature sang you to sleep. And in town, there was such beautiful Southern architecture that people from all over Virginia and parts of North Carolina came to look.

Great Victorian mansions dotted the landscape, and beautiful eighteenth and nineteenth-century churches crowned the many

living much the same way before, during, and after his presidency?

Suddenly, the Kool-Aid wasn't so sweet. Daddy stood and went into the kitchen. As I got up, I sensed the overwhelming despair rocking in the chairs on our porch. The silence gave me goose bumps.

I peeked through the curtains and saw my father putting more sugar in his Kool-Aid. He poured in spoonful after spoonful. I could tell he was very upset, his mind roaming elsewhere. I figured he was thinking about his job on the loading dock at the meatpacking plant, the white man who farmed his land for a fraction of the going rental fee, and the good old days when he could make a good living doing what he loved.

I carry priceless memories of Daddy kneeling in the fields, holding a handful of soil up close to his face, cherishing the deep, rich smell of freshly turned earth. Happiness for me was watching the sunrise while sitting in Daddy's lap, both of us steering his tractor up a field. I would turn around to watch the disc harrow, the cultivator or planter break the earth, and then wave at Mark and Bullet as they ran behind the tractor. Later on, Mark would take a turn at the wheel, driving by himself, Daddy standing on the running board and guiding him along. I would keep Bullet company, puffs of dust flying from our heels as we chased the big red Massey Ferguson up and down the rows.

At noon, Mama would come by with lunch. Sometimes, it was sandwiches. Other times—my favorite times—she would bring a big watermelon, cooled by ice in a tub mostly used for baking hams.

Daddy would step down off the tractor, take the machete he always carried in the fields, and, with one dazzling swipe, split the watermelon in half. And then with a few smaller swings, he split it into little pieces, which the four of us would proceed to devour. Then Mama would leave, and we'd continue until whichever one of us wasn't riding with Daddy was too tired to run behind the tractor. Mark or I would sit with Bullet at the end of the field and watch Daddy drive, tilling the earth, one son at his side, their silhouettes melting into the sunset.

• • •

Daddy finally realized what he had done and emptied his glass into the sink. He refilled it with Kool-Aid, came back out on the porch and sat beside Mama, who was staring out over the field in front of us. In her face I could see the replaying of Bojack's impromptu sermon. To this day, I imagine she was thinking sadly about those many incarnations of Moses who had come and gone without getting the job done. I saw her doubting that we, as a family or a race of people, would ever reach the Promised Land.

Bojack's head drooped guiltily. The Browns simply stared at everybody, and Chauncey Mae sucked hard on her toothpick. Cozy Pitts still held a hand to her heart, looking absolutely crushed. Eugenia went over to hug her, and Rosetta sat on the floor by her mother's feet. Mark and I looked at each other and hunched our shoulders.

No one said a word. It was as if they had finally come to grips with the fact that someone they really loved was dead. After five years of hiding in JFK's shadow, the truth had set in. Their savior was gone, and there was no one to look up to except for the supervisor at the plant or the taskmaster in the fields.

"Lord have mercy," Ethel Brown muttered. "It's a damn tough world."

Another round of "amens" and nodding followed.

"Thangs is bad for a Negro, ain't they?" Jim Brown asked.

"I don't even thank we Negroes anymore," Chauncey Mae replied. "I thank we supposed to call ourselves blacks. Anyway, you right."

Ethel Brown's eyes watered. She sniffed, took a deep breath, and slowly shook her head. "I been praying for most all my forty-five

"Said I was playing nigger. I won't man enough. Well, I wish I coulda been there the minute when you realized you had to play that game, too. And when you realized you won't as much a woman as you believed you was."

Aunt Mary dropped her head.

I wished I was somewhere else. The conversation had turned into something I didn't want to hear. I didn't like it when the adults looked more insecure about life than me. How could I expect guidance or support from these people when I saw such uncertainty in their eyes?

My mind wandered, recalling memories that had been welded shut with pain. Bojack's mouth was the torch that cut them open. I thought about four or five years earlier, when Mama ordered Mark and me into our room, but I sneaked out. Two white men came to the door and called for Daddy. They went outside, and Mama followed out onto the porch. I climbed up onto the sink and peeked between the kitchen curtains and saw Daddy talking to the men.

"Just because you got some land and a house don't mean you can talk disrespectful to white people," one of them said.

"I didn't say nothing except I know them seeds ain't cost that much. He was ripping me off," Daddy said.

"That's my daddy you talking about, *boy*. It's his store. He know what it cost."

"Man in front of me was charged less."

The second white man said, "It's his choice if he want to give a break to who he wants."

"Who he wants mean white people, I guess," Daddy replied.

"And so what if it is?"

They moved closer to Daddy, and he stepped back, which surprised me because he, like Mama, was tall and could be intimidating. At six-four, he towered above those men. He was lean and muscled, weighing close to 230 pounds. He had a broad chest and strong, wide shoulders. I remember being amazed by him on the farm, watching as he tossed hundred-pound feed bags like bags of potato chips. Yet, he was in retreat.

The first white man said, "You going on being disrespectful again." And he started taking off his belt. Then the other white man took off his belt, and they backed Daddy up against their truck. He couldn't run and they started whipping him like he was a misbehaving deerhound.

"Go in the house, Treeny!" he yelled while he fended off the belts. But she froze. I couldn't take it. My father was growing smaller in stature right before my eyes. So, I ran to my room, crawled under the covers and cried. Minutes later my parents came back into the house. I heard the door close and my father yell.

"I told you to go in the house!" he shouted at Mama.

"I was scared for you," she replied.

"You need to mind me!"

"Augustus. I couldn't leave you."

"But I told you to! *I* told you to!"

Then there was a loud bang and a crash, which brought me out from under the covers. Mark was sitting on the edge of his bed looking concerned. It sounded like Daddy'd slammed his fist on the kitchen table. Something broke. Mama started running, and seconds later, she was standing in our bedroom looking out of breath. She closed the door and sat down on my bed. She looked at us and put her finger to her lips. It was the first time I saw her afraid of my father. Daddy was in a rage and stormed down the hall and into their bedroom. He slammed the door shut. My young heart had never suffered such a shocking blow. Daddy was like that for a week or so afterward, and the three of us spent a lot of time in the bedroom. In silence.

about this or that with the confidence of a Greek god. And I would say to myself, *That's my daddy!*

But that June night, after Bojack's rant, I saw a man who looked beaten and tired. Who was confused as to why it had been so easy for them to take his manhood from him before he could gather himself together enough to put up a fight.

The remarks about racism that I'd heard from Mama Jennie and other adults for years suddenly felt real. Now, I fully understood why little white kids could get away with spitting on me when I wasn't even allowed to spit on my own brother. And why my adult mother would have to say "Yes ma'am" to a little white girl that just called her a nigger.

I cried inside that night on the porch as I had aloud the day I saw my father beaten. I closed my eyes, and inside I felt my fists flying in an uncontrollable rage, beating the world and its indignities to a pulp. But when I opened my eyes, there was the world again, smiling and sticking out its tongue.

Bojack was right; we knew our true situation in Canaan, but at that moment I hated him for compelling us to face up to it.

"Well," Aunt Mary said to Bojack. "Now you done ruined our night and made our life seem like it ain't for shit."

"Watch your mouth, Mary. I done heard enough cussing for one night. Y'all do remember there is children here, don't you?" Mama said.

"This ain't no time for manners, Treeny. It's time for this ex-husband of mine to tell us what we supposed to do, since he so God-almighty smart. And why don't you take them damn glasses off so we can argue eye to eye? I want to see what kinda disgust you got for me."

Bojack was sweating but recalcitrant. He calmly took out his handkerchief and wiped his brow. When he spoke, he ignored Aunt Mary's comment about the sunglasses.

"I don't know what y'all all mad at me for. I just done what somebody oughta done for you years ago," he said.

"You ain't doing nothing but raising a whole lotta Cain for nothing," Chauncey Mae said. "You crazy old fool."

"She right," Ethel Brown said. "You just like to upset folks."

Bojack emptied his glass with one swallow, then turned his gaze toward us children.

"I look at myself," he said, "and I'm sad. I woulda liked to been somebody in my life. I didn't want to spend it all being the nothing I am. A lot of it's my fault, but some of it I blames my mama and my daddy for. They didn't tell me I could be something. In fact, they went entirely the other direction. They didn't want me to be somebody, and I tell you why. 'Cause if I grew up to be somebody, then I woulda passed them by, and they couldn't bear to thank I could get more out of life than they did. When some folks' children do better than they did, they feel jealous of they kids when they ought to be happy."

"Bojack, what is it you trying to say?" Mama asked.

"That we got to do something about us as a people in Canaan. We got ourselves a complex as big as Augustus' farm out yonder. We don't thank we nothing, so we *be* nothing, and we pass that on to our children. I'm saying I wish somebody had told me I could get a education. Look at Eliza Blizzard. She got a education, and she making white folks sit up and listen to her."

Aunt Mary nodded quickly, smiled, and pointed a finger at Bojack. It was like she had figured out some great mystery. "I saw that woman's car at your house. You having a thang with her?"

Everybody laughed at how jealous Aunt Mary seemed all of a sudden. She looked a little embarrassed because since she'd divorced Bojack, she tried to give the impression that she never thought about him one way or another. But now it seemed she'd been watching his

"Somebody ought to say something for us," Bojack said.

Up until this point, we children had been quiet. But the subject of Eliza Blizzard was so hot it could make everyone burst out in opinion. Rosetta Jones stepped up to Bojack, stomping her feet into position and slapping her hands against herself.

"Lord, watch out!" Chauncey Mae said proudly. "My little girl done put her hands on her imagination. She mean bidness now."

"Imagination" was what Chauncey Mae called her daughter's hips—as in she was so skinny, she had to imagine that she had them.

"I don't care how much that old biddy talk about equal education," she shouted at Bojack. "I ain't going to no school with no honky children."

"You ought to want to," Bojack said.

The adults gasped.

"For real," he said. "They got all the best books and school equipment. You can use that stuff to get ahead, just like they be doing."

"Listen to this fool!" Daddy stood and yelled at Bojack. "He thanks that if we read they books, we gone get where they got."

"Ah, come on, Augustus. I ain't that big a fool, and I ain't said that. You might not get where they get, but you can get somewhere. Somewhere further than you can get by not reading 'em."

"Bojack, boy, you is a fool. Ain't got good sense enough to pour piss out a boot!" Chauncey Mae huffed.

"Why would I want to?" Bojack said. "You the fool that got the piss in the boot in the first place! Tell me which one of us is crazy?"

"What you crying about, Cozy?" Mama said.

Cozy Pitts' face was streaked with tears. "Everywhere I go, white people cause a stink, and they ain't even got to be in the room with you."

"A little discussion ain't never hurt nobody, Cozy," Bojack said.

"Y'all ain't discussing. That white devil got y'all yelling at each other. Divide and conquer! Ain't that what they say?" Cozy's body shook, and her wig slipped. She adjusted it, the tears drying in little rivulets on her cheeks.

"Tell it like it is, girl," Aunt Mary said.

"Yeah," Eugenia said. "Taliferro say he gone kill him some white folks before it's all over."

"Bojack, you ought to be ashamed of yourself," Jim Brown said. "Way you talking tonight, we ain't good enough for your hind parts. Seem like to me, you'd rather your ass be white. Saying all that terrible shit about your mama and daddy."

"Right on!" Chauncey Mae said. "Ain't you got no respect, Negro?"

"You should ask my parents and other folks if they ain't got no respect for the lives of they children," Bojack replied. "I'll give you a example. Look at all the names of the children in this town. Rayfield Jones. He and his wife name they son Macho. Mason Johnson and his wife name they son Geronimo after the Indian. He ain't no Indian boy. How a colored boy like him suppose to make it in this life with a name like Geronimo or Macho? White folks ain't gone do nothing but laugh at 'em. Seem like to me, that ain't doing nothing but giving they children a death sentence. Putting 'em ten feet behind before the race even starts. Maybe somewhere in the back of they minds, they don't know what they doing, but they sho' nuff making sure they children don't do no better than them."

Bojack kept coming up with good points, but no one wanted to give him credit. They just got their backs up and refused to see the logic.

Aunt Mary spoke up. "We better change the subject before I lose my religion and say something I might regret."

Once again silence overtook the group. No one seemed to be able to look at anyone else. Mama was in her favorite wicker rocker, and it

I got out of my chair. Bullet woke up, went over to Mark's feet, and lay down again. I continued to the far end of the porch and caught another fly. I pulled off its wings and put it on the screen in front of Mantis, but Mantis took wing and flew to another part of the porch. I guess he'd had his fill, or maybe the conversation made him lose his appetite.

So I stood by the screen and looked out over the field. I could not take my mind off what Bojack had said. I turned and looked at my family and our guests sitting quietly on the porch, and I thought about their situation. Bojack was right. They were always complaining about their lives, but they did nothing to escape or to help their children escape. Even though I was only ten years old, it hit me hard and moved something in me to hear a grown man admit that he was sad about his life. He had nothing to show for it, and nothing to be happy about. It jarred me and made me realize that I shouldn't— better yet, *couldn't* end up that way. I couldn't bear to look at my life stretched out before me like a long, empty highway and know that forty years later, I'd be standing in the same spot, looking at the same view. The soles of my shoes would be worn through, but I would have traveled nowhere.

Then I thought of something Mama Jennie had said, something that agreed with what Bojack had been preaching all night. I figured I would say it. No one would say a word against Mama Jennie. So

I walked back to where the adults were sitting. They looked so unhappy that I hesitated.

"Mama, can I say something?" I was never as bold as Eugenia or Rosetta. I couldn't just pipe up in the middle of an adult conversation, so I always asked for permission.

"Sure you can, baby."

Of course, the only problem with asking permission was that everyone stopped what they were doing and concentrated entirely upon you. Whereas, if you just spoke up, you might be able to stick in your opinion before they knew who'd spoken. But now they were all staring at me with anger still etched in their faces.

My voice trembled. "I thank Bojack be right."

"Well, what you know about anythang?" Ethel Brown said. "You ain't no older than a minute!"

"That's right," Aunt Mary said, flipping her hand as if to brush my opinion away like some bothersome bug. "You better stick to riding that bike that you keep covered up like it's Elijah's chariot. That's all a boy your age know anythang about."

"Yeah," Jim said. "You don't even know what you be saying."

"It ain't got nothing to do with what I say," I replied. "It just seem like good sense. I was remembering something Mama Jennie had said one night when we was talking about white folks keeping us down. She said, 'Y'all always talking about white folks acting like the Civil War won't never fought. Well, y'all just as bad. Thangs is different now. Reverend King seen to that. Being Negro ain't gone make you president, but you can still do something with yourself. The handicap ain't being Negro so much as it is y'all's attitude.' That's what she said, to the best of my recollection."

"I do remember that," Mama said.

"The old bitch is senile if you ask me," Aunt Mary said.

"Now, Mary," Mama said, "you can talk bad about a lot of thangs on my porch, but by God, my grandmother ain't one of 'em."

"If she wrong, she wrong!" Aunt Mary said.

"Mama Jennie ain't get to be that old by being no fool," Bojack added.

"I just don't know about all this nonsense," Daddy said.

"I know!" I shouted

can't settle for what they are because that indicates their life is less than desirable. Even though I realized they knew the truth about their lives, I knew they didn't want to hear a ten-year-old kid rub it in their faces. But I had started the thought, so I had to finish it.

"I'll go to school with the white kids. And I'm gonna read and study and get out of Canaan. I'm gonna be somebody!"

They were all silent for a moment before Chauncey Mae spoke. "What you saying is that all of us is nobody, right?"

"No, ma'am."

"Well, what is you saying then?" Ethel asked.

"Younguns is so smart-mouthed these days," Jim Brown added.

I turned to Daddy. He looked mad, and Mama looked concerned. I turned to Bojack, who was smiling.

"I just don't want to be like Bojack," I said while thinking of Daddy, Jim Brown, Arthur Pitts, and other Negro men in Canaan. "I want to like what I am. I want to be somebody."

"Somebody!" Aunt Mary shouted. "Huh, I know what *somebody* mean around here. You be learning soon enough."

"I don't understand," I said.

Aunt Mary replied, "A nigger by any other name still be a nigger."

"And you be a nigger just like us," Jim Brown said.

"A black gnat drowning in a sea of white," Chauncey Mae said.

"No!" I shouted.

I was surprised that I was being so vocal with adults, but I could see Bojack's theory coming to life. I didn't want anyone to put a damper on my life out of jealousy before I had a chance to live it the way I saw fit.

"I'm gonna be different."

"Don't get riled up, chile," Aunt Mary said. "We ain't speaking nothing but the truth."

"You got to realize who you is and where you from, boy," Chauncey Mae said. "Ain't no nigger from Canaan ever done nothing but stay here and work in them fields out yonder, or in them meatpacking plants."

I turned to my only ally, who remained one even though I had looked him straight in the eye and said I didn't want to be him. "I can do it, can't I, Bojack?"

He was still smiling. "You sure can, little brother. You sure can. All of you can," he said, looking around the porch at the four children.

"I ain't learning no white folk's nothing," Eugenia said.

"Me neither," Rosetta said.

"These girls here be talking smart," Aunt Mary said to me. "You learn that shit, you be more a puppet to the white man than we is already. And they control us enough as it is. Keeping us down like a starving dog on a short leash."

"In the end, you probably right," Bojack said. "You can get somewhere in life, but when it all be said and done, no matter how much you learn, the white man can keep you down to a certain extent. After all, he own everythang."

"About time you start to wise up," Aunt Mary said.

"I won't finished," Bojack replied. "So here you is, feeling like the white man is sole responsible for where you at in this life. That's the way it is. And like I say, in the end you may be right. So accept that and then say, 'What do I do about it? Sit here on my butt complaining all the day long about what the white man done to me? Or do I work hard to make the best of what I can get from him?' Studying them books can help you make the best of yourself. The white man can keep you from being senator or the owner of a big company, but you can still be a teacher, lawyer, or doctor. You can use his books to get at least that far over the hump. And you ain't got to give up your

theyselves," Chauncey Mae said.

Bojack frowned. "You live like you want to live, and let these boys live like they wants to live."

"Negro, you making me sick," Cozy Pitts said. "Anythang white folks got, they can keep to theyselves."

"You sho' nuff got that right," Daddy said.

Bojack became quiet. He ate a potato chip, put down his empty glass and walked to the porch door. Then he turned around.

"Well," he said, "I just got me one more thang to say. Then I guess I done said my piece for tonight."

"Well, they is a God after all," Ethel Brown said.

"I don't know the boys real well," he said, ignoring Ethel and looking toward Mark and me. "But I seen Evan sitting up over Morgart's Lake reading them stories in the *Reader's Digest* magazine. One day he went off and left one and it blowed down the hill to where I was shooting my .22. I had a good look at it. I couldn't hardly read none of it. It made me sad that I couldn't read good, but happy that Evan could. I was right proud."

"How you know he was reading it?" Aunt Mary asked. "Mighta been just looking at the pictures."

"He reading alright, ain't you, Evan?"

"Yes, sir."

"Well, keep on reading 'em. If you listen to these folks and stop and don't put up no fight for yourself, you be just like me. Thank hard on that one. Take a good long look at old Bojack. I'm your ghost of Christmas future. Like they say in the story, it don't have to turn out this way for you unless you want it to."

Bojack opened the screen door and took his leave. Bullet scooted out the door behind him and dashed into the cornfield, leaving two cautiously hopeful boys, two very angry girls, and seven twice-as-angry adults. The porch session was over.

• • •

Later on, while we were cleaning up, I noticed that Daddy was only talking to Mark. I knew what was wrong, and I wanted to talk about it, but I had to wait for him to bring it up. If I did, he would perceive it as a challenge, and you didn't push Daddy when he was mad.

The silent treatment kept up until Mark and I said our prayers and were in bed with the light out. I had tossed the bedspread down to the foot of my bed and lay there with just the sheet over me. Mark had opened the two windows in our room to let in a cool breeze. I was just about asleep when Mama and Daddy came into the room. They didn't turn on the light. They just stood there for a moment, two shadows against our bedroom wall. Daddy's anger at me hung heavily in the air like humidity on a 100-degree day.

I pretended to be asleep, hoping that they would decide it was better not to wake me and that we should talk about it in the morning. By then, I knew, he would have calmed down a little. But I was never a lucky kid.

I was so tense by the time Daddy finally spoke that when he called my name, his voice was like what I always thought the voice of God would sound like. I jumped up into a sitting position. I felt clammy all over.

"Evan," he said.

"Yes, sir?"

"If you ever embarrass us like that again, you will be one sorry boy! You understand me?"

"But, Daddy?"

"Don't you but me, boy!" His voice quaked with rage, making

You made us seem like nothing tonight," he continued. "Talking 'bout how you gonna be something better than us. The Walls family is one of the best Negro families in this town. You talked about us like a child that ain't got no respect for elders, particularly his own parents."

"I didn't mean I want to be better people than you. Just to be in a better situation in life."

"Seem like much the same to me," Daddy said.

All of a sudden I felt picked upon, singled out.

"Mark agreed with Bojack, too," I said.

There was a rustling of the covers on Mark's side of the room.

"Well, he won't rude about it, talking back to us and our friends like somebody in this room. And it ain't no need to try and sidetrack me. You just better not let it happen again. Mark my words, boy!"

"Yes sir, Daddy," I replied, and they left the room.

"Why you have to bring me into it?" Mark asked.

"Because it was true. I won't the only one that agreed with Bojack."

"That's true, but they right. I won't disrespectful."

"I didn't mean to be. I just believe Bojack."

"Well, you just ought to watch yourself. Following after Bojack ain't worth getting in trouble with Daddy."

"Yeah, I know you right."

"And I know you are. I didn't need Bojack to tell me nothing. I been knowing all along that I couldn't live like this. I didn't need him to start me dreaming."

I was completely taken aback. I had never heard Mark express what was going on in his mind. Before this revelation, I never knew one thing that he felt deeply about. He never had a Mama Jennie kind of friend to talk to that I knew of, and I knew he didn't confide in Mama or Daddy. He was the loner of our family.

Dumbfounded, I simply stopped the conversation right there. I guess I was afraid that the floodgates of emotion would open if I continued to question him and that neither of us was prepared to handle the onslaught. And later on after we were only brothers in name, it was too late to ask. So I never found out what there was in Mark's past; who he might have seen beat Daddy or make Mama cry, or who had hurt him so much that it showed him that Canaan was not the place for him.

So I took his advice about not making our parents mad. I rolled over in bed, wondering if Mama and Daddy thought I had been frightened out of my resolve. Well, if so, they were wrong. I was even more determined. From that point on, I decided I would avoid any direct confrontations with adults about the issue. And I thought that if I was going to be a black gnat in a big, white ocean, then I'd just have to learn how to swim real well.

Mama Jennie was ninety-five years old and belonged to a group called the Death Club. It was an assemblage of elderly women, of which Mama Jennie was the oldest. The rest were in their late seventies and eighties and had all outlived their husbands and many of their children. They were strong women who refused to live anywhere but in their own homes, despite their many ailments. Every morning they called each other, and if someone did not answer, one of the club members would call that person's family.

On the morning after I'd made my stand, we received a call from Miss Antebellum Taylor. She spoke to Mama and told her that everything was all right. It was just that Mama Jennie sounded particularly tired that morning and she suggested that Mama check on her. Mama said she would later on in the morning, but I could not wait for later on. Mama Jennie had been slowing down, and any sign that she was slowing further worried me.

"I'll be there when you get there, Mama," I shouted as I prepared to leave the house.

There was no answer, but I wasn't surprised. No one said anything to me that morning. We got up, did our chores and ate our breakfast in silence. Daddy was still angry, and Mark, I'm sure, was afraid he would stoke our father's ire by speaking to me. I knew this was only a cease-fire. The gun was still loaded and pointed. One false move and the battle could erupt again.

So I went on quietly through the morning, figuring we just needed something to get our minds off the night before. You know, like you can cut your finger, and it hurts; you think about it until someone stomps on your toe, and suddenly you've forgotten the problem with your finger. I thought that maybe the call about Mama Jennie would be the stomp on our toes, but I was wrong.

Mama slipped out the back door.

"That's a good idea," she said. "You go check on her. Get you out of Daddy's way for the morning. And you think about that nonsense and the trouble you started last night. Get it out of your head, and tell Mama Jennie I'll be 'round the way shortly."

Outside was my prized possession: a metallic-red spider bicycle I had gotten for Christmas. I kept it covered and protected with a big piece of plastic. It was so sleek that it looked like it was moving when it was standing still. It had gleaming, silver raised handlebars with red plastic grips, a slick red banana seat and big black tires like a trail bike. Daddy had taped an old car antenna to the back of the seat. It came up behind me, its tip draped in yellow, blue, and red streamers.

In a minute, I was riding into the wind, which was one of my favorite places to be. I leaned across the handlebars into the oncoming gusts. My shirt flapped against my side like the wings of an eagle, and the streamers swayed above my head. Man, I loved to be on that bike. I let out a yell. I popped a wheelie and held it until I got to the point where the dirt road from my house met the dirt road leading to Days Neck. When my front tire dropped to the road, I heard someone yelling.

"Hot dog! Look there, a damn hot dog!"

I turned and smiled. It was T. Wall, my best friend. With him was the rest of our gang—Beno, Muskrat, and Flak. They were on bikes, too.

"Hey, slick!" T. Wall called.

your place."

"Who told you that?"

"Who you thank?" Beno asked.

I laughed. "Eugenia."

"That's right," T. Wall said.

"That girl got a mouth big enough to swallow my daddy's Massey Ferguson," I said.

We all laughed.

"So," T. Wall asked. "What happened last night?"

Suddenly, he was unnervingly serious, which caught me and the rest of the guys off guard. He stared at me a moment.

"Tell me it ain't so," he said, forcefully.

I smiled at T. Wall. It was the only thing I could think to do that might lighten the somber atmosphere and make them realize that it wasn't a big deal.

T. Wall was my best friend, and I couldn't think of a time when either of us felt unsure of the other's loyalty. I wondered if Eugenia had embellished the truth in a way that portrayed me as a betrayer of friends.

"It won't no big deal," I finally said.

They still looked at me with questions in their eyes. I realized that the adults' reaction to my statement wasn't just an isolated event—that I couldn't dream my dreams in a vacuum while growing up in Canaan.

"Really," I said. "I gotta go see Mama Jennie. Miss Antebellum Taylor say she won't feeling too good this morning. I'll come by after that and tell y'all everythang. The truth! Not what Eugenia probably said."

"Come by the tree house on your way back, E," Muskrat said. "We gone be there. Beno stole some of his daddy's *Playboys*."

"I'll be back there before long." I was still unnerved by T. Wall's skepticism. "For real. Square up, man," I said, although I was starting not to believe myself. "It won't nothing."

T. Wall just stared as I pedaled off.

In five minutes, the air became heavy with the smell of industry, of blood and flesh. I was passing the meatpacking plants. Two huge concrete-and-brick buildings were surrounded by twelve-foot wire fences. They were owned by two different companies, but according to the people who worked in them, only the names were different. Both companies had a reputation for abusing their black employees. Several particularly cruel tales had become legend. I heard many of them at the weekly porch sessions, stories of people working ten to fifteen hours in unsanitary conditions for wages that left them dirt poor. Stories of people who were not trained properly for their jobs. I can't tell you all of the grief-laden yarns I heard about Joe This or Mary That who were ordered by their white supervisors to operate dangerous machinery. If Joe and Mary said, "I still don't quite understand it," the supervisor said, "I ain't got time to waste on you, nigger. Just do it, or I'll just go get one of the other niggers out there waiting for a job to come in here. Ain't no problem. You don't wanna work, there's the door and let the doorknob hit you where the good Lord split you."

Needing a job, they learned how to operate a machine, but only after losing a finger, a hand, a toe or a foot. I heard of a woman who lost an entire arm to a ham-skinning machine. Like the others, she was offered no compensation and could do nothing about the situation. They paid money to a union out of their tiny wages, but the union—also run by whites—never helped them. Beyond the union, there was nowhere to go.

All over Canaan, many evil injustices were inflicted because blacks were ignorant about how to use the system to fight back.

I wanted to be able to one day say, "I can work in the plants if I want, but I think I'll be a vice president. Or maybe I'll go to work for an oil company or a newspaper, and wear a suit and tie to work." I wanted to be able to pick the job out of calm deliberation, not out of desperation. I saw the lines of black people waiting for work and I felt sorry for them and for Daddy.

"The damn place is a prison," Daddy would say when he came home from work smelling like a smoke-cured ham. He spent an hour a night trying to get the odor off himself, and Mama would wash his clothes. They were never satisfied with the results because they were really trying to remove the smell from their souls. No detergent could do that.

I pedaled across the Pagan Creek Bridge and pulled over on the side of the road. To my left was the Colonial Store, Canaan's largest grocery store. To my right was marsh, and down the hill from me, a boardwalk ran over the marsh to where Mama Jennie's house sat up on a hill. The small A-frame peeked out at me from behind tall, stately trees of pine, black oak, and elm. The hillside was covered in dogwood, lilac, crepe myrtle, and magnolia. A rainbow of flower beds graced the hill and surrounded her house. In them were azaleas, violets, blue lobelias, jack-in-the-pulpits, bloodroots, petunias, irises, tulips, and more. The beautiful sight gave me a warm feeling as I marveled at how she managed to keep her flower and vegetable gardens going at her age.

"It's hard work that keeps a woman young," she said to me once. "And I done seen a whole lot of that."

Mama Jennie had worked the fields when she was young and later as a widow. She raised eleven children by taking in laundry. "And believe me, chile. That was a lot of laundry," she once told me.

Not only was she serious about keeping her gardens every summer, she went to church every Sunday, and every other week Mama took her shopping. She cooked her own meals and took a short walk with her cane every day. She loved to tell the story of how her mother had lived to 112 without ever seeing a doctor.

"And look at me," she'd say to Mama. "Old as I is, I ain't taking no pills. You my grandchile. Half my age. Got to take a pill to get up, go to sleep, to feel happy, and to go to the bathroom. I ain't on nobody's pills."

Although her physical endurance was impressive, it was her wisdom that captured me. She seemed to have witnessed more than the sky above. Daddy used to say that the Bible held an answer to every moral problem. I believed the same of Mama Jennie.

"You can ask her most anythang," I once said to Mama and Mark. "She always got an answer, and they all make good sense, too."

"You right about that," Mark said.

"Jennie Lowe is a wise old woman," Mama said, smiling.

"What did Nana used to call what Mama Jennie said?" I asked.

"Your grandmother used to call Mama Jennie's words 'little kernels of truth.'"

I always found hope in Mama Jennie's ancient eyes, strength in her ever-weakening voice and truth in her smile. In me, she found someone interested in the workings of the world. She liked that. She used to say about me, "Chile, you ask more questions than a Philadelphia lawyer. And that be good. More colored chillen ought to wanta know what's going on around 'em."

Every Sunday evening, as regular as the porch sessions at my house, all of Mama Jennie's children, grandchildren and great-grandchildren living in Canaan came by to see her. No one ever told me so for sure, but it seemed like family law that you did not let Sunday pass without stopping by, or you'd have to answer to Jennie Lowe.

News, then later the *Ed Sullivan Show*. After the *Sullivan Show*, we all went home, not to be seen until the next Sunday, except for me.

I called Mama Jennie twice every week and went to see her at least once. I couldn't get enough of her company. Looking at her face was like looking at a beautiful mountain range. It had rugged peaks and smooth valleys, enveloped by clouds of white hair. But in the end, mountains also crumble, suffering the slow pain of erosion. And so it was with Mama Jennie. She had rolled with the punches of life, but their cumulative effect was finally taking its toll.

I got on my bicycle and rode down the hill and across the boardwalk. I carried the bike up the steps Daddy had built into the side of the hill for her. I found her on her knees, digging weeds out of her vegetable garden. She was humming "Pass me not, oh Gentle Savior."

"Hey, Mama Jennie," I said.

She looked up. "Well," she said, smiling. "Ain't you something coming around to brighten up a old woman's day."

"Miss Antebellum Taylor called this morning. She told Mama you didn't sound too good."

"Well, I was a mite tired this morning. Help your old great-granny up from here. I ain't even really sure how I got down here in the first place," she said, laughing.

I dropped my bike and helped her.

"Oh, I guess I'm better now, though. When you get to be my age, you get tired off and on all the time. It ain't no big thang. I just been checking on my chillens. I keeps them alive, they keeps me alive."

"Yes, ma'am." I gave her the cane lying on the ground beside her.

"Now that you seen to it that the old lady ain't 'bout dead yet, what you got on your mind?"

"Nothing but you."

"Ain't what I hear."

"I don't understand."

We started walking toward the house.

"I hear thangs was pretty hot 'n heavy out y'all's way last night."

"Man a'mighty. News sure do travel fast in this town."

"Well, it ain't like it got far to go 'fore it hits the right ear and mouth just waiting to spread it all 'round. I thank both the ear and the mouth was prob'bly on your porch last night, and on the same person to boot."

We laughed at her reference to Chauncey Mae. I helped her up the steps and into the house. She poured iced tea, cut us some pound cake, and we sat at the kitchen table.

"So," she said. "You gonna be somebody, huh?"

Once again, a perfectly amicable conversation turned humorless. I looked into her eyes and thought of T. Wall. I hung my head because I couldn't take what I felt to be the criticism in her expression. I trusted her so much, and because I did, I wanted to leave. I began to fidget. For the first time, I didn't want to hear what she had to say, knowing full well that if she told me I was wrong, I would probably drop it. But as always, Mama Jennie came through for me.

"Ain't no need to hang your head, son. Jennie is behind you. It's 'bout time somebody wanted to stand by theyselves, apart from this crop of shortsighted fools 'round here. I'm just looking like this cause I want to hear the truth. You know me. I'm serious 'bout the truth."

"I didn't mean nothing bad last night. I didn't know I was gone stir everythang up."

"Chile, it's prob'bly blowed over by now. You know how your folks is."

"Yes, ma'am. I hope so . . . blowed over, that is."

She took a big bite of her cake and drank some tea.

wny. Cause we don't know nothing 'bout nothing. That's why. And them folks be walking off with all our little bit of money, and we don't know nothing from nobody.

"Look at Eliza Blizzard. That woman got her a education. It did more than teach her ABCs and what not. Taught that gal how to thank, get her ducks all in a row. That's why she can go up to them school-board meetings and give them folks what-for. She can thank circles around all us."

She frowned and shook her head.

"You know, prob'bly the biggest thang that kept us down all these years ain't been the KKK and shackles on our feet. It's been the shackles on our brains. They didn't keep us down just by divide and conquer. They kept us down by not letting us read. So you be sure to read, read and read some more, chile. That's the key. Get something in that good head a yourns. Can't nobody take that away from you. And if white folks in America can't deal with it, then get on a boat and take yo' educated behind someplace else. You know 'bout Paul Robeson, don't you?"

"No ma'am."

"See there. We ain't even educated 'bout ourselves. He a black man that got black-balled over here. Went cross the sea, yonder somewhere, and lived for a long time. He was a smart, smart man. You be one, too. Look up in the cabinet over there."

I got up and looked in the cabinet. Inside were two tattered books. They were *Old Yeller* and *Savage Sam.*

"I called up Philly and told your aunt Frances 'bout you and them *Reader's Digest* magazines. She sent these books that the white folks she work for had thowed out with the trash. She say they for boys your age."

I was elated to find Mama Jennie so much in my corner. I went over and gave her a hug. Then I told her what Bojack said the night before, that it upset me to hear a thirty-five-year-old man say that essentially he had lived for nothing. Mama Jennie paused.

"You know," she said, "I don't know too many colored folk from that age on up who don't feel the same. How sad is that?"

Many times I'd heard Mama Jennie tell us how even after slavery was legally over, Negro children weren't allowed to read and write. When the Negroes finally found a Negro teacher brave enough to come into Canaan, white people burned down the church they used as a school and lynched the teacher.

Mama Jennie went silent again; I thought she might cry.

"I'll never know what I coulda been or done."

We ate our pound cake and drank our tea in silence. After a few minutes, she spoke again.

"That's why we owe it to our chillen to see that they don't be following in our footsteps. That's why I'm proud of you for standing up for yourself," she added.

"Thank you," I said.

"You know Lost Boy, don't you?"

"Yes, ma'am."

"What you thank 'bout him?"

"He's crazy. Most us just laugh at him."

She looked mad. "Well, what's so funny? He ain't nobody's damn joke."

"I'm sorry."

"You oughta be. Cause that man was just like you when he was your age. Smart as the sun is bright. Had manners to boot. Always say 'yes, ma'am, no ma'am.' Take your bags for you. Always had a smile on his face. The chile was gone go someplace. Then wham! Now he around here talking to the trees."

"...

...g ..., Reverend and Miz Ellis was the Eliza Blizzards of they time. They was in civil rights before anybody even thought of a civil right for colored folk. They was smart folk from up north, and say they gone send Billy to college up yonder. They went out they way to help colored folk 'round here.

"White folks ain't bother them too much, even though they stirred up trouble. For a while, the fact that the reverend was a man of the cloth and she was his wife kept them in a safe zone. But you can push the Klan too far.

"Anyways, when they had enough of the Ellises, they lynched 'em and left they only child, Billy, without a home. And the folk of Canaan, who his parents tried to protect, turned Billy away. Folk said nobody knew the straw what broke the camel's back where the Ellises was concerned and, cause of that, everybody, including me, didn't take him in. We thought the Klan might be coming back after the boy and kill whoever took him in, too. I guess I hoped he would get on a bus and go on up north to his relatives, but then I found out he didn't have none. The boy was so shattered, he didn't know what to do. He wandered the roads for a while. Then he pitched a tent in the cemetery next to his parents' graves. Stayed right there till the church come and made him move. Say they couldn't have no beautiful funerals and thangs if they had to be lookin' at his nasty brown tent. When he wouldn't move, they burned down his tent. Sounds much like the KKK, don't it?

"Before anybody knew it, he done got in the liquor and been stumbling 'round, sitting on street corners crying, lecturing trees and such. Folk say he walked around in a fog, lost. That's how he come about being called Lost Boy."

"That's a terrible story, Mama Jennie."

"You right. And I ain't proud of my part in it neither, but it's so. That's why I want you to keep your head on straight. You done made the right decision, so don't turn back."

"I won't, and I'll make you proud."

"Well," she said. "You just be sure 'n do that."

From that moment on, I considered Mama Jennie my partner in crime. I decided that if things went wrong, if I became depressed because the struggle became too hard, then I would go to her. It would take only one good word from her to set me straight again.

We changed the subject, although it never really left my mind, and finished our tea and cake. Then we played checkers for an hour until Mama showed up, and Mama Jennie decided she wanted to be taken to the supermarket. I told Mama where I'd be, and she smiled and kissed me.

"Go on 'bout your bidness, then. And no more of that talk from last night, you hear?"

I got on my bike and flew across the Pagan Creek Bridge heading for Days Neck and the tree house. I wanted to know what Eugenia had told the guys and what they thought of it all, provided she'd told them the truth.

As I rode, I couldn't imagine T. Wall and the boys not agreeing with me. After all, we were like family. We all liked each other more than our real siblings.

Of course, it hadn't always been that way. We were once just boys passing on the roads, laughing in church and playing hide 'n seek in Days Neck or marbles at school. But two summers ago, we came together as a unit—T. Wall, Beno, Muskrat, Flak and me.

• • •

The five of us made up the Tenderfoot rank in our Boy Scouts troop, run by the Grace Street Baptist Church. Every summer, we

...cepted an invitation from him to bring us to an official scout camp.

At first, our parents balked at the idea of our troop joining white scouts in the remote Virginia countryside. But Mr. Chimes said his friend was trustworthy, and soon our parents gave in. We boys were happy. We were going to spend a week at a real scout camp where we could swim, shoot, tie knots, identify plants, and do crafts for merit badges.

The Tenderfoots decided to study together and stick together once we got to camp. We knew the older scouts didn't want to be bothered with us. We spent months learning our knots and plants and other things in preparation. By June we were ready.

Mr. Chimes piled us into three station wagons. He and his two assistants, Mr. Day and Mr. White, drove us to Camp Smith.

When we got there, all the troops were told to line up on a huge playing field. When that was done, it became painfully obvious to us that we were the only black troop present. And the only poor one, too.

Not all of us had uniforms. I had two, one of which I had loaned to T. Wall. But there were lots of blue jeans and T-shirts and imitation Keds to be seen throughout our troop. We heard the snickers and saw the pointing fingers, but no one among us said anything. We just gave each other a look that said we'd have to stick together.

Everything went fine until the second day, when, out of the clear Virginia sky, a troop from the central part of the state decided to march down to the lake where we were taking swimming lessons. They marched to cadence like a well-trained army regiment. Each of them carried a Confederate battle flag.

Those of us who were swimming stopped. Those who were not turned to meet the angry onslaught. The vision of my father being beaten came back to me. In all of our minds was a slow and torturous fading of dignity, of pride, of any enjoyment at Camp Smith.

The boys in that troop laughed as they passed us by, their flags waving above their heads. The sky seemed to be full of them. An Eagle Scout stood before them and flipped us the bird as a salute, and then the other boys from other troops joined in, flipping and laughing at us. Even camp counselors marched alongside them. We looked to Mr. Chimes, Mr. Day, and Mr. White. They were helpless too, and like most other black adults put in a situation like that in front of black children, their shame was immense. They dropped their heads.

So we just stood and waited for the parade to end. Afterward, we slow-footed it back to our campsite and found it torn apart, a Confederate battle flag flying from a tree in the middle of camp. We were so mentally beaten that no one took it down.

They had also placed trapped skunks under the wooden floors of our tents. We let them out, but already our clothes and equipment reeked. They'd urinated and defecated on our bunks and stole our money. Much of our clothing, of which there was precious little, had been shredded with knives.

Some of us picked a stump here and there to sit on. Others just sat on the ground and stared. For some time, no one moved. We were afraid to investigate further for fear of finding more destruction.

Finally, after some time had passed, one of the older boys took down the flag and set it afire. Muskrat started crying. "I wanna go home now."

"Tomorrow morning," Mr. Chimes said. "Tomorrow morning."

By the time night fell, T. Wall, Muskrat, Beno and I had crowded into one tent that didn't smell too bad. We had taken the two reeking cots outside to let them air out. We huddled on the floor ...

... you gone do then?" Herman Mason asked.

"We can return the favor," Jap said.

"Yeah," Claude Jackson said. "Come up on 'em like a thief in the night."

They made plans centered around the Eagle Scout who had flipped us the bird. They would use him to send a message to the rest of the white Boy Scouts. A message that said the days of sitting back and taking it was over.

"They must thank we still slaves or something," Elroy Meeks said.

"I believe you right," Jap replied. "But we gone put a stop to that thanking in Camp Smith tonight."

"Damn straight," Herman shouted. "It's a new day, baby. A new day!"

I thought of a favorite line of Mama Jennie's from a poem she often quoted.

Sherman's buzzin' along de sea,
Jubili, Jubilo!
Sherman's buzzin' along to de sea,
Like Moses ridin' on a bumble bee,
Settin' de prisoned and de humble free!

I peeked out of our tent and scanned the faces around the fire. I had seen anger in the eyes of black men before, but never had I seen such immeasurable hatred. That night I looked into the eyes of fifteen would-be killers. Scared, I looked to the tent where Mr. Chimes, Mr. Day, and Mr. White were staying. I knew they could hear what was going on. They didn't care; they weren't trying to stop it. Maybe they were happy to hear it. And they weren't the only ones in total support of the plan. The eyes of my friends were red-hot coals in the pitch-black darkness, burning with the excitement of retribution.

Jap Jones dispatched Tom Goode to find out what tent the Eagle Scout was in while we sat in our tent and talked the situation over.

"Ooh," Beno said. "They gone get all up in that white boy's shit tonight."

"Going upside that nasty yella head," Muskrat said.

"I ain't missing it," T. Wall said. "Y'all?"

"Not me," I said.

I wasn't excited about hurting anyone, but if someone else was going to do the hurting, then I was a willing witness.

Hours later, around midnight, every boy in our group left the campsite. We followed Tom Goode through the woods and crept up on the white scout's camp.

In all of the sites, the tents were placed in a circle backing up to the woods, with a big open area in the middle. We went to the back of the Eagle Scout's tent. A boy named Hopewell Long took out his knife and cut open the back of the tent so quietly that he didn't even wake up the two boys inside.

When Jap Jones walked onto the floorboards of the tent, the Eagle Scout's buddy woke up first. He opened his mouth to yell, but Jap Jones had come across a tree branch on our walk through the woods, and there was no hesitation in his swing and no remorse on his face after the branch slammed into the boy's head and laid him flat on the floor.

The Eagle Scout shot up in his bed. Jap, Herman, Hopewell, and some others stuck a skunk-stinking sock in his mouth and dragged him out of the tent. They pulled him into the woods, tied a bandana over his mouth, and tied his arms and legs. Then they ~~~ ~~ ~~~

~~~ ~~~

The boy shook his head, and from the sidelines, the Tenderfoots laughed.

Then they took turns slapping the boy's face until it was beet red. Next, they took off the bandana and removed the sock. They all lined up in front of him, Jap first in line. "You piss on my bed," he said. "I'mma piss on you."

He stood over the boy, pulled out his penis, and pissed right into the boy's face. Next, Herman Mason did the same thing. Then Claude Jackson, Hopewell Long, Tom Goode, and all the rest of the older scouts.

"Open your lily-assed white mouth," some of them said, and proceeded to piss down his throat.

Jap worked up the ability to do it again and stood over the boy, who had urine dripping down his face and pouring out of his mouth. He was crying, but you couldn't tell the tears from the piss.

Jap pissed on him again and said, "White folks can call me nigger from here till kingdom come, but I'm satisfied. Every time somebody call me that and thank they got me cold, I'm gone thank about the day I made a white boy drink my piss. And I'm gonna smile. Y'all want a turn?" he said, turning to us.

We looked at each other. Only T. Wall moved. As he walked to the boy, I thought of Taliferro Pitts and knew that he would have loved to be in T. Wall's shoes. T. Wall did it, right down the boy's throat. After he was finished, he turned and looked at the rest of us. We shook our heads. Though it was the ultimate chance to avenge my father's beating and the stealing of his life as a farmer, and as much as I hated that boy for what he and his friends had done, I couldn't urinate on him.

"Let's go," Jap said. He kicked the boy hard in the stomach as we started to leave. Then, in his big steel-toe boots, Jap kicked the boy hard in the head, and the boy started to throw up. He vomited violently until he had nothing left to throw up and there was only the sound of empty, horrible retching.

Someone must have heard this, or maybe his buddy had finally woken up from the blow Jap had leveled. Anyway, flashlights came on in the campsite, and we all took to the woods like frightened rabbits.

An hour later, when we were all in our tents, two white men came into our camp. One of them was Mr. Chimes' friend. The men got Mr. Chimes and explained to him that two boys had to be taken to the hospital because they had been assaulted. They wanted to know where we had been from the time we left the lake until they walked into our camp.

Mr. Chimes told them that we hadn't left the campsite. That we had been too afraid because of what happened earlier. He showed the men some of our stained bunks, our shredded clothes, and empty wallets. He explained that the afternoon's events had led to us not showing up for dinner and that we planned on leaving in the morning.

The men insisted on having a look inside each tent, and so they did. They flashed their lights in on all of us. We just stared back, having stripped down to our shorts by then. Finally, Mr. Chimes got up the nerve to do what we thought he should have done earlier.

"Where was all yo' concern when we got hit this afternoon? I didn't see nobody coming 'round then," he said.

"I didn't know it had happened," the man said.

"Don't lie to me," Mr. Chimes said, angrily. "I saved your life. You owe me one better than that."

His friend just turned and walked away. The other man followed.

I turned off Highway 10 onto the dirt road leading to the community of Days Neck. T. Wall's house was midway down the main road, which we called "the Track." Behind it was the tree house that the five of us had built with plywood left from a burned-out shack.

As I pedaled into his yard, 5-10, the huge Great Dane that belonged to T. Wall and was named after a local five and ten cents store, came tearing after me, growling like he wanted to eat me alive. But I wasn't fazed. By then, I was used to him charging me. He always choked on the chain that restrained him just before he got to me.

I dropped my kickstand at the base of the big walnut tree in the backyard. Beyond the tree, in a vacant lot, there was a group of men from the neighborhood hanging out around Lost Boy's truck. I ignored them and climbed the ladder. I knocked the secret knock on the trap door, and they opened it for me. "Hey, T. Wall," I said. "You'd thank after all this time, 5-10 would stop barking at me."

"Shit, E. You know he don't like nobody but me. Not even my mama."

"What y'all doing?" I asked.

"Looking at the naked ladies," Flak said, winking at me. "Boocoo tits in here, bro. Come see."

This was typical of Canaan boys. At least, black boys; I didn't know any white boys at the time. There was little for us to do. We didn't have a recreation facility like the white kids. There was no pool, no little league, and very few church functions. We were too young for the pool halls, so we just hung out and talked about the day when we could get laid. Sex seemed to be the only way black men and boys could truly feel like men. So that was pretty much all they thought about.

Older men didn't discourage us young guys, either. In fact, most of the men wore the conquests of their sons around their necks like a Congressional Medal of Honor. Muskrat said that Beno had stolen his father's *Playboys*, but truthfully Beno's father made the robbery an easy one, as he always had. He wanted Beno to be a stud in the worst way. That's just the way it was. Boys became men by getting laid, and girls became women by getting pregnant.

"Look at this one," Beno said. "This the kind they used to hang niggers for."

Flak leaned over and took a look. "Well, hang me, baby. Umph, umph, umph!"

"Yeah," Muskrat said. "You go 'head and fix up the rope. Give me fifteen minutes with that gal, and I hang myself for you. After getting some of that, everythang else in life gone be a letdown anyway."

We roared with laughter, slapping hands all around. T. Wall, who had been cleaning his BB gun, leaned over. "Let me see that."

He handed me the gun, and I looked at it, rolling it over in my hands. I liked the feel of it better than mine. We all had them; that was how you were trained to use the real thing so that you could put food on your family's table. Mostly we shot crows, and we were very proud of our accuracy.

"I don't know about all that," T. Wall said, looking at the *Playboy*. "Yeah, she got a good body, but ain't no pussy in the world worth dying for."

"Well, tell me this," Beno said. "Could you live without it?"

"I guess so, stupid. I ain't had none yet, and I guess I'm what you call living. But if it's like what my daddy say it like, then I reckon you got yourself a point."

"She ain't got enough butt for me," Muskrat said. "Now you take Eugenia. She got a butt that sits up so high and mighty, you could near 'bout fry yo' whole breakfast on it."

"Been in the bushes with one girl, one time, and he the k̲i̲n̲ ̲o̲f̲

........y and stuff like that. I told her she was full of shit and to take her big-butted, crazy-headed self on home."

"Then she said you said you was gone be better than all us," Beno said. "You say that crap?"

"No, I didn't," I said. "Miss Chauncey Mae been spreading the same mess, Mama Jennie said. I ain't said nothing like that."

"See," T. Wall said. "I told that bitch you ain't said that shit. I told her, man, I know E like the back of my hand. He's a brother to the bone and don't want nothing to do with no whitey. Give me five, bro."

He held out his hands, and I slapped them with my hands, palm to palm. "On the black side," he said. He turned his hands over, and I slapped them again.

"What I did say was I wanted an education," I told them, my friendship feeling somewhat renewed after our reaffirmation ritual. "I said I wanted to get out of Canaan. I didn't say I wanted to be better. Just in a better life situation."

T. Wall, who had taken the BB gun back, dropped its stock to the floor. Beno rolled up the *Playboy* in his hands and, along with the rest of them, he stared back at me.

"Ain't that the same thang?" Flak asked. "Better situation mean better'n us."

"Eugenia was right, won't she? You did say you was gone be better than us," Muskrat said.

"No, I didn't. All I said was I wanted to get something in my head so I wouldn't have to worry about the white man taking what's mine, like he done my daddy's right to be a farmer. I want to be like Eliza Blizzard. She says what she wants to say, and they don't mess with her because she smart. She got the NAACP and the federal government behind her with the school stuff, and the hick white people can't stop her 'cause she know how to use they system."

"Yeah, we know 'bout old lady Blizzard and her big-assed mouth," T. Wall said. "If you thank like she thank, maybe Eugenia was right. That woman want us to integrate with them . . . them thangs."

"We can use 'em to study the books, T. Wall. That's all I want," I said.

"E," he replied, looking angry. "I'm disappointed in you, brother man. You oughta be thanking 'bout what you said."

"I have been."

"E, you ain't gone turn Tom on us, is you?" Muskrat asked.

"What you thank? You know me!"

"All I know is you better not. Folks be real pissed off. Eugenia say Taliferro said if he heard you talking that crap, he was gone shut you up by busting up your mouth."

"Taliferro ain't my damn daddy," I said. "Just 'cause he blame everythang wrong in the whole world on white folks don't mean I got to thank like he do."

I was nearly as agitated as the night before.

"You ain't sounding like us," T. Wall said.

"And you ain't listening to what you sounding like," I fought back.

"What you mean by that shit?" Muskrat asked.

"Ain't nothing wrong with people wanting to get ahead. That don't mean I thank less of nobody. Y'all ought to look around. Things is bad."

"It ain't that bad," Beno said. "I thank people doing alright. Look at Earnest Hudd. He ain't been out of school that long. He got a job. Dude got that bad-assed red GTO."

"Yeah," Flak said. "That car is real bad. I seen him race it some. It be standing still and he put that baby in first and hit it. Man, you can see the back of that thang sit down and boom! Burn that dawg!"

"All right!" Beno said. They slapped fives on the black side . . ."

. . . . a job at them plants can't be the best we can do."

"When you get so damn smart? Talking all old, like you somebody's old man," T. Wall asked.

It was a good question. I remember thinking to myself that I was only ten, but I also remember thinking that was just how much Bojack had shaken me up. He'd opened my eyes to the grief around me. Ten years old wasn't too young to realize that it wasn't where I wanted to be.

"I ain't so smart. But I can see. You can, too, if you want to look. I hear Mama Jennie and Bojack talk 'bout Eliza Blizzard and how much respect she get from black and white folks. It don't take no grown person to know that it be better to be like her than to have a bad car like Earnest Hudd."

"I ain't got no respect for her," Flak said.

"You know any black people 'round here smarter than her?"

No one answered.

"See," I said. "And she ain't stuck here neither. If it don't work out in Canaan, I heard Mama Jennie say, Miz Blizzard can just go and leave and work someplace else. Ain't nobody else got enough education or enough money to do that."

"She still ain't getting me to no school with no white folks," T. Wall said. "I'm with Taliferro. Let's kill 'em all."

"That ain't the point, T. Wall."

"The point is," T. Wall said, "is all of a sudden you must thank your ass is white. You ain't nothing special. Your daddy lost his precious farm, and y'all struggling just like everybody else. You coming around here with some pie-in-the-sky dream shit. You better look at who your friends is. One day you be walking 'round here with your dreams and nobody gone be talking to you."

I was shocked by my friends' reaction, suddenly feeling like an outcast, a pariah. No matter what our different desires were, I always thought our friendship would accommodate them. I mean, Muskrat loved baseball, but I hated it. So what? T. Wall loved to fish, but I thought that was as boring as baseball. So what? I wanted an education at all costs, and they didn't. I figured, *So what?*

Just then, we heard laughter outside. It was like a gift from God. We went over to the window, a big hole in the wall.

"What's going on, T. Wall?" Muskrat asked.

"You know how everybody be tired of Lost Boy coming around sleeping on they porch steps and stuff."

"Yeah."

"He been sleeping in this truck for a good while now."

"We know that," Beno said.

"Well, they don't want him sleeping in it no more."

"He ain't hurting nobody," I said.

"That ain't the point," T. Wall said. "Daddy say we can't have no trash like Lost Boy hanging 'round."

"That's the same kinda stuff white folks say about us," I said. "We ought not to say that about our own."

"Why you got white folks on the brain for?" Flak asked. "Like you love 'em or something."

"People like Lost Boy gives black folks a bad name," T. Wall said. "Daddy says he gives white folks a example reason to call all us lazy and shiftless."

Outside the tree house, Lost Boy, his hair in knots, his beard dirty, and his shirt torn, stumbled toward the broken-down pickup truck he called home. The men were laughing.

"What they know that we don't?" Flak asked T. Wall.

"Daddy say they was gone put a black snake in the truck. They was gone hide it somewhere. Lost Boy come on in there and lo...

arms and yelling. Finally, it stopped. So did the laughter of the men. Lost Boy opened the door and tossed out the snake's head. He came out and sat on the ground by the truck and began to gut the snake.

"Damn," Beno said. "He gone cook it and eat it."

Lost Boy was talking up a storm to no one as he continued to clean the snake. The men walked away, shaking their heads and probably planning something else. But for the time being, Lost Boy had won, and I was happy about that.

THREE

When the corn around my house reached a point where it was taller than me, I journeyed into its depths. Even though the crop belonged to the white farmer who semi-rented Daddy's land, I treated it just like I did when it grew for Daddy. In the center of the field, I cut down stalks, creating a circular haven in which I meditated. I spent most of my daylight hours there, spinning wonderful webs composed of fascinating dreams about who and what I would become.

It was in that place of refuge that my love of reading blossomed. The first novel I ever read was *Old Yeller*. The second was its sequel, *Savage Sam*. Mama Jennie spoke to Aunt Frances again, and she sent more books that had been thrown away by her employers' children. I carried a dictionary into the field with me to help me through them. I devoured those books and any other fiction I could get my hands on. My vocabulary grew faster than the corn in the field harboring me, and little by little my speech began to change. Through an unwavering practice schedule, "thangs" slowly became "things," and "ain't" practically disappeared. At first, I just pretended I was one of the characters I read about and spoke as I thought they would. Pretty soon, I was speaking as myself, and although I slipped a lot, I did well.

"Why you talking all proper and stuff for?" Mark once asked.

"Because it's the way you're supposed to speak, I think," I said

fed my appetite for knowledge. I was already moving beyond them.

In early August, Mark and I talked Mama into buying the books we needed for our school year early so we could get a head start. I read most of them before Labor Day.

T. Wall and the gang stayed clear of me for the better part of the summer. The first time I saw them after the argument in the tree house, they asked me if I was still thinking that same crazy stuff. I said yes. They shook their heads and walked away.

It's funny, though. I didn't miss them and hadn't really thought about them much. I was totally preoccupied, learning and enjoying it like nothing before. On the Saturday before I started fifth grade, I sought out the man who was responsible to finally thank him.

Bojack was exactly where I expected to find him, sitting at the edge of Morgart's Lake, wearing his reflector sunglasses, and shooting his rifle. An empty bottle of Boone's Farm Apple Wine lay beside him.

I approached him from the rear, down the embankment, through the pine and maple trees. I snatched a honeysuckle blossom from a bush and sucked on the back end of it as I sat down beside him. He nodded and unloaded his chamber on a piece of wood bobbing in the water.

"Ain't seen you at the sessions lately," he said without looking at me. Another shot rang out.

"Mama and Daddy won't let me come no more. *Anymore.*"

"I reckon I shoulda kept my fat mouth closed and you wouldn't be in that ole doghouse."

He ran out of bullets and stopped to reload.

"I wish I weren't in the doghouse either, but I'm glad you didn't keep your mouth shut."

"Weren't!" he said, turning toward me, playfully mocking. "You say . . . weren't?"

"Yes, sir."

"Where you learn to talk like that?"

"I've been doing what you suggested. I've been reading the paper and books and most everything I can get my hands on. I've been studying."

"Well," he smiled, "ain't you something? Maybe I ain't so sad no more that I talked up."

He began to shoot again.

"Can you tell me something?" I asked.

"What?"

"Can you tell me why you got mad all of a sudden? Why you've been coming for years and then all of a sudden you got real angry? I guess I've seen you stewing in your juices, but—?"

"Well, ain't you a little lawyer. Coming up with a question like that. Right personal, too."

"I'm sorry. I didn't mean to get too big for my britches."

"Oh, hell, I know that. I'm just kidding with you. Lighten up some."

He laid the gun across his lap and gazed out over the lake.

"Let's see here now. I guess it was Eliza Blizzard what done it. Yeah, that's right. I had just seen her that evening before I come over to your place. I reckon she got me riled up and such."

"Aunt Mary said you were shacking up with her. Is that right? The school principal?"

Bojack laughed. "Naw, that ain't true. Why would that lady want to shack up with me? A man like me ain't got nothing she want. The truth of the matter is that Negroes 'round here don't like the woman. She been going 'round to house after house trying to get a petition. She trying to change thangs 'round here for the better. Trying to

"Ain't you heard?"

"No. A lot of people ain't talking to me so much these days. And I can't remember Miss Blizzard coming around to our house."

"Oh, she been there. She told me. Your folks run her off just like all the other peoples."

"I guess I can see why. After listening to folks on the porch that night, I guess Miss Blizzard won't have much luck anywhere."

"Well, she got plenty luck with me. That's why folks be seeing her car at my house. I'm probably one of the few Negroes in this damn town can see she right. I help her any way I can. I can draw a little bit. I got some posters in the shack behind the house."

"How come some people can see, and some people can't?"

"I be damned if I can figure that one out," he said.

He took aim and began shooting. The piece of wood split again and bobbed in the water.

People said shooting made Bojack happy, but he didn't look happy then as he ripped through a few .22 longs. It didn't seem that he was concentrating on the shooting. It was like it had just become a part of him. A natural rhythm like walking. Something a person can do without concentrating, which allows the mind to be free. Bojack's mind might not have been on his marksmanship, but it didn't seem free, either. Just like the night he exploded in anger on our porch, he seemed burdened.

"You shoot good," I said when he finished that round and began reloading.

"I do, don't I?" He turned and smiled. "Good technique and good equipment. Got the technique in the Army and the equipment right here in Canaan."

"Can I hold it?"

"Yeah. You can shoot it, too, if you wants."

"Oh, I never shot a real gun before. Just my BB rifle."

"Well, if you gone start, you might as well start shooting with the best. This here's a Springfield semi-automatic .22 rifle. Feel that weight. Ain't it nice?"

I nodded as I took the gun. It had a strap, and Bojack showed me how to wrap it around my arm to help stabilize the rifle.

I was surprised at how little it kicked, and I hit the wood on my first try. Bojack seemed impressed.

"I'm pretty good with my BB," I said.

"I bet you is." He smiled.

"Where'd you get a rifle like this in Canaan?"

Bojack paused. He took the gun from me and began shooting. In hindsight, I think he took the gun because it was his security blanket, which he needed in order to talk about the ghosts in his past. He let it rest across his lap after he'd finally disintegrated the block of wood. His face—what I could see of it—reminded me of pastures in the middle of winter. Pastures covered with dead, brown grass, bereft of livestock or any other kind of life.

He caressed the barrel, and his voice quavered when he spoke.

"I got it from a man I really looked up to. More a daddy to me than my old man ever was. Reverend Ellis was his name."

"You mean," I replied, "Lost Boy's . . . I mean Billy Ellis' daddy?"

"That be the one. How did you know Billy's real name?"

"Mama Jennie told me."

"Oh. I see."

"How come he gave you the rifle and not Billy?"

"He gave us both one. We used to hunt squirrels and rabbits with 'em. Man, could Reverend shoot!"

"Could he shoot cherries off a tree from as far away as you can?"

"Way farther," Bojack said. "Billy could too." He paused. "I

out of Canaan and being looked at as a nigger by white folks. See, he figured if he went off and fought his little colored heart out on the battlefield, then they would respect him. Well, he went alright, and he fought. He came back with medals, but when they gave a vict'ry parade for the vets coming home to Canaan, they wouldn't let no colored march. Then he realized he coulda died over there and nobody white woulda give a good goddamn. Probably woulda been happy he was dead more than ole Hitler. And he thought he was fighting for some freedom. Sheeeeeit!

"Only thang much I remember 'bout him now was watching him sitting in the backyard one day, building a fire. And drunker than a skunk too, boy I tell ya. He sat down and watched the flames for a while and then he went in the house and come out with the American flag he come home with from the war. Next thang I knew, he thowed it on the fire and watched it burn.

"He ain't never had no love for me or nobody else after the war. Folks say 'nobody else' included my mama, too. These days, I don't remember much about her. I just remember her being there. Nothin' special, just there. Anyway, them days I was goin' nowhere fast. Billy kinda adopted me, and we become fast friends. Then Reverend and the Mrs. adopted me, too, and it was like family . . . till they got lynched."

My head dropped. I couldn't believe he was telling me all of this. Since Aunt Mary left him, he'd been a recluse. He probably found a kid easier to talk to and less judgmental.

"If you know Billy's name, Mama Jennie musta told you how he ended up like he did."

I nodded.

"Well, I turned my back on him, too," Bojack said.

I looked up at him. He was staring out over the lake, the water reflecting on his sunglasses, making me think of that river you often hear about people crying.

"I know," I said.

"I was afraid," he said.

"I understand that."

"Oh you do, do you?"

"Yeah. I mean, I reckon I probably woulda done the same thang—*thing, the same thing*. It's the way things were."

"That don't make it right."

"Nope. I reckon not."

"It's a bad thang to live with. I tried to talk to Billy three days ago. I seen him sitting on the street corner by the bank on Main Street."

"What happened?"

"He ain't even know who I was."

"I'm sorry."

"Me too," he said quietly. "Me too."

There was a moment of silence, and then he patted me on the head and smiled again, as if to thank me for listening.

"But," he continued, "I bet you ain't come here to hear no old dude cry the blues."

"Nope. I came to thank him for turning me on to being something. Maybe you let Billy down, but you started something with me. Maybe I'm your turnaround. Like I said, I've been reading a lot. The newspapers, books. I practice speaking a lot. That's why I'm talking like I'm talking."

"Music to this old fool's ears. You got a big smile all on your face. Must be liking it all."

"I do. I love to read."

"Well, ain't that some shit? What your mama and daddy thank of that one?"

"Not much."

everybody's still upset. Even T. Wall, my best friend."

"Ummmm."

"Mama Jennie says they'll probably get over it soon. Just like with everything else. I can't figure out why they're not mad at you, though. You can still go to the sessions."

"Well, I ain't no threat, that's why. Dig this. See, I done already had my life pass me by, just like them. We sinking in the same old rickety-assed boat. But you ain't. You can still be more than most all the colored folks in Canaan ever had a chance to be. That makes 'em jealous for the chances they never had. They mad at you 'cause when you become something, you toss all them lost chances right back up into they faces. It hurts."

"But they didn't fail at life. They didn't have the same chances I do. There won't no civil rights movement before they were born."

"That don't matter none. All that matters is that most of us feel you ain't got but one chance at life. If you don't get a even-Steven chance to take your best shot, then you gets mad. And when folks come along after you, getting what you shoulda got, you gets even madder."

"Shouldn't they be happy for them?"

"Life ain't that simple."

"Well, now I feel bad for wanting more."

"Ain't no need for that. If somebody dies, you ain't gone stop living, is you, 'cause you feels bad for 'em? Course you ain't. You got to go on living for yo'self, or you just grow up to be old and bitter like us. Somewhere, sometime, somebody got to break the circle."

"I'm sorry," I said. "That you didn't get the life you deserved."

"Well, thank you, but I learned to live with it. It weighs me down so sometimes that I finds myself shuffling instead a walking, but I gets by."

"How do you learn to live with something so unfair?"

"Black folk," he said, "have always learned to live with what they ain't been able to rise above. And no matter where you go and how far you get, one day you gone hit a wall and know that the only reason—and I mean the *only* reason—that wall is there is 'cause you black. It might be that you go all the way till you want to run for president, but folks gone say, black folks included, that America ain't ready for no black president. But that ain't your worry now, 'cause all that be way down the line. You just got to trust Bojack and Mama Jennie, and believe that Canaan ain't your stopping point."

"I believe you, but I can't understand why some people like T. Wall believe it is."

"I don't know. Black folks been living behind bars for so long they done got used to it. And when some bars get lowered enough for to get over 'em, folks ain't looking hard enough to see they been lowered. And if they do see that the bars been lowered, they probably afraid to step over and face what's out there 'cause they might fail. But I don't really know. I ain't much on no philosophy and shit. What you thank? You be the reader 'round here."

"It sounds right to me."

"Well, okay then. Reckon we oughta write us a book on it?"

"Could be some day," I said, smiling. "Thanks, Bojack."

"Aw, it ain't no big thang."

"Then you won't mind doing me a favor."

"Like what."

"Teaching me football. I think I want to play someday."

"Son," he said, "you have touched my heart. You know if football was whiskey, I be drunk all the time."

He wrapped an arm around me, threw his head back, and laughed. As it echoed off the lake, I knew I had made a friend.

FOUR

It was the middle of December, almost a full four months into the school year, before I woke up from my fits of fancy. I had been living in a protective bubble, concentrating entirely on schoolwork, football and my romantic notions of fate. I was blind to the repercussions of my declaration of independence and the resentment it had seeded. A sobering blow eventually came in the form of two scratches on the front fender of my beautiful bike. Two long scratches from the beginning to the end of the fender, deep and destructive, exposing scarred silver beneath torn, red paint. Two scratches I knew I hadn't made.

I hadn't ridden the bike in a long while. But it was an unusually warm day, so I decided to skip the bus and ride to school. Everyone knew the bike was mine, how special it was to me, and how much care I gave it. I should have realized my fondness for it made it the perfect target. And I should have left it at home.

As I sat there on my banana seat, my books across my shoulders in my Boy Scout backpack, I began to cry. I thought how the two scratches dirtied the whole bike. I thought of the polishing, the cleaning of the wheels, the greasing of the chain, and the special heavy plastic for shelter. It all seemed an incredible waste of time; the scratches had ruined its perfection.

I thought I could have prevented this minor tragedy if I'd only faced reality. Now someone had forced me to face it. I had to wonder if

into my head with each angry peddle stroke.

In the course of the summer, T. Wall, Beno, Flak, and Muskrat became distant acquaintances. And at the beginning of the school year, I didn't help myself any by declaring my thirst for knowledge out loud.

At least the teacher loved it. I had studied all the books and was ready for almost any question she tossed my way. Because I seemed so excited about it, she called on me more than anyone else. I was so busy impressing her that I must have come off as a smart-ass to my friends. That was not my intent; I just wanted to learn.

My teacher, a small-framed older woman, decided to make other uses of my ambitious nature. She'd ask me to empty the trash can for her, erase the blackboard, move books. Soon I became the teacher's pet, which was a badge of dishonor in my world among adults and kids alike.

Stories of my being a little rat quickly came home to roost. Chauncey Mae and Cozy brought Roberta and Eugenia over to fill Mama in. I overheard the girls happily telling stories about the classroom turncoat. Embarrassed, Mama used Mark to combat her feeling of being failed by a child. She stressed how well he managed to make good grades and get along with everyone all at the same time.

"I think you better be taking a hard look at ole Evan," Chauncey Mae said.

"Sho' nuff," Cozy concurred. "Sound like he becoming a problem child."

Back in my bedroom, I decided that the problem was them—not me. I thought of an encounter during recess when I was accosted by a classmate.

"The problem is you. I'm just trying to be a good student. It's not my fault the teacher likes me."

"Oh, you just the teacher's pet," my accuser had said. "Kissing her butt, and she always putting you up in our faces."

"It ain't true neither," I shouted. I tended to slip into old speaking habits when I got mad. "She likes me because I do my work instead of playing around like you."

"You just get good grades and stuff 'cause you always kissing up," he said. "Cleaning the blackboard, emptying the trash, trying to talk white, and all kinda shit."

"I'm not speaking white. I'm speaking correctly. And she asks me to do that other stuff."

"Yeah, 'cause you her pet."

"No, because she can depend on me. That's why."

"Get outta here with that shit, boy. You ain't fooling nobody."

I looked around thinking I must not have been fooling anybody, because there were many kids standing around looking as if they wanted to torture me.

I became the one excluded from most student activities. I suddenly realized what the word *pariah* meant.

I got the evil eye when we all went out to play baseball at recess, so I backed away. But my subconscious protected me. It told myself that I hated baseball and that I ought to be bettering myself intellectually instead of wasting time with balls and bats. So I'd go off in a corner and do homework from the morning's class while the other kids played.

I got the same treatment when it was time to play football, which I had grown to love. My subconscious, however, told me that what they were doing was boring, that my Sundays with Bojack had placed me eons ahead of them in the understanding of the game. Off again to my corner, where I could read a book.

I didn't discuss the situation with any of the kids and so I'd

My parents had become proud all of a sudden of Mark. We both had decided to be excellent students, and we both were doing so, but because Mark hadn't embarrassed them, Daddy dubbed him the favorite.

After the first six weeks of school, we both came home with straight-As, but a chocolate cake was made only for Mark, spending change given only to Mark. When Daddy managed to acquire a used set of World Book Encyclopedias, a bookcase was built over Mark's bed, and his encyclopedias were placed there. I was never told directly, but I knew that they were off limits to me.

Mama and Daddy spoke to me only when they were giving orders or scolding me, which they often found reason to do.

• • •

Pulling my bike into our driveway, I decided to talk to my teacher the next day. So, I showed up to class early.

"Well, now, Brother Walls," Mrs. Leggett said. "I know you like school, but isn't this a bit much?"

I smiled. "I came early because I needed to talk to you."

"Okay, then," she said. "You go sit down, and I'll be right with you."

She finished writing out something on her desk, and then she walked over to me and sat.

"What's on that bright little mind of yours?"

"It's about the other children."

"Oh?"

"Yes, ma'am. See, they don't like me very much. Just last year, I was one of the gang, but this year everything has changed."

I explained it all to her, but she didn't take it seriously.

"It's just children playing their little games. It was happening when I was your age, and it'll be happening when your children are your age. It'll blow over, and you'll be back in with the rest, wondering why you ever gave it the first thought."

She patted me on the head and sent me out to the playground, where I found my corner and read my book.

When I got home that afternoon, I decided to try Mama. I was banking on the fact that mothers, when truly pressured, sympathize with their children.

I looked at her through the kitchen window, scouting her mood. She was on the phone and laughing. I opened the door as she was saying, "Girl, could you believe what you was hearing? Ain't he the lyingist fool you ever did see?" She laughed again.

I walked in and shut the door. Instantly, she frowned. I placed my books on the table and stood there waiting for her. After a few seconds, she told whoever was on the other end of the line to hold on.

"Ain't you got nothing better to do than to stand around looking at me?"

"I need to talk to you," I said.

We looked at each other for a second, each of us waiting for the other to do something first.

"Well, spit it out then!" she finally shouted.

"I wanted to talk to you alone," I replied, pointing toward the phone. My face trembled a little.

Mama's frown softened, and she told her friend that she had to call her back.

"Come on over here," she said. "Now, what is it?"

I started to tell her about what I was going through, but she quickly cut me off.

"Look, Evan. Don't be wasting my time with this foolishness. You have got to stop causing trouble. Here's what I want. Y...

to, but I started to cry.

"Go on now," she said. She was not about to console me because that might cushion the blow she'd just delivered. She'd inflicted tough love and was standing by it.

I bided my time until I could call Mama Jennie and explain my situation.

"Meet me at the school right early in the morning," Mama Jennie said.

"Why? What are you going to do?"

"Mrs. Leggett ain't from around these parts, but she been here a good while. Long enough to know who I is. I reckon she'll listen to me."

"How will you get there?"

"Don't you worry 'bout that. You just be there."

I arrived even earlier than the day before. I beat Mama Jennie by only a few minutes. She had gotten a ride from her son, my great-uncle Brother. He spoke to me as I helped her out of the car, and I said hello back.

"It ain't gone take long," she said to him.

"I ain't going nowhere," he replied, and we went inside.

When we got to the classroom, Mama Jennie made me wait outside. The door had a small window in it, but it was too high for me to reach, so I put my ear to the door, hoping to hear something.

I didn't, but Mama Jennie was right. Whatever she had to say didn't take long, and she came out smiling.

"What did you tell her?"

"Nothing for your ears is what. Just a couple a old biddies talking is all."

"And?"

She laughed. "Everythang is all right, chile. She see how important it is to you now."

"Is she mad at me because you came?"

"No, she ain't mad. So stop your worrying, and walk me to the car. Brother out there waiting in the cold."

When she turned and took a couple of steps, I peeked in the door; Mrs. Leggett smiled at me, and I returned it. I felt pretty good inside.

"Now, she say Christmas vacation be starting up next week. That ought to give thangs time to come together. Maybe when school start up again, all your friends be in a better frame of mind."

"Thank you, Mama Jennie."

"Don't mention it."

When we got to the car, she handed me a package off the seat.

"I was gone wait to give you this at Christmas, but I reckon I'll gives it to you now. It ought to help with all that loneliness you was talking about on the phone yesterday."

I kissed her, helped her into the car, and waved at Uncle Brother as they drove off. Then I opened the package. It was a transistor radio.

Once in a blue moon, Mama's image-consciousness actually worked to my benefit. For Christmas, I had asked for my own .22 rifle. Daddy told me when I asked that I would be lucky to get a piece of candy, and he meant it. So I prepared myself for the worst holiday of my life. Usually on Christmas Eve, I could hardly sleep. Once I nodded off, I was up with the chickens and into my presents. I tried to brace for disappointment by telling myself, *This year it's just another day.*

Relief came with a visit from Reverend Damon Lee Walker, who was over one night working on church business with Daddy, who was a church deacon. Mama was making them tea when I walked into the kitchen. The reverend spoke to me.

"Hello, young Evan."

"Hi, Reverend Walker. How are you?"

"I'm fine, son. Just fine. You ready for Christmas?"

I paused for a moment because I didn't really know how to answer. Mama gave me a hard look—a don't-you-dare-say-something-to-embarrass-me look.

"Yes, sir," I said. "I am."

"Good, good. What is ole Santa bringing you?"

Now I was stumped. If I said he was bringing me nothing, I'd certainly embarrass them by making them seem cold. If I said a rifle, it would look as though I was using the reverend to put pressure on them to buy the gun. I looked quickly from Mama to Daddy.

Mama broke into a big smile. "What's the matter, Evan? That ole cat got your tongue. Tell the reverend about the gun."

A little out of kilter, I pushed out a sentence. "A .22 rifle, uh . . ."

"Yeah," Mama said. "Santa is struggling to get a rifle so this young man here can shoot groundhogs and such." She smiled at me.

"Well, that's quite a nice present," the reverend said.

"Yes, sir."

"Well," Mama said, rubbing my head and kissing me on the cheek, "he deserves it."

So I got my gun because Mama couldn't bear to let the reverend go away thinking there was anything wrong in the Walls' home.

After Christmas, I spent the remainder of my holiday shooting rats in the barn, watching football playoffs with Bojack, and listening to my radio. I usually went to sleep with the radio, listening through the little white earphone, enjoying the tunes and memorizing lyrics that I thought gave me some great insight into life.

I didn't see T. Wall or any of the other guys over the holidays. I wanted to, but since Mama Jennie had told me to use this as a cooling-off period, I did. Although I didn't see them, I thought about them a lot.

With some song blaring into one ear, I took time to appraise what was left of my friendships. Had I been truly insensitive? Or were they insensitive? What about being an individual? Was it more important than going with the flow? I guessed so, if the flow only took you to a roadside ditch. I planned to soldier on.

• • •

When school resumed, some things were different. Mrs. Leggett still asked me to clean off the blackboard and to help her with books, but she asked other kids more than me. She didn't call on me as much in class, choosing more often than not to overlook my outstretched

dinner. Shoulders as cold as the January air were turned to me every time I looked like I was about to say something. Children do not forget things easily. I sat quietly in my seat and stared out the window.

Weeks went by, and nothing changed. Even Mrs. Leggett's new mode of operation was taken as a criticism of me. A group of kids walked up to me one day at recess. I was, of course, reading. I didn't look up to see who it was because I was tired of seeing the intense emotion in their eyes.

"You notice she ain't calling on you no more in class?"

"I do."

"Well, what you thank of that, smarty?"

"I try not to think about it."

"She thanks you a asshole, too."

I recognized all three voices, but I was shocked by the last one. Never before had Rosetta Jones spoken in anger to me. I couldn't resist looking up at her.

"You spent all those nights on my porch eating my mama and daddy's food. Now you throw that crap in my face?"

"You ought not to be such a asshole," she said and walked away with the group.

I began to break down.

By the time spring came, isolation had defeated me. I tried hard to make new friends and recapture old ones. I stopped going off into my little world at recess and attempted to participate in their games. But they were having none of it. I figured they were just being tough, basking in the glow of their obvious victory over me. I figured they were making me sweat a little before letting me back into the gang. Once, I even apologized to T. Wall and Beno for this silliness I had cooked up. It hurt me terribly to do that. They just laughed and walked off.

Some days I would find myself kissing up to them, almost willing to go to my knees and beg for some friendship. By the end of those days, I'd always feel nauseous. I rode home on my no-longer perfect bike, completely uncomfortable with myself. It made me sick to know that I had offered to trade my dignity for friendship.

How desperate did I become over that spring? I am embarrassed to think about it. I contemplated all sorts of measures to get back into their good graces. I let my grades fall by flunking a couple of tests. But they didn't take it as a sign of good faith. They took it to mean that they had successfully broken me.

Home was no better. Mark was busy giving me hell because I had failed tests, and I began to hate that he was my brother. That, as well as our competitive nature, caused me to stop flunking. Maybe Mrs. Leggett yelling at me influenced me a little, too.

The days wore and wore on me. Finally Mama Jennie got tired of hearing me complain, and she sat me down to talk. We were on her screened front porch, looking out over her hill and her flowers.

"I always did love the spring, though I can't enjoy much of it 'cause somebody always be sitting beside me complaining about this or that. I can't even hear the little birdies singing."

"I'm sorry," I said.

"It's okay, son. The ole lady just toying with you. Let's have us a discussion and see if we can't get all this stuff offa that chest of yours."

I settled into a big wicker chair, and she rocked in her favorite porch rocker. I took a big swallow of her sweet, sun-brewed iced tea.

"I don't understand, Mama Jennie," I said. "I want to be their friend, but I don't know what to do. I love reading. I love learning. I tried to apologize, but they won't let me off the hook. But I'm not dropping my grades anymore. And I ought not to be blamed for th

"What can they possibly be afraid of? And so what if they are? It ain't their life."

She turned away from me, raised her eyebrows, and took a deep breath. I looked out over the boardwalk and watched an old man crossing it, carrying a bag of groceries from the Colonial Store.

"Once," she said, bringing my attention back to her, "they was these two colored boys living up near what's now Porter's Trailer Park. Use to be nothing but a bunch a ole shacks all lined up in a row that was slaves' houses. Anyhow, not too long ago, these two boys was there, and they liked each other in the way mens and womens suppose to like each other. You know, falling in love and all that. More than just being friends. You know what I'm getting at, son?"

"Yes, ma'am."

"Well, maybe you *is* reading too much these days," she replied, smiling. "So anyways, some of these no-account Negroes 'round here decided they was gone teach them boys a lesson. Went on and beat 'em bad and then took and run 'em right out of town. Some say they used a broomstick on 'em in a certain way. The thang was, them boys won't bothering nobody but theyselves. If you was to find it unnatural, then that be fine for you, but that's all the far you should take it. But some folks can't hold theyselves back with thangs of that nature. Thangs that go against what they feels is the natural grain. And more important than that even is that they afraid that they might see something of theyselves in there somewhere, and they can't handle that, so they got to get it out of they lives."

"Well, I don't see how they figure that trying to educate myself is against the natural grain."

"You see anybody around here trying to do what you doing?"

"Mark is."

"I mean somebody like you. Talking up about it and ain't ruled by what people be thanking about you. Mark is just like his mama. I ain't saying he ain't going no place, 'cause he's a smart child, too, but he ain't sure of himself, or he wouldn't be trying so hard not to offend nobody by going full force after what he want. No, I'm talking about a shining star."

"Well, if I'm that, I'm not the first. There was Billy Ellis."

"And look how folks helped him out."

"Why would they be afraid to see themselves in me or to be like me? I don't think I'm anything special, but I'm not bad, and to want what I want isn't bad. I don't see how it can hurt."

"Maybe some of them want to do what you doing. Some of them probably afraid of trying and falling on they faces and being embarrassed in front of everybody. Some of them look at what you doing and see a big, nasty dark forest staring back at 'em. They might know that they is something good on the other side, but they afraid of what's in them woods they got to go through to get there. Along with a whole bunch a other thangs, folks 'round here remember the Applegates being found dead in that cornfield over yonder near your place. They remember what the Ellis family was and see what it is. It just look like something they can't handle, something that ain't worth stirring up white folks for and maybe getting killed over and all. Some Negroes just feel all that reading and studying and trying to be a big lawyer or something ain't a Negro's place. Like I say, against the natural grain."

I nodded. "Aunt Mary told me that a nigger by any other name is still a nigger."

"Well, there you go, then. She don't believe Negroes oughta be nothing. Talk like that just back up what I say."

"Why do they believe that? When they go around saying stuff like that, don't it just keep other people from trying? H

"Funny how they don't teach you nothing about Negroes in them school books," she said angrily. "Nat was a slave. He led a rebellion. Got a bunch of slaves together and went on the run killing white folk from plantation to plantation. Even the white children. Now, I ain't for no whole lotta killing, but in times of war—and that is what it was—you gotta do what you gotta do. I don't fault Nat none. He was trying to free hisself and his peoples. But don't you know, one time he went to a plantation, and they was a waiting for him and his mens. They started shooting at 'em soon as they rode into the plantation, and don't you know that most of the shooting from the plantation side was from slaves. Negroes killing Negroes for the white man. Helping them crackers keep them in they place, all because they been brainwashed into believing that's where they belonged. Been going on for a dog's age, chile." She shook her head and sighed. "My Lord!"

"I guess I had figured out that we do this to ourselves. I just didn't want to believe it."

"Well, believe it. 'Cause if you don't believe it, you can't fix it for yourself or nobody else."

"Huh! I couldn't fix it for me or anybody else long as they keep treating me like I'm the evil white man."

"I reckon they thank you trying to be white and all."

"I don't see how they figure that."

"Look at the way you be talking and all. Doing that studying and stuff. They thank you trying to act white, so they tries to act white back at you in they own way."

"I don't see how they feel the way they're acting is white."

"Well, lotta folks feel like most of being white just include a person being powerful enough to dump on anybody he wants to. So maybe they trying to look at you through them kinda white eyes, like they big enough to keep you down in your place, so you won't get up'ty. If they can keep you down, then they done showed you they in control of your life. Just like white folks been keeping us down, afraid of what might happen if they takes they heels offa us. Maybe we might show 'em that we smart, too, and start running some of the stuff they been running all these long years."

I didn't want Mama Jennie to see me fighting off tears, so I got up and walked across the porch and stared out the other side. I heard her rocker begin to creak, and I knew she was doing what I had seen her do many times before. She was rocking back and forth, gathering enough momentum to help propel herself to her feet. Then I heard the familiar tapping of her old, thick-heeled, black lace-up shoes against the wooden floor. I felt her behind me and then her hands on my shoulders. I could hold it in no more.

"Go ahead and cry, baby," she said. "Ain't nothing to be ashamed of."

"I'm so tired of being called an Uncle Tom."

"That hurt, don't it?"

"Yes, ma'am. A lot."

"See, the white folks got the word nigger. They use it when they want you to feel like you lower than the nastiest insect alive. They use it 'cause they know it makes you hate yourself when you hear it, and you got to fight against it. But sometimes it takes all the strength you got and wears you down to a nub. When colored folks want to make another colored person feel like they ain't nothing, they use Uncle Tom. It's colored folks' words for nigger. Same meaning, and it ain't no easier to listen to, I swear."

"I hate thinking they know they have me beat."

"Ain't nobody got you beat, child. You too young to be beat in a lifetime type of struggle."

"Become a quiet man. Hold to yourself. I don't just mean in body, I mean your thoughts, too. Keep them inside yourself. Don't beg, whine, or nothing like that in front of nobody. Keep you to you, and don't let nobody know you but so well. Make people wonder what you is all about. Then, they be respecting you. People always respect what they don't know good. It might be out of fear of what they don't know about you, but that be alright too. Just as long as they respects you."

I listened to her good sense. I understood it, but I still didn't want to believe all of it was necessary.

"Why do I have to go through so many changes? All I ever wanted was to try and make something of myself."

"Let me tell you something now, Evan. You ever hear the crabs-in-a-bushel-basket theory?"

"No, ma'am."

"Well, listen up, and listen up good."

I turned around to face her. She kept her hands on my shoulders and looked right into my eyes.

"Negroes," she said, "is sometimes like crabs in a bushel basket. See, if you catch about three-quarters a bushel basket and watch 'em, you see 'em trying to climb to the top to get out."

"That's natural, ain't it?"

"Sho' it is. As natural as you trying to get ahead. But if you was to watch carefully, you be seeing that every time one crab gets just about to the top, another one'll reach his ole claw up there and snatch that first one back down into the crowd. Negroes is sometimes like that; don't want one to get ahead if the rest can't. Just like them crabs. You hear what I'm saying?"

"I understand."

"Good," she said. She pulled a tissue out of her pocket and wiped my eyes. "But don't you accept none of this mess, now. When they grab you by the leg and try to keep you down, you take that loose foot and kick 'em right in the face. You hear me?"

"Yes, ma'am."

"And then don't even look back. That's why you need so many changes. It be the only way for you to be getting where you want to get."

"I hear you," I said. She hugged me tight and kissed me on the top of my head.

"All right then," she said softly. "That's *my* man. That's *my* Evan."

1969

CANAAN, VIRGINIA

G oing to church was a big part of life in Canaan. I can't think of a person from my community that didn't participate in the Sunday ritual, and there were plenty of congregations to accommodate them. It felt like the town had one church for every fifty people. There were the traditional churches like ours, Grace Street Baptist, and several holy-roller churches headed by, as Daddy called them, "jack-leg" preachers who "woke up one day and decided they was called or something or other. Jumped up in the first pulpit they could find and commenced to yelling about nothing. Can't preach a lick, but they right good at passing the plate!"

I enjoyed that Sunday custom, except during football season, when Reverend Walker seemed to sense that my favorite team, the Dallas Cowboys, was playing and would preach well into the first quarter. His sermons, football season or not, were not the reasons I enjoyed being there. He had been preaching practically the same sermon for years. It would start out slowly, usually with the picking of a verse or two upon which to expound. Somewhere in the middle of the sermon, he lost sight of the particular verse and fell into the general "God is good and Satan is bad." The hellfire-and-brimstone portion came at the end, with stomping, hopping around the pulpit and flailing his arms. He would point to the choir director, and the choir would sing a song while he wiped his brow. This routine was broken, though only slightly, on holidays.

On Christmas you could expect the usual sermon and likewise on Easter. But I guess nobody minded much. Just like people seemed comfortable with their lot in Canaan life, they seemed fine with Reverend Walker's monotony.

One thing I did like was the choir. Only when it was in the midst of a robust, body-swaying, hand-clapping, tear-jerking gospel did I truly feel the presence of God. I remember well one special summer night during revival services. A minister from a church in Norfolk was visiting. All through his sermon about Job, you could hear a rumbling in the sky. Just as he finished and the choir was into one of those famous gospels, a thunderstorm hit us in full force. The organist played louder, and the choir sang with a new intensity. I heard an old woman shouting from the balcony, "Sing it to him, children! I do believe he's a-talking back!"

Outside, the thunder roared. Lightning flashed so brightly that the holy scenes on the stained-glass windows seemed to come alive. Christ's eyes flashed a certain comfort to me from a glowing cross. I felt like I was on Calvary, too, looking up at him as the storm turned the day into night.

This choir was swaying and Reverend Walker had joined in. I felt something I couldn't put my finger on, but I knew it was good and it gave me goose bumps. I rocked from side to side, clapping, stomping and sweating. My young voice rang out. Then, in a flash of light and a great boom of thunder, the electricity went out and with it went the organ. Afterward, some people swore that it wasn't the storm, but the organist; she played the organ with such feeling that the rest of the electrical system overloaded. Whichever, the organist didn't miss a beat. In the dark, she slid over to the piano and the gospel continued. The choir couldn't be seen, but you could feel them moving and singing. Before it was all over, the congregation was standing, clapping and singing in the dark. It went on for the

then "Preach on, brother!" then "Tell the truth, Reverend!" right on into the crescendo of "Thank you, Jesus!" and "Hallelujah!" Then, when words could no longer use up those relentless feelings, the true act of "getting happy" usually took place. The ladies got physical, standing at their seats or in the aisles still screaming, but also jumping, throwing their arms about, crying and fainting. Just before the fainting point, a group of younger women would grab the older women and take them back to their seats and fan them. Miss Betsy Williams was famous for "getting happy." You could predict her crescendo moment as accurately as a Reverend Walker sermon.

I also liked the deacons who fell asleep during the sermon. Especially Deacon Tadd Wells, who would sleep every Sunday and wake up suddenly and shout "Amen" at the top of his lungs, usually at the most inappropriate moments.

Eugenia was also fond of resting through sermons. Once, she began to snore loudly. People looked at her with disgust, as if the looks alone would wake her up. But Eugenia was a heavy sleeper. Taliferro would nudge her to wake her up; he once nudged so hard she fell off the pew and onto the floor with a huge thud that stopped Reverend Walker mid-sentence. Everyone in the church became quiet, waiting for a sign from Eugenia indicating that she was all right. Up from the floor of Grace Street Baptist Church came another healthy and obnoxious snore. The children could not restrain their laughter. But even that couldn't compare to the day Eliza Blizzard made rounds.

I was sitting with Bojack that day, up front and close to the pulpit. One row behind Mama and the deacon wives, who were one row behind Daddy and the other deacons. I really didn't want to be there. None of us kids liked to be that close to the deacons and their wives, or Mrs. Walker and other authority figures. Such proximity compelled you to pay attention to the sermon, which meant you ran a greater chance of getting into trouble for falling asleep. Bojack assured me that the risk was well worth it—that I would want to see what was going to happen from as close a position as possible. "Something you be telling your children 'bout one day," he said.

I questioned him, hoping to get him to tell me what was in the offing, but I had no luck.

Things were going on as usual. Deacon Wells had awakened from a deep sleep twice to yell "Amen!" I had to turn all the way around in my seat to keep tabs, but Miss Betsy Williams was well into the rocking back and forth.

When it all finally began, I was fighting sleep. Reverend Walker was preaching that Negro children should be directing themselves toward a good trade, having started the sermon with the verse, "Blessed are the meek, for they shall inherit the earth." Bojack elbowed me in the side, and I looked up to see the most notorious and the smartest black woman in Canaan storming down the middle aisle. Immediately, like everyone else, I tried to figure out why she was heading toward the pulpit with no indication that she would stop short of it. I turned to Bojack.

"What's she gonna do?" I asked.

"Just wait and see," he said.

What she did was simply outrageous. She stepped up onto the pulpit during the sermon and interrupted the minister.

"Excuse me, Reverend Walker. I need to speak to the congregation."

"You can't just be walking up here taking over as you please, woman. Where is your respect for the Lord?'

"In my heart, and when I see him, I'll give it to him."

"Well, I'm his representative

 got to interrupt my sermon, but now you trying to rewrite it, too!"

She put her hand on his chest and shoved him out of her way.

"Step aside, Reverend," she said.

A great roar of confusion overtook the sanctuary. Miss Betsy Williams stood and yelled, "Six six six! It's her! Revelations is coming to pass, and that woman be the anti-Christ!"

Eliza Blizzard raised her hands and asked for quiet. Reverend Walker stood behind her, embarrassed and amazed. It took a few minutes, but people finally calmed down, though many remained standing and angry.

"Now listen up," Miss Blizzard said. "I have some surprising news for you. At the last school-board meeting, Mr. Bojack Johnson and Mr. Ezra Thomas from this church, along with a few from other churches, some people from the federal government and myself, watched the white board members, much to their disgust, make the integration of Canaan schools official. Yes, that means all of your children will be going to school with white children."

Another roar of confusion took place as I turned and faced a truly astonished congregation of popping eyes and dropped chins. I realized how sad it was that many members of this church did not know about the integration plan, that they had to be told by Eliza Blizzard, that black parents hadn't had enough interest in their children's education to keep tabs on who they would be in school with, that Bojack's constant pestering at the sessions as to how much black children might benefit from integration didn't make the adults suspect that it was in the works.

To me, all this was the ultimate example of how the blacks of Canaan had accepted their place and never looked beyond it. I was outraged that they were angry at someone who was trying to help them escape. Maybe they were mad that someone was deciding this for them—although they weren't interested enough to find out about it and go fight it. Or maybe they knew in their hearts that it was good for them, but they were afraid. Either way, I wasn't in the mood to offer sympathy. All my feelings were with Eliza Blizzard, who was trying to restore some order. In the middle of the continuing bewilderment, I asked Bojack what he had to do with it all.

"Nothing but general support!" he yelled, even though he was sitting next to me. "That's one helluva woman. I told her about you. Gonna get you to meet her one of these days."

"Listen to me!" she shouted from the pulpit. "It's over now. We might as well talk about how to deal with it."

But if anyone was willing to listen, I couldn't find them. Some people shouted back at her, and others yelled at each other back and forth across the sanctuary. It reminded me of the roar you would expect in a football stadium when the home team scores the winning touchdown at the last second. Even Bojack got caught up in the fray. He was standing up yelling. "Y'all let the lady talk. Shut the hell up, goddamnit!"

When it was obvious to him that no one was going to listen, he sat back down and shouted in my ear, "Whole lotta no-counts hollering like a bunch of stuck pigs. They don't even know the whole of what they hollering about."

I had never seen anything like it. There was so much going on that I couldn't focus my attention on any one particular thing. I did hear Betsy Williams still calling out to her anti-Christ, and I did see Cozy Pitts with tears in her eyes, standing next to Taliferro, who looked as if he could kill Eliza Blizzard.

From Eliza, I only grasped bits and pieces. Someone trying to shut her up had cut off the PA system. Her voice was strong, th and still carried proudly into the barrage of an her. From her I heard fragments of ruling . . . Integration Equal ed

...ay, she had ...y of Canaan into chaos. ...he session members still in an uproar. ...he kitchen after Kool-Aid and potato chips had ...n distributed. First I overheard Aunt Mary.

"That bitch must be crazy," she said. "It's a wonder somebody ain't knocked her upside the head by now."

"Yeah," Chauncey Mae said. "How in the hell do she get off deciding for us what's best for our children?"

"You ain't been showing nobody that you interested," Bojack said. "Whenever they was looking for parents to come to PTA meetings, y'all always got something to do. Whenever they was looking for a PTA president, y'all always be passing the buck. 'Naw, not me. I'm busy. I ain't got time for no nonsense such as that.' When what you was really saying was you ain't had no time for your own children. Now all of a sudden you act like you give a good goddamn."

"Don't you be lecturing me, boy. I'll sho' nuff put a cap in your black ass. I'm fired up now."

"I ain't having no shooting talk on my porch," Mama said.

"'Scuse me, Treeny," Chauncey Mae said. "This fool done got me all upset now."

"At least when we was on our own, we could do what we wanted," Ethel Brown said. "Now the children got to be right up under 'em. And they gone be stepping down on our children, too."

"I agree with that," Daddy said.

I couldn't see him, so I don't know for sure, but I felt Bojack shaking his head.

"Is y'all blind or what?" he asked. "You ain't doing what you want. You doing what they gives you. What they allows you. Old books and bad equipment to work with. They got you right where they wants right now, and you running around saying how happy you is to be treated inferior. On one hand you complaining about crackers keeping you down, and on the other hand you helping 'em out."

I thought about Mama Jennie and her story of crabs in a bushel basket.

"White folks got everything. If we stays to ourselves and keep doing what we doing, our kids be just as bored with life as we is. We got to get in there and fight with them white folks for a piece of the action."

"And you crazy if you thank they gone give our children something just 'cause they go to school with 'em," Jim Brown said.

"Well, let's hope that if we gets to school with 'em, that it'll be kids learning to like each other. Then when they grows up, they won't be hating each other like we do. Maybe they might even help each other along the way."

"Is you shitting us or what, boy?" Aunt Mary huffed.

"No, I ain't shitting you. I'm trying to look at this hopefully. If I can't look at it that way, then I might as well be dead, 'cause otherwise what hope has we got? What choice do we have?"

"I ain't going to school when it open," Eugenia said. "Taliferro, neither."

"You'll go if your mama say you will," Bojack said.

"And I might not tell 'em they has to," Cozy shot back at him. "Ain't by myself, neither. Lotta folks be feeling this way."

"How long, Lord?" Bojack said. "How long?"

"I hope you don't be living to regret helping that lady do what she done to us," Cozy replied.

Things were never the same again in Canaan. New lines in the battle of the races had been drawn, penned with deep resentment, increased fear, and even deadlier hatred from both sides.

But both sides also took more interest in th
myself.

Before, I did

... town library. It was an old ..., which sat on a little hill next to the post ...nd looked down on Main Street. It stood three stories tall, square with cylindrical towers at the corners that reminded me of farm silos but with big windows. In the front, there were balconies between the towers off the second and third floors. It was painted white, with a burgundy roof, trim, and shutters. A grand covered veranda, decorated with all sorts of spindle-work ornamentation and lacy spandrels, wrapped completely around the house. It seemed to be as wide as the street.

I had passed this place all my life, never really noticing it until I fell in love with reading. Then, I couldn't keep my eyes off it. I craved it, but I didn't go inside. I felt I couldn't. There were unwritten laws in Canaan; it was understood that no black people went into this building even after the *Whites Only* sign came down.

The library was like the tennis courts, the football fields with goal posts, the nicely manicured baseball diamonds, the swimming pools and golf courts throughout Canaan. They were built as "public facilities" and were kept up with public money, but only for a specific public. These places, like the white churches, were sacred to whites.

I haven't been the first at many things, but I was the first black person to break the rule and set foot in the Canaan library. I decided that since we were going to go to school together, we might as well read together. Also, I had run out of books to read with school being closed and my aunt Frances without any more throwaways to send.

The day I did it, I remember walking up the wide, front steps. I looked all around, trying to detect whether or not any white people saw me, and if so, were they coming to stop me? But no one came, and I opened the big mahogany door. The smell of old books and dusty silence greeted me.

It was not what I expected. No walls had been knocked down to make wide-open spaces for rows and rows of bookshelves. The house was still a house, and as I would soon find out, each room had a certain type of book. The living room held autobiographies and biographies. The dining room had the classics, and so on.

I waited in the vestibule by a table that looked to be the desk of the librarian. In a few minutes, a white woman and man came into the hall, looking at a book. When they looked up, they stopped in their tracks. The woman slapped the book closed, tucked it under her arm, and marched toward me, her shoe heels pounding against the floor. I backed up, afraid and thinking that I had made a huge mistake.

She was tall and skinny, maybe fifty. Her shoulder-length hair was streaked with gray. By the time she got to me, her face had gone from pasty white to a deep pink.

"What are you doing in here, nigger boy?" she said.

I didn't get too mad. It wasn't as if I had expected her to call me anything else.

"Are you the librarian?" I asked.

"So what if I am!" she shouted.

"I want to check out a book."

The man joined us. He was young and stocky, wearing a business suit, and his face was red. "Why don't you go somewhere and get some nigger book to read?"

I didn't know exactly what he meant by "nigger book." As far as I knew, black people didn't write the kind of books I was looking for. That is how isolated I was in Canaan.

"We don't have a library."

"Because y'all so ignorant you can't put a bunch of books together in a room somewhere," he said. "Do you realize that you have dirtied this place? It

threw it back onto the table.

"What makes you think I have to let you in here?"

"I don't guess you have to, ma'am. It says it's a public library, though."

The man shook his head. "I guess it was going to happen. The damn federal government give the niggers the right to go to school with white children, and now they want more. Give 'em an inch, by God."

"Can I check out a book?" I asked.

"No!" she yelled. "You can read something here, but I'm not letting you take a book out of here. I know you people. Either you steal and never come back, or you'll come back crying about how you lost it. Thieves and incompetents is what y'all are."

"Yes, ma'am," I said.

What was I to do? I couldn't convince her otherwise. This woman wasn't important enough to argue with and lose my opportunity to read more books.

"Go on in there and find something," she said. "And don't let your black ass out of my sight."

I walked into the parlor directly across from her. I was looking for children's stories, but it was just general fiction. The first book I focused on was *Stoner*, so I picked it up and sat down to read. As I began, I heard the man say, "We gone have to do something about things like this."

There was a heavy threat lodged in that statement, and it made me afraid. I thought of days before my time when people like Reverend Ellis and his wife could be lynched and left hanging from a church steeple. It was the first time that I wondered if Bojack and Eliza Blizzard were indeed wrong.

I went back every day, though, with my dictionary in hand. I read that book and more. I hoped that little by little I would change the woman's mind. That she would see that I was honest and fairly competent. She didn't speak to me much, so I never knew if I made any headway with her. I doubted I ever could. Some minds cannot be changed, I figured. Minds like the ones that built the town's first private school, Canaan Academy.

• • •

Its foundation was laid the week after it was announced that schools would be integrated. By the third week of August, enough prefabricated buildings were in place to get them started. It had a full complement of teachers, many of whom were hired away from the public school system. Many Canaan whites wasted no time in creating ways to keep their children away from blacks, no matter what the federal government said.

Blacks, who had no money to build an academy, had no choice but to attend the public schools. So, throughout the black community, people set out to prepare their children for their upcoming meeting with the whites. Churches held seminars at their summer Bible school sessions, teaching children what to expect from white people. Mostly, they taught them to expect to be treated like dirt without exception, and how to band together for support when said treatment began.

Daddy took Mark to our church's seminar. I heard about it all secondhand because my presence was not welcome.

One Saturday morning, just before noon, I was sitting in the cornfield with a spiral notebook that was my diary. In it, I held conversations with an imaginary friend who I called Martin, after MLK. But I wasn't writing. I was just sitting there looking at the shadows from the stalks bend in elegant ───

listening to the ───

─── sitting. "In my time, I done searched ── peace and quiet in all sorts of fields. Besides, I saw Bullet coming out of the field." He smiled. "What you up to?"

"Nothing," I replied. "How about you?"

"Well, I had to work early this morning. Had to get a truck of meat loaded and out. Fellas all talking about what the churches be teaching the kids in Bible school about what they oughta be looking for when they goes to school in the fall with the white kids. Telling them to walk in groups to and from they classes and to not talk to nobody white unless they spoken to. Telling all the boys 'specially not to talk with no white girls. But I don't know why I'm telling you. I reckon you know all about that."

"No, I don't know." I said.

"Ain't you going to Bible school this summer?" he asked, looking concerned.

"I tried."

"What you mean, tried?"

"I rode there the first day on my bike, and when I was getting off it, I got hit by a rock. And then another rock and then another rock. I looked up, and it was Beno, Muskrat, and Taliferro Pitts. They kept on throwing 'em, and the other kids just stood around and laughed."

"Ain't no grownups out there?"

"Yes. There were some."

"And?"

"They laughed, too," I said, thinking painfully about how I had stared at a group of ladies who had known me since I was born. One lady, Mrs. Wharton, bandaged me and took me home when I fell off my bike one day in town. Now, she and the rest of the ladies returned my stare with one of their own, which said, *"I know you ain't even looking at me for no help."*

"What you do then?" Bojack asked.

"Got back on the bike and came home."

"I'll be damned," he replied. "You gone go back come Monday?"

"I don't think so. I mean, I had to put up with being turned away by my friends at school because I had to go to school. But I don't want to spend my summer going back for more."

"Your boys done completely turned on you, then?"

I nodded. "I don't ever go to T. Wall's tree house no more. I miss them a lot. I miss playing with them the way I did before I was the teacher's pet. I guess I get lonely."

"You got me and Mama Jennie," Bojack said, opening his arms wide.

I didn't want to hurt his feelings, although my silence probably did anyway. I couldn't tell him that while I had them both, they were adults. I wanted someone to run with like before. Someone to fight wars with in the backyard, someone whose marbles I could win in a heated playground match, someone to sulk with when our parents punished us. But that was not to be. I often saw T. Wall from a distance, either at church or passing on the road. Our eyes would meet, but only for a second before he turned away.

"I reckon I understand," Bojack said, looking down and twirling the football.

"So when I'm not at the library or shooting rats in the barn with my .22, I just come out here. I study my textbooks for the fall. I had to beg Mama to get them early, and I only got them after Mark decided to ask for his, too. I do that, and I write in my diary."

"What you say in there?" He pointed to my tablet.

"Mostly about my wish that I could leave Canaan."

"Well, you can't leave yet. We got to finish learning your football. We got to practice more. I got to ~~~

~~~ up, and he returned that with an even bigger smile and a laugh.

"What is it?" I asked.

"I thank I said it was a surprise. Which means I get to deliver when I feel good and ready."

"Well, I hope you get good and ready real soon."

We both laughed, and he reached out and brushed a hand across my head.

• • •

As it happens, I didn't have to wait very long. Three days later, I was riding shotgun in Bojack's truck, smiling grandly with anticipation. I had been worried that Mama and Daddy wouldn't let me go off to some undisclosed destination, especially with Bojack. But Daddy's unexpected eruption of temper made it easy.

During the week, something bad had happened to him at the meatpacking plant. To this day I'm not sure what it was because neither he nor Mama would say. But on the night it happened, he was in such a rage that she made Mark and me stay in our bedroom with the door closed. The three of us ate dinner on the floor between our beds while he ate alone at the kitchen table. She stayed with us as we did our homework and waited until he'd gone to bed before she ventured into the kitchen to clean up. Before she went into their bedroom, she made us promise to be scarce for the next couple of days.

"Y'all got to give your daddy some time and space now," she said.

So when Bojack came to ask permission to take me for a ride, she happily consented. I was conflicted about feeling bad for her and feeling so excited to see what Bojack had in store for me. After a while, I just decided to go with the moment and worry about home when I returned.

Silence took over the cab of the pickup because Bojack got tired of me asking where we were going. He instituted a gag order, which remained in place until we ended up on the outskirts of the other side of town. When his truck finally came to a stop, it did so in front of a little clapboard house in the woods. Swaddled in flowers and shrubbery, it was a well-cared-for home that made me feel good just looking at it. Mama Jennie would have loved it.

"Are you ready, little brother?" Bojack asked as we made our way to the front door.

"I sure am," I responded. "But can you tell me who lives here?"

"Well, why don't you knock and find out for yourself?"

So, I did and was subsequently frozen in place when Eliza Blizzard opened her front door.

"Well, hello, young Evan," she said.

And she knew who I was, which immediately had my head spinning. This was the one and the only Eliza Blizzard standing in the doorway, and I could not find my voice. Positively or negatively and for as long as I could remember, her name and her presence had evoked the image of a larger-than-life figure. Unreachable. Untouchable. Unbeatable. As far as I was concerned, she might as well have been the quarterback for the Cowboys, and as I stepped inside her home, I wondered why she'd want to have anything to do with a lowly boy like me. I thought about asking for her autograph.

But then I got a hold of myself, and I noticed something unexpected. Every time I'd seen her before, she'd been dressed for the carrying out of some serious business. But on this particular day, she was wearing faded jeans and a man's shirt, untucked, with the sleeves rolled up to the elbow. She wore Keds just like many of us kids. After all of this worship or fear from afar, could it be that she was just regular folks?

"Yes, ma'am"—my voice a little stronger.

"Well, alright then. You are welcome into my war room."

She draped her arm around my shoulders and walked me toward two pocket doors closed against each other. I'd never heard the phrase "war room" before and it made me nervous. I looked at Bojack, who was still smiling, so I tried to relax. Eliza slid the doors apart, and we followed her into her dining room. There were a dozen people present, some working at the table and others huddled off to the side in twos or threes. When we walked in, they all began to smile. One man stood and lifted a champagne bottle from a bowl of ice on the table. He popped the cork, poured the champagne into canning glasses, and then passed them around to the others. Eliza dipped another glass into the bowl of ice and filled it with Pepsi. She handed it to me as the adults raised their glasses. I followed suit, and they laughed.

"You just hold yours regular," Bojack said, and I complied, lowering my arm.

Eliza Blizzard began to speak. "We are gathered here today to toast the liberator of knowledge."

I looked around to see which adult she was referring to, and I was stunned when I saw her turn to me.

"Here's to the brave black boy who freed the Canaan library all by himself."

"Hear, hear! Amen to that!" they shouted, and they drank a hearty toast to me.

To me. Evan Walls.

Bojack told me later that I zoned out. That I seemed to be in a trance. I don't know what I looked like from the outside, but inside I was thinking how different this experience was from that life-altering night on my back porch. This was the complete opposite. When Eliza Blizzard's friends shook me back into reality, I wished I could replace that night and those people with this day and these people. When I came to my senses, I spilled some of my Pepsi, but no one seemed to mind. I couldn't remember ever receiving that kind of praise, and it touched me deeply.

Eliza Blizzard sat me down at the table and put my drink in front of me.

"Evan," she asked, "do you know that you have done more to fight institutional racism than almost everybody in this town? You should be so proud of yourself. I am proud of you. We are proud of you. You are like us now. You're an activist. I hope you will always find a way to help your people."

The ladies came around to give me hugs and kisses. The men shook my hand and looked strongly into my eyes.

"Bless you, baby," one lady said.

"You're the Lord's treasure," another said.

"A brave, brave young man," one of the men said.

I guess Bojack could see that I was overwhelmed. He suggested that I take another drink.

They left me alone for a little while to get myself together. Then, Eliza Blizzard laid white poster boards on the table in front of me. She placed some markers on top of them.

"So, I need a sign, Mr. Liberator," she said. "It should say, 'Equal Education is Freedom for All.' Can you do that?"

"Yes, ma'am. I can."

"Well, carry on then, soldier of the cause."

I was never more careful with a project than I was that day. I carefully made the outlines for big letters in black. Then, I colored them in with red. While I worked, I listened as the adults. wh- ' gotten back to business, planned for othe-
school integration and th
the fr

                                                        . .oi a new age in

. uay was done, Bojack didn't have to order quiet in the truck as he drove me home. I was at peace absorbing the fact that somebody had actually shown me respect. And that somebody had been Eliza Blizzard. At that moment, I felt like I could do anything, and I carried that feeling throughout the summer.

SEVEN

The night before that much-dreaded first day of school, I was stuffed from the Labor Day picnic at Mama Jennie's house. I lay on my stomach close to the edge of the bed, my right arm hanging over the side to the floor. I was playing with the weave of the scatter rug, not the least bit sleepy.

It was a warm September night and the windows were open. Through them came sounds of crickets, the comfortably haunting hoots of an owl, and, every once in a while, Bullet's bark from somewhere in the fields.

I was thinking that although it was a larger and better-planned Labor Day celebration than usual, it was pretty much unsuccessful. It was larger because Mama and Daddy and my many aunts and uncles wanted to give us children something extra special to enjoy before we went off to school—integrated school—which in the minds of some was like sending a child to war.

All sorts of games had been set up. Badminton, Twister, a softball and bats, card games, checkers, Monopoly, and a football that was thrown around a bit. The football tempted me, but I knew my cousins wouldn't be thrilled if I tried to join in. Dirty looks and some not-too-subtle body language made clear that nobody wanted to play with me. But in the presence of Mama Jennie, nobody attacked me overtly, so at least I could eat in peace.

The games just like the

Fear of the next day left most of the adults without much of an appetite. Instead of eating, drinking beer, and telling stories on one another, they sat around solemn and frustrated, talking about what they expected to happen to their kids. Some discussed holding their children out of school but decided against it because Mama Jennie told them it would only end up hurting their own.

"The white kids still be getting they education, and you can be damn sure they ain't gone care that you sitting yours at home protesting. At home getting nothing in them brains is exactly where they be wanting our chillen."

After that, some fantasized about having enough money to start a Canaan Academy for blacks, but those kinds of dreams always flew by empty and quick. The kids just sat around, dabbling at the games and eating a lot, mostly out of anxiety. By the time we got home, I was depressed.

Across the bedroom, I heard Mark rustling the covers and guessed he was also suffering through a sleepless night. Finally, I heard the covers being tossed off, and my brother practically jumped off the bed. Since we were barely speaking to each other, I know he was surprised that I called out to him.

"What's the matter?" I asked, sitting up.

He turned toward me but said nothing. Maybe he wanted to but in the end decided that I wasn't trustworthy enough. After a moment, he left the room, and then I heard him knocking on Mama and Daddy's bedroom door.

"What is it?" Daddy said quickly in a sleepless voice.

"Mama, it's me," Mark said, his voice quaking. I knew he was struggling with his emotions because he called to Mama even though Daddy had answered. We always went to Daddy for cuts and scrapes, and to Mama for wounds of the soul.

"Come in, baby," she said.

He opened their door, and I heard him burst into tears. All of a sudden I was terrified. This boy, fifteen years old, who had always seemed a rock, had broken down in the middle of the night.

"I keep thinking about the terrible things white people have done to us," he said through the darkness. "I'm scared."

I heard Mama get out of bed quickly and run to him.

"My baby," I heard her say in the dark, and I knew she was hugging him. Knowing Mama, she was holding him tight against her chest, rocking him gently, and caressing the back of his neck and head.

"I know, baby. Mama knows."

And then I heard her begin to cry. My own tears made their way down my face, dropping onto my bed. Mama began to hum her favorite spiritual in Mark's ear. I added the words in my mind.

There is more peace somewhere
There is more peace somewhere
I'm gonna keep on til I find it
There is more peace somewhere

I imagined Daddy on their bed. He hadn't uttered a sound. I figured that maybe a tear of anger had swollen. Anger at the things Mark was crying about, and surely anger at the fact that he could do nothing to protect his son from the white man and white kids. I remembered the shame of our Boy Scouts leaders the day the white scouts flaunted their Confederate flags.

How does it feel to be him? I wondered. I imagined there was no frustration greater than that of a black father helpless to fight for his children. No wonder so many black men became like Arthur D...
beat their wives, left their families...
alcoho...

...ears of integration.

• • •

I tried to suppress my fears that summer, but as school neared, storm clouds of anxiety settled over me. Just a couple of days before the Labor Day picnic, I visited Mama Jennie to vent the fear in my heart. She was preparing a tipsy cake while I watched from the kitchen table. A homemade sponge cake rested on a sheet of waxed paper next to her stirring bowl filled with a custard made of milk and egg. She was adding to it sherry wine, whipped cream, and almonds.

"Everybody is real nervous about school," I said. "Folks at the session don't seem to talk about anything else. Mama and Daddy act like they're sending us to Vietnam or something."

"Different kind of war. I catch the meaning," she said, nodding as she poured the custard into a larger pan.

I thought about that as she lowered the sponge cake into the custard and put a cloth over the whole thing. Then she sat down beside me and wiped a napkin across her sweaty forehead.

"I reckon folks got reason to be afraid," she said.

"Are you afraid? Of white people, I mean?"

Her face sagged; her eyes became sad and unfocused. It was like watching the brightest sun you could imagine dimmed by sinister clouds. She began to perspire again.

"Hand me another napkin, baby," she said.

As she gently patted it over her face, I felt bad. I had put her in an awkward position. No black person liked to admit that they were afraid of white people, but I had to know if she was. I felt her answer would help me understand the proper level of concern needed to deal with the upcoming school situation.

"Yes," she finally said, nodding, staring off into her past, gathering the evidence that supported her fear. "Yeah, if I'm gone be honest with you, I have to say that I am."

I guess I expected that answer, but at the same time I was surprised to hear it. I never thought she was afraid of anything.

"Why should you be afraid?" I asked. "Everybody says white people in town respect you more than any other black person."

"Huh," she replied with a disbelieving laugh. "If they respects Jennie Lowe, it's 'cause she old and set in her ways. They figures they ain't got nothing to worry about from her."

She became indignant at that thought and tapped her hands angrily against each other in her lap.

"Why is I afraid? I tell you why." She pointed out the window. "'Cause they controls everything. With the snap of they fingers"— and she snapped hers—"they can change who you is and who you gone be for the rest of your life."

"Is it really that easy for them?"

Of course, I knew it was, but I guess I hoped I'd be surprised by her answer.

"Who you thank you talking to?" she asked.

I didn't understand where she was going. I thought I had upset her even more.

"You mean, you?" I asked, pointing to her.

"Yeah, me."

"Mama Jennie. My great-grandmother."

"Well, you got it half right anyhow. The right part being the last part."

"I don't understand."

"My name is Cora. Cora Lowe. It ain't Jennie."

My eyes widened.

"I guess you feel like you don't know who you been talking to all these years. Like you b———

. . . . amount to much. Colored folks began to take pride in the little thangs that come with they freedom. Thangs like naming they own children. So that's why my mama ain't wait for the missus to name me. She called me Cora. But my papa, he told me that the missus come down to see the new baby, me, that is, and they told her my name. But she say, 'I'll call her Jennie. Don't y'all think that's a good name for a nigra girl?' *Jennie*, by the way, was a regular name they give to mules back then. What that tell you?

"Papa say ain't nothing they could do but nod they heads, and I been who I ain't really been from that point on. They ain't much different about the names. One could be a slave name as well as the other, but I reckon it say something 'bout control when it comes down to people telling you who you is and what you all 'bout, naming your children and stuff. That old woman, she come down to the house and branded me as sure as I was a damn cow or something. Umph."

"Why don't you go back to 'Cora,' then? Be who you were supposed to be?"

"The damage already done, chile. Inside and out. Ain't worth thanking 'bout."

I handed her another napkin, and she dabbed the corners of her eyes.

"Do you think any white people are a little afraid of what's happening?"

"They built that academy, didn't they? And the ones who can't afford to go there probably afraid they children gone get beat up. That they happy little nigras gone turn out to be not so happy, and the colored children gone have too many chances to get some revenge. They probably afraid they little white girls gone be falling for the colored boys, and that ain't nothing new. I could tell you some stories, and maybe I will someday. And most of all, I reckon they afraid to tackle that old myth they been talking up lo these many centuries."

"You mean that blacks aren't born as smart as white folks?"

"That be the one. I reckon more than a few of 'em is thanking, what if it ain't true? What if the niggers got brains after all?" She chuckled a little. "You know what they says. Hard to keep 'em down on the farm then."

"I think some of us are afraid of that myth, too."

"Naturally. They been brainwashed. I know plenty of colored folks what believe that. Yeah, chile. Lots of them. They thank that we ain't up to snuff in the book department just like the white folks be thanking. They probably afraid that going up against the white chillen will prove that they is dumb. They wants to believe that they is as smart as any white folks, but you know in they hearts they ain't completely sure. Some would rather stay home and not find out for sure."

"Do you think it's true?"

"No, baby. Course not. They ain't born with no more sense in they heads than us. I know that. I done some mammy work in my day. Remember Dr. King and all them other Negro men and women what changed this entire country? Don't you thank they outsmarted a few of these crackers along the way?"

"I guess so."

"Sure they did . . . You want some iced tea?"

"Yes, ma'am."

"It's out there on the porch, brewing in the sun."

She continued as she pulled glasses from the cupboard, sweetened the tea, added ice from the refrigerator and poured.

"It ain't what you born with, but what you be exposed to," she said, handing me a glass.

"That's what I thought—I mean, about being exposed. But I heard Miss Chauncey M

, ...t gonna study anything they try to teach them."

"Well, that's just plain stupid. What they gone stop studying for? What do they thank they been studying before anyway? It was all from books written by white folks about white folks. We just got to teach our children to read between the lines." She shook her head in disgust. "When folks get carried away about something, the first thang they do is stop thanking right."

"Why do you think they'd cut off their noses to spite their faces?"

"I reckon it goes back to what I said 'bout the myth. And I guess it's 'cause they hates the white people so much, they don't want to have nothing to do with 'em. It's just like I said, though. You can't escape 'em even if you don't go to school or church with 'em. Just being alive puts you in touch with 'em. You paying 'em when you pay your bills, they build your house for you if you can afford one, you gots to shop at they stores, you drive the cars they be building. Just ain't no way to get 'round it. Might as well let some of that evilness out and go on and deal with the devil as he is."

"I think it's right and all, the integration. But I'm still afraid."

"Rightly so, I guess."

"What can you tell me about white people? You know, about what to watch out for. What do you know about 'em?"

"Chile, I don't know nothing 'bout 'em really. I been around 'em a lot, but all I know is how to gets around 'em, to sweet-talk 'em up and get what I wants out of 'em. Most colored folks know that. I can tell right away how much rebellishness each one of 'em might have in 'em, and how to deal with that accordingly. But I don't know nothing 'bout who they really is. The only thang you can predict 'bout 'em is that they probably ain't gone be treating you like family," she said, chuckling.

I told her how weak I felt going in, like the underdog in a prizefight. I told her how I kept reaching for something stable to hold onto to give me some strength, but that I couldn't find it. I told her how I had read my textbooks from cover to cover, but how I still didn't feel confident. I explained that I kept looking over my shoulder for something, some precedent on which to base my choice of how to enter this battle.

"I know what you mean, son," she said. "I know exactly what you looking for, but we all got a big hole in our past. A big emptiness. Like I said, I just missed them bullwhip days, but Lord, Lord I can hear the echoes of leather cracking against dark backs. Umph!" she said, unconsciously wrapping her arms around herself. "Chile, I can feel it in my *bones*. I always could. It's in your bones, too. I thank you feeling it a little now, too.

"You hear it when you need to feel some pride and you look back for something to draw on like the white folks do. They be saying thangs like, 'I'm descended from George Washington' or one of them rebel soldiers which I ain't gone dirty up my mouth with they names. 'My great-grandfather was a great general in the Civil War; he signed the Constitution.' That gives 'em pride to stand on. When colored folks looks back, all they sees is a string of slaves in chains. *Chattel.* All of a sudden, they pride is gone, chile. Just like water through your fingers. You say, why it got to be this way? And you start to hear them bullwhips a-cracking."

I thought of Daddy getting whipped by those two white men.

"What if they beat up on me?" I asked.

"They just do."

"Can't anybody do anything about it?"

"Like what? And who? Shoot, all I can say is that I'll be there for you when your wounds need tending to, whether it be wounds of the body or the heart.

[illegible — text obscured] ...and thoughts. All the dignity we got is in our own community. But that ain't no good. A thang like that is useless unless it's respected through all communities. You can't have dignity in just a little section of society without having it in the whole shebang. And we lose a little bit of that every time we got to go up against some cracker. When that happens you realize that it just ain't complete.

"Just the other day, I was with yo' mama shopping in the grocery store. Ole man Thompson was in there with his little great-granddaughter. I don't reckon she no more than seven, and she was drinking some juice. She took one look at yo' mama and throwed the juice right on your mama's dress. Then she say, 'Nigger bitch.' Folks turning all 'round looking at us and stuff. Ole man Thompson just smiled like she just finished a piano recital or something. Now, it really hurts when a child does it to you.

"You always want to knock somebody upside the head when they calls you names and thangs, but then you feels guilty for thanking about how you wants to beat that child to death. You look at something so innocent, and this vile mess comes out. It stays with you. You know that this child is just a seed of hate that's gone sprout more branches of hatred while she grows. With a whole another generation of that staring you in the face, how you figure you can hold on to some kind of dig-ni-ty?"

The story made me feel bad for Mama, and for my future.

"I keep hoping that the racists are all old and dying out. That only a few might be left."

"Don't be holding your breath on that one," she said. "Racists is like roaches. Where they is one, they is a thousand."

"Well, that wasn't what I needed to hear," I replied. "I have a whole life to live next to these people."

"Like many peoples before you, with you, and after you."

"While we're talking about it, you know I read somewhere that if there is one of those nuclear explosions, one of the few things left living will be roaches. Now, you say racists will be around, too."

She laughed. "That is bad, ain't it? Roaches ain't deserving of such company."

We both laughed.

"I don't know," I said, coming down from the laughter. "I guess I just wish I could understand them a little bit. I'd feel better going in."

"Wish I could help you, but I don't understand 'em, neither. I just know the range of white folks, from the paddy rollers to the Klan, and to them what helped with the civil rights. A Negro needs to be able to tell the difference so they'll know who to go to in the times of strife. Sometimes seem like your life depends on knowing which type of white folks is which. But as far as knowing what it's really like to be white, how they see the world, hell, don't even waste your time. We can't do that no more than a man can know what it is to birth a baby."

"It's too much," I said, overwhelmed by it all. "Maybe people were right. Maybe Eliza Blizzard was wrong. Why go into it just to have to deal with more grief? I wonder if an education is any good to us anyway."

"Look at it this way. Ain't no need not to try. You ain't got nothing to lose. If you try hard and you still don't get nowhere, well, it ain't no skin offa yo' back. You still be where you at. Just a little bit smarter.

"Education ain't all just about what's in them books," she continued. "Going to school with them white chillen will help you get to know 'em better. And if it's gone be that thangs ain't gone get no better, at least you know something 'bout the enemy you didn't know the day before, and that can't be bad. It helps to know a little bit about the devil in your life. H

...get it out of his head that you still on this *somebody* kick. When he look at you, he see a boy that ain't got no respect for his daddy. The white man don't respect him, and he thank his son don't either. But the deal is that he need to open his mind and put his children before his pride. Your mama, she just afraid of things coming apart. I done talked to her two times already. Calmed her down. Last time I told her that she better be looking out for you. If she don't, I'm gone have to come out to that farmhouse and throw down!"

We both had a long laugh, and I leaned over and gave her a big hug.

• • •

That night before school began, Mama held Mark until his tears had dried up. When he finally came to bed, he fell right to sleep.

The next day, Mark and I stood side by side. I was going into sixth grade and he into tenth. We watched the big yellow school bus come down the road toward us. He looked down at me, and neither of us spoke. No need. We knew what the deal was—that no matter what had gone before, we were family. We were up against the greatest evil in our lives, and we had to stick together.

The bus stopped, and thankfully the driver was black.

"Come on in, children," she said, attempting a comforting smile. But I could tell that comfortable was the last thing she was feeling or could help others to feel. I knew this woman, Mrs. Cotton, through my parents. I knew the cadence of her speech, the way she normally held her head, the way her smile normally looked. It was all out of whack. She was working so hard at her saying her words the way white people talk. I guess she had been doing it all morning, trying not to let the white parents or children think badly of her. I understood.

I walked onto the bus behind Mark. Although I had expected them, the white faces confused and disoriented me. Mark turned and whispered, "I feel it, too."

I nodded and moved down the aisle. Practically all the seats were taken. Mark took a seat next to two black kids. The only empty seat left was one next to a young white boy. I looked at the seat and at him and waited for him to slide over. He just stared back at me like he was in shock. Mark pulled me to him and squeezed me into the seat beside him.

"You know what?" I asked.

"What?"

"I think *he* was afraid of *me*."

"I know," Mark said. "Bojack said that white people are as scared of us as we are of them when it's one on one. They think all black people carry knives."

• • •

I was placed into what used to be the white middle school. For me it was like going into the Canaan library again for the first time. Most of the white teachers wouldn't look at us and considered a request for help to be loathsome. The black teachers seemed much like the black students. They walked softly, their eyes shifting from side to side, their backs raised in preparation for battle like a few cats strolling through a den of German shepherds.

I wondered about Eliza Blizzard, thinking that this day must be toughest on her. She had helped set it up, and many blacks and whites hated her. They were probably happy to see that she had been demoted during the merger of schools. She went from being principal to a regular teacher at the high school. But soon we would realize that she had taken this in stride and already moved ~~ ~ greater goals.

It took me ~~~

~~~ ~nd they had so

~~~~

~ou just been used to they leftovers," Bojack replied.

"I guess so."

"Did it scare you? I mean, everythang being so nice and in good shape?"

"It made me more mad than scared."

"Tell me about it."

"Yeah, I was mad that I didn't have all that stuff before. And I was scared, too. Sometimes, it was sorta like being in a doctor's office. Everything was shiny and cold, you know?"

"Oh, I know. But I reckon that was more the peoples than the place."

"You reckon right. How'd you know that?"

"If I had a education, I reckon I'd call it a educated guess."

He was right; things had been particularly cold. I finally arrived at my homeroom, feeling rushed and late, but it turned out that most of the class was having the same difficulty, and I wasn't the last to turn up.

It was noisy when I entered, but as soon as I passed through the door, the room fell silent. I was the first black to arrive. Glancing into a sea of peach-colored faces, I made my way through a maze of red, brown, black, and blond hair. I took a seat in the middle after a quick survey. There was something unsettling about the front.

Maybe it was just that I'd be too close to the white teacher. There was something demeaning about sitting in the back, as if it was expected. After a few minutes of staring, the painful silence lifted. I guess they figured by then that I didn't have a knife. A boy across from me leaned over the left shoulder of the boy in front of him.

"Think we ought to slide over some?" he asked. "If we stay this close, our hair might kink up."

A group of them laughed. The teacher looked up, but she didn't seem ready to engage. She was white, old and wrinkly. Her hair sat up on her head in a thimble shape that I imagined you couldn't have bowled over with a rock. I figured her ideals must be equal to her age. I guessed that she probably hated blacks, and from that I deduced that I'd never be able to keep my grades up in her class.

I sat there stewing in my juices as the jokes continued. Something here or there about my lips, my nose, a few things about my mother who screwed dogs and pigs, some discussion of my body odor and how I probably couldn't count to ten. Of course, I knew this kind of thing was coming. So I was extremely happy to see Rosetta Jones, Flak, T. Wall and a few other black kids enter. They glanced at me and sat on the other side of the room. We were allies in skin tone only. Couldn't they, like Mark, overlook all that other stuff just this once? How long were they going to carry on with this nonsense?

"Good morning, class," the teacher said. "I'm Mrs. Jones."

She stood and walked in front of her desk. Mrs. Jones tried her best to calm the nervous class. She delivered a warm monologue, saying that everyone was aware of the new situation and that all should try to make the best of it; that this was how it was going to be from now on. A couple of the white kids groaned, and she ignored them.

She began to call roll for the seventeen whites and seven blacks. She had to go through it twice before she got everyone to answer, or to answer loud enough for her to hear. Mrs. Jones gave a short orientation for those of us not used to the school. Then she moved right into the first lesson, which was history.

She familiarized everyone with the particular item to be discussed and then posed a question. She looked at us waiting for answers, but none came. Black kids stared at the white kids, and the white kids stared back. Who would t~l~ ~ ~

~~~ ~~~ seemed genuinely surprised. I was amazed at how dumb white people thought we must be.

She asked a few more questions, and I answered them all, determined to let her know that I was as smart as the smart-assed white kids next to me. She was simply astonished.

I felt like a god, but out of the corner of my eye, I saw the stares. Much colder even than when I had first walked into the room. Stares of *uppity nigger* and stares of *Uncle Tom*. I was in a crossfire of hate.

When class was over, I was met outside the door by T. Wall and Rosetta.

"You oughta be goddamned ashamed of yourself," T. Wall said.

"For what?" I asked.

Rosetta spoke up. "You gone kiss that white lady's ass, too, so you can be her pet, too, ain't you? Get out my face, Uncle Tom!"

They both stormed off down the hall, and I stood by the door, trying to be tough, trying to show them that I wasn't bothered in the least, but I was, and I am sure they knew it. *As if things weren't bad enough*, I thought. In one direction I'd be the nigger, and in another, I'd be the pet, the traitor, the Tom. I guessed it wasn't so safe in the middle, after all.

When I got home, a message had been left for me. All the spokes on my bike rims had been broken out, the frame had been bent by a sledgehammer, the fenders had been ripped off and the tires cut up.

There it was. My beautiful bike, finally completely done in. I ran in to tell Mama, but she was ready for me. News did travel fast in Canaan.

For the next fifteen minutes, I heard about how I had disgraced the family by kissing up to the white lady and putting down the other black children. Did I enjoy making Daddy crazy? Did I enjoy turning this family upside down?

I couldn't get a word in, so she never knew that I figured I had been doing just the opposite.

When she finished being angry and pleading with me at the same time, I walked outside to eyeball my bike. I felt heavy-hearted. To this day, I don't know who destroyed it, but my money was on T. Wall. I stood there thinking, *But we were the best of friends.*

S ummer turned to fall, the leaves changed, the nights chilled. My Friday nights were dominated by high school football, my Sunday afternoons by the NFL. Outside of class, my school days were spent searching for private places of refuge from my ever-resentful classmates. During classes, when I wasn't answering a question, I kept my eyes on my desk or on Mrs. Jones. At home, I searched for a warm haven from the cold silence of my family. I found it in the woods across from our house. One day I happened upon a small area that reminded me of my circle in the cornfield. A haven of tall, skinny, pines. I liked to lie on the ground in the middle of them and stare upward. Especially, at night.

But not everyone was hiding out, concerned about making waves as they pursued their mission. Eliza Blizzard continued to boldly move forward.

Not long after school started, she began a crusade against the four grocery stores and the two meatpacking plants. She put leaflets in the mailboxes of as many black people as she could, asking them questions like, "How many black people work at the checkout counters in your favorite grocery store? For that matter, how many black people have a good job in your favorite grocery store? Of the thousands of black folk that come and go in the packing plants, how many have been supervisors? The answer to all of the above questions has to be a big ZERO. The next question is, black people of Canaan, what do we do about it?"

The resounding reply from black Canaan was "Nothing." As usual, I eavesdropped on that week's porch session.

"You can tell that fool won't born and bred in Canaan," Chauncey Mae said as she sucked on her toothpick.

"Yeah," Ethel Brown said. "She won't 'round when they was hanging our behinds from trees for all kinda trivial-assed thangs."

"She don't remember what happened to Nate and Cora," Aunt Mary said.

I thought about Reverend and Mrs. Ellis hanging from the church steeple.

"She don't know these crazy crackers like we do," Jim Brown said.

"It ain't enough," Mama said, "that she done turned the whole town upside down with her craziness with the schools."

"That's a fact," Daddy said.

Everyone became quiet, because they all knew that the school business was touchy with Mama and Daddy. One son was a traitor who spent time kissing up to white teachers and trying to embarrass other black children with how much of the white folk's nonsense he knew. The other wasn't a Tom, but he was still too smart for his own good. Mama and Daddy played the part of injured parents so the others would take pity on them.

Eliza Blizzard got little support from people. What help she did get came from the same few who had helped her with the integration of the school system. Even still, Eliza would not be deterred. She figured out how to get the people on her side. She set her sights on Ray Coon, who was the most hated white man in town. Ray owned

Canaan's largest gas station. It was called Ray Coon's Gas & Oil, and it had six pumps, sold maps, cigarettes, sodas, chips, and other snacks, had two hydraulic lifts and three full-time mechanics.

He was vilified because when it ca...

offen...

... what the fool's problem is. It's a good bit of justice, though, that a white man as hateful as that be named *Coon.* Come to thank of it," she said, laughing, "maybe that be the crux of his problem."

Eliza Blizzard began to frequent Ray Coon's gas station, which was something of a struggle for her. She usually went elsewhere because, as Bojack told me, "She can't stand being called 'nigger gal' every time she go to get some gas. Folks who been born and raised up around that cracker are used to it."

But Eliza Blizzard stuck it out. Every time she got some gas and he called her "nigger gal," she called him "Ray" instead of "Mr. Coon." Then her few supporters started doing the same thing. He was outraged that blacks presumed to call him by his first name— so incredibly outraged that he eventually changed the name of his station to Massa Coon's Gas and Oil, his thinking being that blacks who dared to call him by his first name would have to call him Massa. People say he had quite a chuckle thinking about it. When Eliza Blizzard drove up on the day he put up his new sign, he strolled out of the building with a huge smile.

"What you want, nigger gal?" he asked. Then he tossed back his head and winked at a couple of his mechanics who had come out to witness the moment. They prepared to yuk it up when this uppity black woman called him "Massa."

"Fill it up, Coon," she said.

He was stunned. "You know what my new name is, nigger gal!" he shouted.

"Yes, but Coon is more official. Don't you think?"

Massa Coon went into a wild rage and refused to sell her gas. Eliza Blizzard got out of her car and shoved him aside as she had done with Reverend Walker the day she announced the integration of schools. Then she cussed him up and down as she filled her own tank. This wouldn't have been so bad except that the gas station was on one corner of the only intersection with a traffic light, which meant it was the most traveled intersection in town.

Black people who were passing on the street or sitting in their cars waited for Massa Coon or one of his boys to strike her down. Never before had they seen white people stand for anything like that. But nobody did anything to her. It was then that Canaan blacks came to believe that white people were afraid of Eliza Blizzard because she had almost single-handedly changed the school situation, which must have meant she had some powerful connections with the federal government. Massa Coon didn't want to be the first to attack her in front of a crowd and then suffer humiliating—even criminal—repercussions.

Later that night, Coon suffered a near-fatal heart attack. Within a few months he sold the station, and after that blacks came and went with relative ease.

The struggle continued. Newly energized blacks boycotted the local grocery stores and in the end forced the owners to hire black stock and checkout people. After that, they boycotted all food produced by the packing plants and forced them to hire black supervisors. Four were picked, and Daddy was one of them. He bought a new car and new clothes for Mama, who now wouldn't be seen outside the house unless she was dressed "sharp as a tack."

"Lord God, thank you so much," Mama prayed at the dinner table every night. "Thank you for the many blessings you have bestowed upon us. Thangs is really turning around for black folk in this town. Once again you have kept the Walls family out in front."

Things even got better for Bojack. In the midst of all the excitement, he and Aunt Mary stole away f

back remarri~

~~~u some time

....~, anu the way I was acting was one of them problems."

"Well, you haven't changed much that I can see."

"Nope. But now she understands why I had to play nigger, so to speak. You know, shuffle, give up them yes'ums, look at the ground, look weak and dumb. Just to get through the day with the white folks. Thangs was hard. I had to get by. And when she went off by herself, she found out she had to do the same thang. I thank that restored what little manhood I got in her eyes."

"You think it will last?"

"I believe so. She done learned some thangs, and I done learned some. I reckon both of us be better off now."

"I hope you're right. If you're happy, I'm happy for you."

"Thanks, little man. Thanks a lot."

It got on my nerves that everybody seemed to be doing well besides me. Only Mark was having similar problems, but he was working his way out. Black kids gave him grief for being such a bookworm, and he was afraid that this would lead to him being called an Uncle Tom, too. He began to spend more and more of his study time in front of the new color television that Daddy bought.

I resented Mama's prayers of thanks every night at the dinner table. Every night before Mark came into our room, I knelt by my bed, my stomach on fire, and prayed for God to lift the burden that He must have known was too punishing for a boy my age. But nothing improved, and I began to think that maybe white people were right. That God wanted us to be a subservient race, and that he was punishing me for trying to overcome the odds. I figured he, as well as my old friends and new foes, had decided it was open season on Evan Walls. I became about as popular as a fish hook dropped in the Chesapeake Bay without bait.

• • •

One Sunday afternoon, I was riding an old bike that Bojack had fixed up for me. I had my transistor radio in my shirt pocket, and I was listening to Joe Tex singing about a woman with skinny legs. I felt what I thought was a bee sting on my leg and then one on my back. I stopped the bike and looked around. Coming out of a clump of bushes were the barrels of BB rifles. The boys, T. Wall, Flak, Beno, and Muskrat, had opened fire on me. I was getting hit all over, and some spots started to bleed. I wanted to ride away, but I had placed my hands over my eyes to protect them, and I was afraid to take them away to put them on the handlebars. So I sat it out, although it was incredibly painful. BB rifles hold a lot of ammo. When a couple of them stopped to reload, I uncovered my eyes and rode away, covered with welts.

Another day, I was walking home from Bojack's after discussing how my Dallas Cowboys beat the Washington Redskins, a team I hated because people said that they were one of the last pro teams to allow blacks to play. As I crossed Bojack and Aunt Mary's long front yard, I heard a familiar bark. I turned and saw T. Wall and Beno at the edge of the woods bordering Bojack's property. In front of them, lumbering toward me, was the big Great Dane, 5-10. Quickly, I thought of all the times I had stood out of range of this dog and not feared him at all because of the chain he was tied to. I thought of all the times he almost choked himself to death trying to get to me. Well, it had all come home to roost. His bark seemed twenty times more vicious, and he looked fifty times stronger. Before I could move, I began to cry, because I knew I'd had it. This dog would tear me apart.

I turned and ran toward Bojack's, chants of "Sick 'em, dog" and "Get him, 5-10" coming from the ~~~

~~~ged to Bojack, who ~~~ from his house at full speed. Beer sloshed out of a bottle he didn't think to drop, and he was growling like Dick Butkus, his favorite linebacker. He got to 5-10 before the beast reached me.

Bojack threw his bottle at the dog and kicked 5-10 to the ground. When the dog got up to attack him, I saw something extraordinary. Bojack fought the dog like he would a man. He grabbed it by its collar with his left hand and began to punch the dog's head with his right. It was furious and fast, and when it was over, Bojack stood watching 5-10, squealing, run flat out back toward T. Wall and Beno. The dog passed right by them on his way home.

"Yeah, that's right!" Bojack yelled at them. "Carry your butts on home and tell yo' daddies all 'bout it. And tell 'em if they wants to get ugly, I got something for they asses, too!"

Bojack picked up his bottle and turned to look at me. Once again, I wished I could see behind those reflectors. I wanted to see his eyes. He raised the bottle and threw it at a big rock in the ditch by the road. The bottle shattered with a *pop*. He took a deep breath. Breaking the bottle brought him relief from the quickly accumulated stress. I took note.

"You go on home now," he said softly.

I watched Bojack walk away, and then I searched for unbroken bottles in the ditch. I found a ten-or-so-pound rock and took it and the bottles to my circle in the woods. I set the rock between two of the trees and took the first bottle in my hand. *This is T. Wall*, I thought. And I threw T. Wall into the rock and he shattered. Then I threw Beno and Flak. Then I threw Mama and Daddy, and I started to cry. It felt so good. The constant burning in my stomach that had become so much a part of me eased up a bit. There was a release, and I started to laugh while I cried, because I had found something to take off some of the edge, and that made me happy.

For the next week or so, I was as meek as a country mouse. As often as I could, I headed to my special place in the woods. Inside the house, I floated through on my tiptoes, listening for footsteps, quietly checking around corners and running back to my room if I noticed someone coming my way. It was sort of like those special nights of old, only without the thunderstorms, flashlights, and the security of my grip on Daddy's pant leg. Sometimes I had to become part of the family, or as much a part as I could be. For instance, I had to sit at the dinner table and not be talked to. Other times, when we were all getting ready in the morning, I passed my family in the hallway without being acknowledged. I had to ask my mother for my clean shirts, which she all but threw at me. I had to ask my father for milk money, which he gave to me while saying something beneath his breath like, "Useless as tits on a boar hog."

I would just go back to the woods and study my schoolwork, read library books, listen to music, and stare at the sky. There was nowhere in my world more comfortable for me.

• • •

Two truly interesting and different events took place during this time, the first of which was the transformation of my brother. It had been going on for a while, but I hadn't noticed it because I was so busy fighting the world.

The first clue came on report-card day. I walked into the house behind Mark, who was holding his card out to Mama. She was cooking, so she stopped, wiped her hands on her apron, sat with a smile, and took his card. I could tell Mark was nervous, but I didn't know why because Mama read the card and then gave him a big bear hug.

"That's real good, baby," she said. "Real good."

Mark took his card back and walked to the bedroom. I gave Mama my card. She frowned, and that really got to me because I had brought home straight As. She slapped it shut and handed it back to me.

"Getting As," she said as she stood to resume cooking, "don't mean much if you got to kiss a white lady's feet to get 'em."

"I didn't," I replied. "I earned them fair and square."

Mama turned on me. She held up her wooden spoon. "Don't you be getting on my nerves this day, boy. I ain't got time for none of your nonsense! Hear me?"

"Yes, ma'am."

"Then get out my face."

"Yes, ma'am."

I passed Mark on my way into our bedroom. When I heard the television come on in the den, I pulled out his report card. He'd gotten three Bs and two Cs. That was not like Mark. Even though we never talked about it, we had an informal yet intense competition as to who would fall off the straight-A pedestal first. It made me mad that Mama would hug him for that, that she would be happy he had fallen, but I guess it played into her image of how things should be. Now her friends would feel less intimidated by us, and they would feel that they had at least gotten one of the Walls boys back on the right track. Mark obviously wanted it that way because he was playing the correct political game. One that would hopefully place him back into the graces of the black community.

Even so, Mark was really ~~feeling~~

~~...~~ped—an exaggerated ...method of walking. You made a quick step with your left leg, then bent the knee (a quick dip), then dragged your right foot past the left and repeated. It also required a specific swing of the arms.

Anyway, I heard shuffling in my parent's room one night while they were out. When I peeked through the cracked door, I saw Mark in front of the full-length mirror, trying desperately to master pimping. He looked awkward and tortured, like a person trying to walk for the first time after a painful physical-therapy session. He was in that room for hours. After that, I saw him trying to pimp around other kids his age. He also started using a lot of profanity. Not that he didn't say "shit" once in a while, but now every other word was "fuck" and "cocksucker." It seemed like I just looked up one day and he had gone south on me and the declaration that he'd made to me on my infamous night with the session.

I, on the other hand, had no delusions of being cool. I never tried to pimp. I never could "hang," never could "do the push and pull" or "the bump" quite right. I never found the nerve to "smoke some shit, man," never was called "bro" by any black male my age, never was "down," and never could say "muthafucka" with the accent in the right place.

All of these shortcomings left me isolated. At the point of Mark's transformation, the loneliness had begun to get to me, and I began to doubt myself again. So, I found myself pouting on Mama Jennie's porch. She had been cooking a ham, and I could smell it on her apron as she sat beside me. She held my hand.

"It's not working," I said.

"What ain't working?"

"You know what we talked about? Keeping to myself and not begging for their friendship? I keep studying and doing things the way you and Bojack say I should, but I don't get anybody's respect. Not even Mama and Daddy's. I just keep getting more and more ignored. They don't accept me any more than before. I still watch the kids play football, and dodgeball, and baseball. I just sit against the wall with a book. I'm still making good grades, as good as any white kid in my class. How come nobody praises me? How come I have to be nothing special to be treated special?"

"My baby." She turned my head so I looked right at her. "Honey, you just got to give it some more time."

"How much?"

"It don't matter. Time is all you got, anyway."

"I don't understand."

"If you go back to begging for they friendship, it ain't gone do you no good. You'll still be a up'ty nigger and a Uncle Tom, and nobody will speak to you anyways. So you might as well be quiet and work at what's good for Evan. Respect will come in time."

That was easy for her to say. After all, it was me who was suffering. I felt I didn't have time to wait and that Mama Jennie couldn't really see the scope of my problem.

"I know all this may sound small to you, Mama Jennie," I said. "But it's big for me. Ain't people meant to have friends? I always figured so. I just can't take all the enemies. It wears me down. Sometimes I just hate life. Sometimes I think I wouldn't care if I wasn't around. You know, like dead."

Mama Jennie took a deep breath. Her eyes looked empty, like someone who had nothing left to give.

"I ain't gone sit here all holier than thou and tell you not to feel that way, baby. I have walked many a day with the same kinda feeling on this ole heart," she said, patting her chest. "Maybe this is the first time you done felt it, but it ain't gone be the last. I tell you, I survive [illegible] something special about Evan Walls."

She was usually right, but I had my doubts on this one. "Someday" seemed like a long time from then, and I needed some support right away. It was hard for me to go from home to school and back home again, being treated with disgust. I got teary thinking about it. I asked her something I had been thinking about for a while.

"Can I come live with you?"

"You mean leave yo' mama and daddy altogether?" she asked, shocked by my question.

"Yes, ma'am."

"Oh, baby. Is it that bad?"

I fought back the tears. "Yes, ma'am. I feel like it is."

"Baby, I don't believe in takin' you from your family. I'm too old anyways. I ain't gone be around that much longer. But I will take a bigger interest in how you be getting raised if you wants me to. Would you like that?"

"I don't know. They'll just get mad."

"I think I can handle your mama. Can I call her again?"

"Yes, ma'am."

"Good. Let's try it this way for a while before you go moving out on 'em."

Weeks later, the first breakthrough in my solitary confinement came. I was reading, sitting in my usual lunchtime space, when two shadows dimmed the light. I looked up to see two white boys from my class, gazing down at me. One of them looked to be about my height but was stocky. He had brown hair and a pleasant enough expression.

"Hey," he said. "I'm Dee Brown."

The second boy was probably the same height but was blond and skinny.

"And I'm Eddie Gleason."

I already knew their names, but the fact that they felt they had to introduce themselves shows how isolated I was. They frightened me. No white people, aside from my teacher, ever spoke to me. I looked at these boys, and I kept seeing the two white men who whipped Daddy.

"I'm Evan Walls," I finally said.

"We were just wondering," the one called Dee asked, "why you're always so quiet and keep to yourself except in class?"

Right away, I thought, *Okay, they're just messing around with me.* How could they not know? They were the ones not talking to me. They ought to know why I stayed to myself.

"Is there a law against it?" I asked.

"I guess not," Dee said. "We was just wondering."

"How about that nobody talks to me, so I don't have anyone to talk to."

"You don't talk to us, either," Eddie said.

That baffled me. "You were there that first day when all you white kids were making jokes about my hair, my lips, and everything else. You didn't stop anybody from picking on me so, I assumed you agreed with them."

"Well, I reckon that was a justified assumption."

"Me too," I replied.

"I'll admit," Dee said, "on that first day, I was afraid to stick up for you, even though I thought you were being treated wrong. I was never raised that way. Really. My folks take a lot of grief around here for not being that way."

"I'm not from around here anyway," Eddie said. "I'm from Northern Virginia. They already had integrated schools before I left. I was surprised when I came down here two years ago and there

but why come to me?" I asked. "You don't need me for anything but trouble."

"You just piqued our interest," Dee said. "What can I say?"

"You don't have to be friends if you don't want," Eddie said. "I guess we can all live without each other."

I laughed. "Yeah, I guess we could. But we can be friends."

They smiled and Dee asked, "Whatcha reading, friend?"

I have to admit that I was still afraid of them. I had always heard not to trust a white person any further than you could throw 'em. Once at the session, Cozy Pitts said, "If a white man tell you it's Friday and you yourself knows it's Friday, you still ought to go look at a calendar, 'cause with them, you never know, child. You never know!"

I thought about that, but I realized I had nothing to lose. I figured that no trick they played on me could be any worse than the tricks the black kids played on me. I looked at Dee Brown and Eddie Gleason and thought, *Mama Jennie was right.*

Respect will come in time.

• • •

I armed myself with a sentence that I would use when a black person came up and asked why I was running around with a couple of white boys.

"I went where I was wanted," I planned to say.

Funny thing was that nobody ever asked. I guess they just took my action to be in the natural progression of a black person who they thought wanted to act white.

Dee and Eddie treated me as an equal. It was the little things that tipped me off. One day while waiting outside our school for our respective buses, I was drinking a Coca-Cola.

"Let me have a swig," Dee said.

Without thinking about it, he grabbed the bottle and drank right after me without even wiping off the bottle, which even my own brother wouldn't have done. It wasn't calculated, some attempt to prove his acceptance of me. It was careless, like there was nothing to fear, so he didn't think to wipe it off. That made a big impression on me.

And they always talked to me no matter where we were. They could be walking toward me in the middle of a group of the baddest rednecks in the school, and when we came close to each other, if they didn't drop off to chat, they were always yelling something like, "Hey, E. Check you after school, man."

Most whites in Canaan would never speak to blacks when other whites were around. Dee and Eddie always did. It was great to have someone to talk to about Friday's and Sunday's football games, someone to tell dirty jokes with and to casually punch on the shoulder to show how much you liked them. I even stopped reading all the time during my lunch break. Sometimes, we'd just hang out. Other times, we'd throw a football around or lift a few barbells in the workout room. I still never played in either of the big lunchtime games because the black kids didn't want me in theirs any more than the other white kids. I didn't hold it against Eddie and Dee, though, when they wanted to play with the white group. I just found my space and a good book. They always came back for me at the end of the period so we could walk to class together.

One Friday, I was sitting in my usual spot, reading about the Battle of Bunker Hill for history class. Joey Green, who was white, and I were working on a project that included maps and drawings of the famous battle for presentation to the class. I'd wanted to work with one of the black kids. I approached Rosetta, but she laughed in my face.

way, with the black person laughing in my face, calling me "Snowball," and me walking away ashamed of being stupid enough to think I'd be included.

Snowball was a new nickname given to me by the black kids. I don't know how it came about. It just started being fired at me in the halls. Then adults started calling me "Snowball" at church. Pretty soon, the white kids started calling me by the name, probably feeling it would do as much harm if not more than the word *nigger*. They were right.

Anyway, I was sitting there reading about Bunker Hill when the bell rang. Dee and Eddie came running over.

"Let's go," Dee yelled.

I picked up my books and walked toward them.

"Hey, you know what?" Eddie said.

"What?" I replied.

"I think y'all should come over and play basketball tomorrow. It's gonna be too cold to before long."

"Okay," Dee said. They looked at me.

I stopped dead in my tracks. I didn't believe he'd actually meant to include me. No white kid had ever asked me or any other black kid that I knew about to his house. That, like so many things regarding race, was just unheard of in Canaan.

"I don't know," I finally answered.

"What do you mean, you don't know?" Dee asked.

"Just that. I don't know," I repeated. I knew that Mama and Daddy would not let me go. In fact, I might get punished just for mentioning it.

"You been here all your life, Dee. You know stuff like that doesn't happen."

"They say there's a first time for everything," Eddie said.

"Yeah, well, *they* won't be around when I get lynched by your neighbors, or your parents, for that matter."

"My parents don't care," Eddie said.

"*Sure*, they don't."

"They don't. I mean it!"

"I bet they do," I said.

"I know my own parents!"

"Children are always the last to really know their parents," I said.

"I'm telling you it's okay," Eddie said. "Think about it some more."

I didn't learn anything else that day. Instead of listening to teachers, I argued with myself over the possibilities of going to Eddie's house. When I stepped off the school bus that afternoon, I was still arguing with myself. I don't know why, because I knew I wouldn't be allowed to go. I guess I was trying to figure out if it was right that I wouldn't be allowed.

Later that night, the phone rang, and Daddy came into the den.

"Turn down that TV," he said. "It's for you, Evan, and listen up. I'm getting enough stink raised at me from folks 'round here about you and them white boys. Now they calling the house. You go in that kitchen in there and take this call, but this better be the last one. I don't want no more white folks calling this house. You catch my meaning?"

"Yes, sir," I replied, which was about all I said to Daddy in those days.

"Get on it then."

It was a white boy all right. It was Eddie.

"What are you calling for?" I asked.

"What do you think?"

Silence.

"Are you coming tomorrow?"

"I . . . I don't know."

"Wait just

. . . beyond belief that Eddie would set me up like this.

"I know what you're thinking, but you're wrong, hon. My husband and I aren't those kind of people. So, if you really want to come, we'd be happy to have you. I know the attitudes around here, but we don't share them. *All* of Eddie's friends are welcome."

"Okay," was all I could get out. I was still a little too stunned to speak.

"Then you'll come?"

I thought quickly. I didn't want to tell her that my parents were the problem. That they hated all white people and didn't like me associating with them. I didn't want to tell her that Daddy would punish me if I asked. So, to avoid her asking questions like "Why won't they let you?" and then saying things like "Let me talk to them," I said yes.

I didn't go back to the den to watch TV. I just went to bed at seven thirty on a Friday night. I lay awake for a long time wondering. I had to go. I told her I would be there. But then again, I also thought that maybe I could run away and never come home again. That way, no one would be asking me why I didn't show up or where I was all day. In the end, I figured I'd just have to get on the bike and go—then hope that, as usual, Mama and Daddy wouldn't care enough to ask where I'd been. Even though I thought I had it all figured out, I still woke up with my stomach on fire.

I never thought I'd find myself appreciating my parents' disdain, but that next morning I felt lucky when I got the usual cold shoulders. I went about my business trying to keep things as normal as possible: watching a few cartoons with Mark, feeding and playing with Bullet, and practicing punting the football. About eleven, I told Mama I was going to ride to town. She grunted at me, and I got on my bike.

Thirty minutes later, I arrived at Eddie Gleason's. Believe me, riding through the all-white neighborhood of West Hill was no picnic. I'd worn one of Mark's baseball caps and pulled its brim down over my face as far as possible, as if that would keep people from noticing that a black boy was riding through their neighborhood. Of course, it didn't work. Nobody said anything to me, but I got lots of long and intimidating stares from some simply amazed people. Kids dropped toys and stopped mid-game to scurry into their homes, I presumed to tell their parents. I expected at any moment to see adults come running out with guns to mow me down.

After reaching Eddie's house, I stood on the steps second-guessing myself. I was afraid because riding through West Hill had changed my concern from Mama and Daddy to white people in general. Maybe Cozy Pitts and Chauncey Mae were right. Maybe white people were not to be trusted. Maybe Ethel Brown was right that night she was at our house gossiping about me. I had heard it from the den.

"Is it true what they be saying, girl?" she had asked Mama.

"I ain't much in the mood to talk about it," Mama replied, but Ethel being Ethel continued.

"Evan better be learning that ain't no white cracker around here no friend of no Negro. That child better open his eyes."

"We done told him that."

"What he say?"

"He want to know how we thought they was using him. Augustus told him off right good. For his smart-assedness."

"Good for Augustus, then. What he be talking about, how they use us? White folk don't do nothing but use us every which way. Hell, sometimes I thank that's all they be around for."

"Amen, girl. You ain't gone get no argument from me. Mark told Augustus and me that Evan say th—

...before me. She had ...own hair and brown eyes and a porcelain face. I remember thinking how smooth her face looked, and that she probably never had a pimple in her entire life.

When it looked as if I couldn't speak, she did.

"Hello. I'm Elizabeth Gleason."

"Hi, Mrs. Gleason. I'm Evan Walls, but I reckon you had that already figured out."

"I did," she said, smiling while pulling up the brim of my hat. "You have a nice face. Don't cover it up so much."

"Yes, ma'am," I said. "I mean, thank you, ma'am."

Then she put her arm around my shoulder and pulled me into the house. It was the first time a white adult, except a doctor, had ever touched me. Before Elizabeth Gleason, there had never been so much as a handshake. When she touched me, I felt very warm inside and sensed that there was as little prejudice in this woman as there could be in any person alive. She guided me through the house into Eddie's room. Noting the difference between this home and the houses of the black people I knew, I tried not to hold it against the Gleasons that they had so much.

"Evan's here," she said as we entered the room.

"He made it!" Dee said. "I can hardly believe it."

"Dee," Mrs. Gleason said. "Don't be so hard on Evan. This is not as easy as it seems. You boys behave, and I'll bring you something to drink in a while."

"Your mother is very nice," I told Eddie after she'd left.

"You can say that because she's not your mom. Everybody else's mom is nice."

"I guess you could look at it that way. Though I don't believe it's necessarily so."

We played around in Eddie's room for a while, among other things talking about the kids at school that we hated. By the time that conversation was exhausted, I realized that the great majority of the people I hated were black. I was embarrassed, and I wondered what they thought about that. Afterward, Mrs. Gleason fed us lunch and sent us out to play basketball.

And we played well together. I took on Dee, one on one. I won and then took on Eddie, who beat me. We laughed and joked like crazy, saying stuff like "Swish" when we hit nothing but net or "In your face, sucker" when we scored a basket on one another. The last time I'd felt that kind of camaraderie was in the good days with T. Wall and the fellas. Thinking about them made the moment bittersweet.

I leaned on the trunk of Mrs. Gleason's Chrysler New Yorker and watched Eddie play Dee. Dee made a lucky hook shot and started rubbing it in.

"You see that, E?" he shouted. "'Cause Eddie sure didn't. He just saw the smoke off the net."

I laughed with them, looking for the smoke from the fancy red-white-and-blue nylon net while thinking of the chain-link net T. Wall and the rest of us had played with. Though I didn't want to, I couldn't help contrasting the two worlds to which I had been exposed. Of course, I felt I belonged to and, more importantly, wanted to belong to the world of the chain-link nets. But I felt separated from that simply by the acceptance of my white friends. I mean, if they liked me and the blacks didn't, didn't that mean I was more like them than the blacks? Didn't that mean that I had no link to great people like Martin Luther King Jr. or Jackie Robinson or to my heritage in general?

Before I let myself get too down, I jumped up and suggested we play HORSE, because we could all be involved, and I wouldn't have time to sit around and think.

While we were playing ~~~~ ~~~~~ ~~~~~

~~~~~~ Eddie laughed it off. I laughed because it was one of those things at which you either laughed or cried, and I didn't want to cry. I felt separated from my heritage, and now, because that couple had reminded me of who I was, I was feeling separated from my new friends. As they walked around laughing at the couple, I realized that no matter how close I came to these two boys, I could never be a part of them. I'd never see the world as they did and never have the world react to me in the same way. They were regular white boys who liked to yell, wear John Deere hats and go hunting. They had the comfortable swagger of white boys. The kind of stride that came with the knowledge that the world was yours to explore and to own. Later on, I would hear John Denver singing, "Life ain't nothin' but a funny, funny riddle. Thank God I'm a country boy." I would think about Eddie and Dee, and how they could walk through life with an ease I could never touch.

I was in the world with these black people, some of whom were my family, and these whites, some of whom were my friends. Yet, I felt close to no one.

• • •

That evening just before dinner, Daddy went to town to pick up something from the hardware store. When he came home, he was as mad as I had ever seen him. I knew he'd found out. How stupid of me not to remember how small Canaan was.

"I was just at the store," Daddy said, "and Michael Beauchamp stopped me. He said ole man Taylor saw a colored boy playing basketball with two white boys over in West Hill. Said it was at somebody Gleason's house. Ain't that one of your little honky friends?"

I saw no reason to try and lie my way out of it.

"Yes, sir," I said.

"You went over there?" Mama jumped in. "Today?"

"Yes, ma'am."

"And you didn't tell us where you was going?" she continued.

I got mad. "You never care where I go. I didn't think I needed to tell you."

With that, Daddy slapped me across the face. I fell against the kitchen table, knocking a stack of dishes on the floor. Mama screamed because they were her good set. Mark came running and saw Daddy pick me up and slam me against the wall. He slapped me again and then held me by my shirt collar with one hand and pointed at my face with the other.

"Didn't I tell you to leave them white boys alone?"

"Yes, sir," I said, before spitting some blood.

"Well, is it something wrong that you can't listen to me?"

"No, sir. It's just that they are the only boys who will play with me."

"I wouldn't play with you neither if you was with them stone crackers. And I don't care if nobody ever plays with you; you leave them white boys alone. You hear me?"

"But they're my friends!" I shouted.

"Don't you raise your voice at me, boy. I'll slap you to hell and gone. And furthermore, I don't give a good goddamn about that *friend* business. You gone stop it or else."

I didn't respond, pretending I couldn't hear him. How could my father be denying me something as simple as friendship? It was all I had, and I wasn't going to let it go.

"Well," he said.

"I can't," I finally said.

He slapped me again.

And again.

"Say you ain't gone see 'em," he shout-

"Evan!"

...ut and never

"Say you ain't gone see 'em!" he shouted between slaps.

"I won't!" I yelled. "I won't!"

"Don't talk white talk to me, boy. I said you ain't gone see 'em."

At first I just didn't get it. You don't think too clearly when your head is being beat in. So I just said once more, "I won't."

He slapped me again. "I said for you to say you ain't gone see 'em no more."

I finally understood that he wanted me to repeat what he'd said word for word. He wanted me to say *ain't*. This would be a symbol for him, a sign that he had beat the fight out of me, a sign that would be the denial of my friendship with Eddie and Dee. A sign that would be the denial of my quest to become somebody, a sign that he had finally put me back in my place, which was beneath his thumb, behind the images of Augustus and Treeny Walls. When Bojack spoke about parents who didn't want a better life than their own for their children, I never thought he meant Mama and Daddy. I thought he meant people like Chauncey Mae and Arthur Pitts.

I could stop seeing Eddie and Dee, but I would not give up my desire for an education and my dreams for being something special in my life. I shook my head, no.

This time I got hit harder. I realized it was Daddy's fist—not an open palm. I heard Mama scream.

"Evan, please!" she pleaded. "Please just say what he want!" Tears were streaming and she was trembling. When I didn't respond, she ran away, quick footsteps disappearing down the hall. Mark ran, too.

"Say ain't," Daddy said.

I opened my mouth to say no, but blood from my nose ran into it and choked me. I couldn't speak, so I vigorously shook my head again, and as they say, the lights went out.

• • •

Hours later, I woke up. It was dark and Mark was asleep. My face hurt so much I began to cry. I got up, went into the kitchen, saw that it was one thirty in the morning but called Mama Jennie anyway. She tried to calm me down and said she'd have another talk with Mama in the morning. I went back to bed, where I stayed all the next day, resting and hiding my bruises.

No one bothered me until Aunt Mary came into my room. She sat on the foot of my bed and told me that she heard about what had happened, and didn't I think it was time to stop all the nonsense and stop troubling Mama and Daddy so much? I just hunched my shoulders. I wasn't in the mood to hear about it, but she was intent on making me see the error of my ways.

"Let me tell you a story," she said. "I used to be like you. Trusting and all. I had this white friend. A little girl down by the beach. She and I got real tight when Daddy was chopping weeds in her daddy's peanut fields. We was both sixteen, and she just got her driver's license, so she took me to town for a sundae. She went in and brought out the sundaes 'cause I couldn't go inside. We was in a truck, so we drove out to one of her daddy's fields and then sat in the bed to finish the sundaes. Her two brothers showed up and jumped in the truck with us, shucking and jiving and stuff. Then, before I know it, she said she wanted another sundae, and her brothers say for her to take the car since we was all comfortable in the truck."

There was a pause. "What's wrong?" I asked.

Aunt Mary had started to cry.

"You don't have to tell me this if it's gonna hurt," I told her. I meant it, too. I didn't feel like I needed any kind of lesson from a person as full of hate as Aunt Mary, but I

I couldn't

. . . so I do that they

and not one thing woulda been done about it. Nobody but colored folk woulda blinked a eye, and they woulda been too scared to do much more."

"What happened?"

She took a deep breath. "Them two boys . . . now, I know you ain't but eleven, but I know you gone know what I mean. Them two boys, they took my virginity. For six straight hours they took turns raping me. *Raping* me. And my *best white friend*—huh! That bitch, she set me up."

"Does Bojack know?"

"No, and don't you tell him. He thanks I'm the only thang he got that the white man ain't tainted. And them two boys, they still around. Mens now. They gives me a dirty, degrading smile every time I passes 'em. If I could get away with it, I'd kill 'em dead as a stump."

I sat there stunned. *You never know what kinds of pains people carry around with them,* I realized.

"Well, what you thank 'bout that?" she asked.

"I'm sorry."

"Teach you anythang?"

"Yes. It teaches me another reason why life is so hard for black people. It teaches me about how we get used and hurt. In our minds and in our bodies."

"And don't it teach you that you got to stay with your own, and leave them that would hurt you alone?"

"Yes," I replied, thinking of people who wanted to be with me as "my own." Color didn't factor in.

She smiled. "So you gone let them white boys alone then?"

It would have been so easy to appease her, but I could not give up Dee and Eddie, even in sympathy for Aunt Mary's lifelong pain. Without those friends, my life was painful, and I didn't believe I should suffer just because she did. Besides, Dee and Eddie didn't rape her. I couldn't imagine them ever raping anybody.

"I'm sorry, Aunt Mary. I wish it hadn't happened to you or anybody else, but Eddie and Dee didn't do nothing to you. They can't be guilty for something somebody else did."

Aunt Mary stood quickly and stared down at me with such hatred you would have thought I was one of the rapists.

"If you can forgive them for what they done to me, then you can have 'em!" she yelled. "Just don't expect no love from me."

"But I don't forgive the men that raped you," I said, shaken by the entire moment. "But my friends don't even know you. They never touched you. Why should I hate them?"

"Because they is white," she said forcefully. "Because they *all* is the enemy. Every damn one of 'em."

She stormed out of the bedroom.

S unday mornings at our house meant sausage, applesauce, sweetened iced tea, and Mama's locally famous homemade rolls. Probably every black person in Canaan knew about the rolls. Mama got calls to make them for all kinds of events, from church bazaars to weddings to after-funeral dinners. But on most Sundays, she made them just for us. I loved waking up and smelling them baking, my mouth watering with the thought of butter melted in them and then dunking the whole thing into some cold White House applesauce. It was the most pleasant meal of the week. We all woke up fresh and happy.

"There's just something special about the Lord's day," Mama would say before turning on the television set to a station airing her favorite religious show. The gospel music and the minister's hellfire and brimstone became a backdrop to our breakfast and a prelude to Reverend Walker's rote sermons. We would chatter about last week's goings-on and about what the week would hold. It had all been very nice and very family-like—until everything changed.

I didn't wake up to the normal Sunday morning delights the week after my beating from Daddy and Aunt Mary's revelation.

Mama wasn't singing the gospels along with the television. In fact, the TV wasn't even on. There was just a deadly silence broken every now and then by the clinking of silverware. I heard Daddy shuffling around his bedroom and Mark turning on the shower. I took a deep breath and shook my head, still feeling some pain, wondering at the whole mess I'd brought on.

Aunt Mary had left after our discussion and told everybody about my going over to Eddie Gleason's and the beating I got. She added other things that never happened but were, in her mind, the appropriate embellishments to make steeper my fall from grace.

The black kids at school became even more vicious. It was a daily bloodletting. I dreamed of Christmas vacation, thinking I would be rid of the steely knives in the other black kids' eyes. Every time I passed one of them or a group of them, my wounds opened deeper. There was never enough time between stabbings for the wounds to heal. They passed me in the halls singing their arrangement of the guards' chant from *The Wizard of Oz*. "Oh-reee-oh. Ohhhhh-re-oh!"

The teachers, especially the black teachers, were no help. Like the adults at my church who allowed me to be stoned on my way to summer Bible school, the teachers turned away from my pleas for help until I no longer pled. Some white teachers tried, but they made only a small effort. I think they thought I deserved it, too, but they didn't matter much to me. I never expected anything from them anyway.

Dee and Eddie expressed their friendship even more vigorously. They knew my penchant for going off alone to sulk my way back into shape, so they allowed me to come in and out of their lives as I pleased. They put no pressure on me and remained good friends.

Those friendships helped some, but I still felt that my life had no center. I just wasn't whole. I spent most of my time alone at home and at school groping in the dark for something that would make me feel at home with myself. Mama Jennie and Bojack urged me to struggle forward. Mama Jennie sang "Onward Christian Soldiers" to me, but I was tired. I was wilting.

I tried to appear aloof when others were looking me over, hoping
for a sign that they were getting to me. At night, I found my spot in
the woods and shed my emotions, which ping-ponged from tears

• • •

By the time everyone got to the breakfast table that Sunday after
my beating, I was reminded of why I spent more time in the woods
than in the house. Everywhere I went, there was incredible tension.
I began to hope as hard as I could that Mama Jennie would relent
and let me live with her. I had to settle for the fact that she had
threatened to turn Daddy in to the police if he beat me again. He
knew they'd jump at any opportunity to lock up another black man,
especially one who saw himself as special among local blacks. I tried
to ease things by forcing a conversation.

"How come everybody is so quiet?" I asked.

No one answered.

"Don't you want the TV set on, Mama?" I asked.

She stared at me for a while with so much anger in her eyes that
I had to drop my head. I saw that she had burned the rolls, which
she'd never done.

"I ain't in the mood," she finally said.

I guess that was the first time I realized what I had done to them.
The incredible squeeze play I had put them in. I hadn't thought much
about how Daddy wanted to become the head deacon, which was
something I knew he wanted badly. But that was becoming less of a
possibility; Reverend Walker had told Daddy, "If your own children

can't look to you as a model and then do the right thang, how you expect my sheep to follow you as my lead shepherd?"

Mama suffered, too. Chauncey Mae had been infested with Rosetta's hatred. She called Mama to tell her that she wasn't sure she could come to the porch sessions in the upcoming summer. "Child, I gots me a reputation to be concerned about. I can't be coming 'round to no house with no Uncle Tom in it," she told Mama.

Ethel Brown threatened the same thing and only said hello whenever the two met. Cozy Pitts didn't even bother to call. I'm sure it was scary for Mama to be losing her friends.

And Mark's situation was pathetic. He was trying desperately to become a true *brother*, and I was standing in the way. No one would take him seriously as long as I was his little brother.

We got dressed and went to church. Mama and Daddy still sat with the deacons and their wives but otherwise didn't mingle much. Mark's friends seemed to barely tolerate him, so he unhappily sat beside me. We were all depressed and isolated. We stood with our hymnals open at the appropriate moments, but we did not sing.

Reverend Walker took to the pulpit and absolutely stunned me with a sermon titled "The Little Boy Who Thought He Was Better Than All His Little Friends." He read the title twice before he went into his sermon, which tore me and my dream apart. He never mentioned my name, but the entire congregation knew where the message was aimed.

I tried to tough it out, but I couldn't. I looked at all those Jesuses in the stained-glass windows and remembered the comfort they had given me in those days of revivals, but they were of no help. So I decided to run out, no matter how embarrassing. I stumbled standing up and stepping over Mark, but I quickly gathered myself and ran as fast as I could out of Grace Street Baptist Church, trying my best not to notice any more of the laughing faces than I had to. Bojack met me outside, and I fainted in his arms.

I guess it must have been about a half hour later that I woke up at home, with Bojack sitting on my bed beside me. I woke up looking at my reflection in his mirrored sunglasses.

"I ain't never going back!" I yelled before I burst into tears.

He put his hand on my shoulder

"I guess," I said, breaking the silence, "I never thought nothing like this would happen. I didn't think I would be pushing folks' noses way out of joint. All I wanted was to be somebody."

Bojack turned back to me, his face sagging around the sunglasses. He looked as if he wanted to say something, but couldn't, having come up empty.

"They think I'm trying to be white," I continued.

"Yeah," he said with a big, depressed sigh. "I reckon they do."

"Isn't it possible to be somebody and still be black? How come they figure you have to give up your blackness if you want to get As? Do they want us all to dig ditches forever?"

"Yeah," Bojack said. "I reckon some do."

• • •

The next morning, I felt uplifted, even though I had gotten on the bus with embarrassingly ashy, gray skin, which was a sign of real backwoods, low-income black folk. As we left the house, Mama took the time to rub some lard on Mark's face and hands. When I came behind Mark, ready for the same treatment, she just looked at me and said, "I ain't studying 'bout you, boy."

But it was the last day before Christmas vacation. All I had to do, I told myself, was to make it through one more day. Then there would be two weeks of rest from school, and I could spend most of the time at Mama Jennie's.

I was in homeroom when I realized that making it through that one day was not going to be easy. I noticed the other black kids were extremely restless, shifting in their seats, stealing quick glances at each other, nodding and staring at their watches. Mrs. Jones didn't notice, but she didn't pay much attention to most of the black kids.

I kept my ears open all morning while passing kids in the hall, hoping for some kind of clue. I got caught staring, too; as I remember, a couple of them yelled at me, "What you staring at, Snowball?"

I got nothing out of my heightened awareness, so I was taken by surprise when, at two minutes to twelve, right before the lunch bell, all the black kids in the school except me left their classrooms. Later, I found out that this was happening at the high school and even the elementary school.

They lined the hallways and took everyone else in the school hostage. They banged on lockers and chanted, "Death to whitey!" and "Say it loud. I'm black and I'm proud." They threw books and folding chairs at every white person who dared peek out of a classroom. Some of them brazenly faced off with white male teachers who tried to stem the tide.

Much of this was happening right outside my classroom door. I sat in my chair, shocked and entranced. Outside were T. Wall and Flak. I saw Rosetta run by, enraged. She shouted loudly, "Death to whitey!"

All of a sudden, I woke up, quickly looked around and realized that I was the only black kid still in the room and probably the only black kid in the entire Canaan school system who didn't know that a protest had been scheduled. I was crushed. This was the ultimate slap in my face.

White kids looked at me as if to say, "Well, nigger, what are you sitting here for?" And I wondered why I was there. Slowly, I got up out of my seat. I walked tentatively toward the door, knowing that once I went into the hall, I would be treated just as if I were white. But I didn't feel comfortable sitting in the class, either, because I could tell the white kids didn't want me there. My stomach was on fire.

I made it to the door and stuck out my head. Sure enough, a book just missed my face as it ~~~~~ ~

~~~~ ~~~~~ white kids had drawn the line. Up until that point, many of them, by virtue of my friendship with Dee and Eddie, had begun to accept me. I was invited to a couple of other houses of non-Canaan natives, but I didn't go because I was afraid of Daddy. At that moment, though, they thought of me as the enemy. I felt them all thinking the word "nigger." I couldn't stand it, so I turned away. I was in the middle again. My stomach pain inflamed.

Eddie emerged from the door at the far end of the hallway, which was open. I had forgotten that Mrs. Jones sent him on an errand. Now, he was running back to the class, afraid, ducking books and chairs.

I turned to Mrs. Jones. "It's Eddie," I shouted. "He's out there!"

She ran to the door along with Dee.

"Over here," she shouted.

"Run, Eddie, run!" Dee yelled.

Angry black students rained books upon us. We ducked but looked back out to find that they had grabbed Eddie. Two boys held him as another started shouting in Eddie's face. Then, the one shouting punched Eddie in the stomach. I just couldn't stand it. I thought, *Maybe their gripe is legit, but this isn't right. This makes us blacks no better than the men who beat Daddy.*

Bojack had taught me to body-block the way the pro football players did it. So, I sprinted and threw my body into the two boys holding Eddie. He was released in the collision and was able to make it safely into the classroom. I was slammed to the floor and tasted blood in my mouth. That was all I remembered until I woke up in the hospital to find Mama Jennie sitting by my side.

· · ·

Coming out of that long, drug-aided sleep was quite difficult. Though I was still on the edge of sleep, I twisted my head back and forth, fighting the urge to drop off again. Little by little, I won the battle. Where there was darkness, there was soon fuzzy light. Where there was numbness, there was excruciating pain. Where there was nothing, there was a smell I couldn't put my finger on.

When my eyes were finally able to focus, I saw Mama Jennie snatching an arm back from around my face, covering up something and then shoving whatever it was in her purse.

There was a lot of pain. I was forced to take a deep breath in order to deal with it. Mama Jennie assumed I had taken the breath to hold back on an avalanche of tears. I guess she expected me to wake up, see where I was, and then let the rivers flow.

She leaned over to me and whispered. "You go ahead and cry, baby. Ain't nobody here but me."

I thought about it for a while and actually searched myself for some tears, but I came up empty.

"Right now, I don't think I can cry anymore."

"Well, I guess I ain't surprised at that," she said. "I reckon you done cried enough already for one childhood."

"I guess."

She gave a sad smile, kissed the palm of her hand and put it on my forehead. I closed my eyes as she held it there. I enjoyed the warmth as much as I could through the pain.

"How you feel, baby?"

"I hurt pretty bad."

"Let me get the nurse, then."

She went to the door and called the nurse, who checked my chart and brought in a cup of water and some pills. It took everything I had just to sit up enough to swallow them.

Mama Jennie sat there, smiling and rubbing my forehead. I began to wonder about what was causin~ ~

"Th

..... even notice it," I said, looking down at the cast on my left arm.

"And you got two broken ribs," she continued. "And finally, you got yo'self a full-blown ulcer. Bleeding and everythang."

"An ulcer!" I shouted, and then winced from a sudden blast of pain. I knew what caused ulcers; I knew people who had them. Overworked men and women, desolate and full of anguish, trying to keep themselves and their families above water in a world they knew was stacked against them. I didn't want to be included in that inconsolable group. I mean, Cozy Pitts had an ulcer. I had nothing in common with her. But then, the more I thought about it, the more I realized that I sort of fit the description. And then I felt the melancholies coming on, as Bojack used to say. I felt like I had finally gone over the deep end.

I just lay there thinking about the ulcer. I simply couldn't believe it. In the middle of these thoughts, I realized that something else was wrong. *Where's everyone else?* I wondered. I knew the answer, but I asked Mama Jennie anyway.

"Are you the only one here?"

"Brother out in the waiting room . . ."

"I mean Mama and Daddy."

"No, son. They ain't come with us." Mama Jennie looked heartbroken.

"Why not?" I asked.

She took her hand off my forehead and sat back in her chair. Her fingers played nervously around her purse.

"I reckon," she said, "your daddy figure this is good for you. It won't bad enough that you was out there making friends with white folks, now you out there protecting 'em against colored folks. Your Mama and Daddy so embarrassed they can't leave the house."

"You mean I could've died, and all they would've cared about was their reputation."

"I reckon. But it ain't quite that simple. All of the *somebody* stuff. Your daddy's troubles, your mama's troubles, and her being afraid of what you and everything else is doing to your daddy. She's trying to hang on to both of you, but it ain't easy. I'm feeling like she thank she gotta make a choice in her heart. You know, between you and him. Between the life she had and you."

I nodded. I didn't know what to feel except guilt.

"How did you hear about it?" I asked.

"Chile, you talking 'bout Canaan. I knew about the whole thang before you hit the school floor."

"So everybody knows?"

She nodded.

"You know," I continued, "I think they wanted to kill me."

"Sounds that way."

"What stopped them?"

"White po-lice who took the opportunity to break some of them boys' heads. You know the po-lice loved that."

"And I bet black folk are blaming me for the police."

"You right."

"I knew it."

"Well, you did give 'em that chance to enjoy they favorite pastime. But none of that change the fact that them boys what done this to you deserved some of they own medicine."

"What else are they saying about me?"

"Oh, baby, don't beat yourself up over this now. You know what they be saying. The same ole, same ole."

I took a deep breath and stared at the ceiling.

"It's hard being a N̶e̶g̶r̶o̶

"You know what I don't understand?"

She shook her head. "What might that be?"

"Is how a little eleven-year-old boy can stir up so much trouble. Most of the time what a kid thinks don't matter much at all."

"You right. Most of the time what they thanks don't matter, but this is different. Prejudice here is so thick, it's like one of your aunt Mary's pie crusts."

I smiled.

"The wound was opened when the first one of us became a slave and through the Civil War until emancipation. Then, it kinda healed over, just enough to maybe get a scab. Before that scab could heal over, people like Dr. King and Eliza Blizzard come along and ripped it off and left that sore wide open with a whole bunch of sensitive nerves. You might not be but eleven, but that's plenty old enough for you to be able to pour salt in an open wound. And you know how salt on a cut can hurt."

"Can I do anything to make this whole mess easier?"

"You just keep on doing like you doing, baby."

"Then, I got a few white friends and no black friends."

Mama Jennie looked sad. "Baby, I don't know what else to tell you. But I think you got to keep on moving on. You done gone too far for folks to be changing they minds as far as I can see. Ain't no turning back now."

I got tired of talking all of a sudden. Mama Jennie and I had been down that road over and over again. I lay in that bed feeling like I really wanted to give in. Maybe it wouldn't work. Maybe they'd still hate or maybe they'd accept me. There was always that chance. So I wouldn't be somebody; so what? Maybe, though, I might find a little peace. I had to decide which was more important. And if I backed down, how would Mama Jennie and Bojack feel toward me? I hated the thought of disappointing them. After all, when no else cared, they did. But I wondered if I hadn't been backing down because of them. Was I really following this dream for me, or them?

"What you thanking, baby?" Mama Jennie asked.

"I was just thinking," I said with a frustrated chuckle, "that I don't even know what *somebody* means. Here I am running around studying myself to death, learning how to speak correctly, trying to outsmart everyone and everything, and for what? To be *somebody*? What is *somebody*? I almost got myself killed over something I don't know anything about. I can't put my mind around it. It's almost like heaven, the way I've built it up. You know what I mean? It's like someplace everybody's supposed to want to go, but you don't really know it's there. Do you?"

"I guess you really don't, but you keep living like it's a heaven out there."

"But why?"

"Well, look at it this way. If you live a life good enough to get to heaven and there is a heaven, then it's all gravy, right? If you live a life good enough to get into heaven and there ain't no heaven, well then you just led a good life, which ain't hurt no one. You just go wherever it is you going, knowing you done some good in this world. You can rest easy. Same goes for being somebody. I don't thank many folks that goes on to be somebody actually knowed what kinda somebody they was gone end up being. They just did all the right thangs, so when something come along that pointed 'em this way or that, they got the basics, you know? So many of our folks ain't even got the basics. Ain't got the foundation they can build on later. *Somebody* is out there for you somewhere, if you can just keep hanging on."

"I just don't know anymore. I just want some peace. I don't know who I'm living for."

people tries to make you lessen yourself and accept something less than what you wants out of yourself, you decide what you gone be in this life: a follower or a leader. This ain't the kind of thang you can sit on the fence 'bout and just sorta exist without making a decision. Peoples is gone make you make a decision, and you has to live with the consequences. It's decision-making time, my son. Either you stands for something, or you'll stand for anything."

"I understand," I said. "And I know what I want. I just think I need some rest. Things always seem worse when I'm tired."

Mama Jennie nodded and helped me with my blankets. I was trying to find the position that caused me the least amount of pain when Bojack walked in, followed closely by Eliza Blizzard. I couldn't believe it. I tried sitting up again as she walked straight to Mama Jennie and held out her hand. Mama Jennie took it.

"How do you do, sugar?" Mama Jennie asked.

"I'm honored," Eliza said. "Honored to finally be in the same room with you. You are a legend, you know?"

It did something to me to witness this highly educated, politically astute and socially powerful woman pay her deferential respects to Mama Jennie, who threw back her head and howled.

"Girl, you sho' do know how to make a old woman feel something good 'bout herself."

Eliza smiled and let go of her hand. "I hope you don't mind that we stopped by. I was out of town. I came back early when Bojack called, and we came running over."

"No, sugar. I don't mind. Fact is, you might be the perfect medicine," Mama Jennie replied. "I think this does ole Evan some good. Look here now." She turned to me. "You got the three of us. The three people who believes in you the most, here together. Just for you."

"Yes, ma'am," I replied and smiled genuinely through my pain.

Eliza said hi to me and took a seat on the foot of the bed as Bojack walked around to the other side and knelt next to me.

"How you doing, little man?" he asked.

"I'm in pain and trying to figure out why I can't be somebody and be liked at the same time."

I felt Eliza rub my leg, and she smiled at me sadly.

"I think you can," she said. "And on the way here, I got an idea. When you're better, I want to take you on a short trip. If your folks will let me."

"Oh, I'll see to that now. That I will," Mama Jennie said.

"Thank you, Mama Jennie," Eliza said. "If I may call you that."

Mama Jennie nodded proudly, and we all talked for a while. Eliza told us about some job offers that she was considering, which made me sad. Bojack had us laughing with stories from his daily life. He could be hysterical when he wanted to be. Pretty soon, though, I got tired again, and they all noticed.

"Well now," Eliza said. "We don't want to overwhelm you, Evan. But we had to come by to let you know that we love you and stand by you."

"Yes, ma'am," I replied.

They both gave me hugs and waved as they left my room. I lay there quietly, digesting that visit. I wondered about where Eliza Blizzard might take me as I began to fade in and out. Mama Jennie getting out of the chair brought me out of it.

"Baby, I'm gone get up on out of here now. They gone keep you in here for a week or so, they say. Doctor say they want to watch you for a while. So you just close your eyes when you feels like it. Take the time in here to get a good rest. I'll be coming back and forth until you go home."

She leaned over and kissed m~

"You put a stick of butter in your purse when I woke up, didn't you?"

"Well," she laughed. "I cannot tell a lie."

"Why would you have a stick of butter in the hospital?"

"I reckon I oughta be embarrassed at this mess," she said. "But what the hell. Back in slavery days, the peoples used to rub butter on they noses when time came around for Christmas and New Year's Day."

"Why?"

"Considering all the troubles they been having, they figured it might help them slide on into the new year just a little bit easier. A little smoother."

"Thank you, Mama Jennie," I said, remembering at that moment all she had meant to me. "I love you."

"I loves you too, honey. God knows you'll never know how much. Close your eyes now, and tell that ole sandman I be coming at him shortly myself."

1973

CANAAN, VIRGINIA

I woke up looking at a bunch of feed sacks and flicking ants off my arm, which had been outside my sleeping bag and stretched across a bed of freshly fallen leaves. The five sacks filled with broken glass I had shattered over the years looked purple in the September moonlight. They were stacked between two of the trees that made up my circular haven in the woods. Nearby was a big seventy-or-so-pound rock that had replaced the much smaller one I first brought here.

Things had gotten worse for me in Canaan, but no matter how much I cried and shook, and no matter how blurry my vision got, I could usually zero in on the big rock and successfully smash up T. Wall, shatter Aunt Mary, or totally disintegrate the likes of Eugenia Pitts.

I rolled over and flipped open the latches on my toolbox. It was a rusty old Craftsman that Bojack had given me. I kept all my essentials in it. I reached in and grabbed a flashlight, flipped it on, and pointed it at my watch. It was one o'clock in the morning. I laughed because I had watched a four o'clock preseason football game that was over at seven; I had come out to the woods to rest just for a little while, but it turned into six hours. It didn't matter much, though. No one at the house would have cared if I didn't come home. In fact, I spent many nights outside in the woods because I was uncomfortable at home.

I put the flashlight back into the toolbox and lay down again. I zipped up my sleeping bag, which was actually Bojack's from the Korean War. I thought about how much things had changed in the four years since the beating I'd taken on the day of "Death to Whitey."

. . .

That mugging had kept me in the hospital for three and a half weeks. For the first half of that time, only Mama Jennie, Bojack, and Eliza Blizzard came to check on me and to keep me company. When I was alone, I read books left for me by candy stripers.

When Mama and Daddy finally came to visit, they were a couple of happy chatterboxes. Mama kissed me. Daddy shook my hand, asked how I was doing and told me that they missed me around the house.

Mama told the nurse, who happened to be checking my vitals, that she and Daddy had been out of town and that my great-grandmother, whom I had been staying with, had a terrible time reaching them. The nurse smiled, looked at me sadly, and left. She had often heard Mama Jennie talk about how terrible it was that parents would sit at home and let a child suffer alone in a hospital.

Deep down, I wanted to forget that it took them a week and a half to come see me. I wanted so much for the care they exhibited to be real. But just the same, I knew better. It turned out that they were pressured to see me because of guilt. Not their own, but that of the black community at large. "He a honky wannabe for sho', but I don't reckon he deserved all of that mess they done to him," is what one old lady had said to Mama Jennie.

With this in mind, they couldn't continue to act like they had no sympathy for their own son, especially when they were benefitting from his misfortune. Reverend Walker bestowed upon Daddy the title of chairman of the deacon board. He also made Mama president of the missionary circle. And on top of all that came appreciation from some white citizens of Canaan. Daddy received another promotion at the packing plant, and M—

job selling girdles and b—

...   ... the damn

...... yonder before I let that cracker

...... plow anywhere near my land again."

Mama and Daddy were now hanging around the Canaan middle class, and they began to act as if they had always been there. They spent a lot of time talking about their many new purchases and how bad they felt for the pitiful folk. One night during the summer after my school beating, I tiptoed into the kitchen, filled a glass with Kool-Aid and peeked through the kitchen curtains at the session conversation. Although several members had threatened to boycott our porch, they didn't. Maybe it was tradition, or maybe it was the addiction to gossip. Maybe, like before, they wanted to be near those who had something in this world. I'm still not sure.

"Child, you say your paycheck was spent when you got it. Huh! Mine is spent way before I even earns it," Ethel Brown said.

"And half mine, too," Jim added. "If both us won't working, we'd be in some kinda trouble."

"Yeah, I knows the feeling," Aunt Mary said.

"It's a damn shame," Chauncey Mae added.

"It's pitiful," Ethel said.

"Lord knows, I pray every night thanking Jesus for our many blessings and praying for the pitiful," Daddy said.

Mama delicately kissed him on the cheek, the way a rich wife would kiss her rich husband who showed such sensitivity.

"You ought to pray," Jim said. "Y'all sure is lucky."

"Yes we are," Mama said, acknowledging the luck in such a way as to suggest that only certain people were deserving.

• • •

Cozy Pitts had become increasingly irritated with Mama and Daddy because of "they high-minded, nose-in-the-air ways," as she said to Ethel Brown one night after they passed under my bedroom window on their way home. Another night, she let them have it face-to-face.

"Well, at least some of us got children where we can stands to look at 'em. Not one that's near about messed up in the head as Lost Boy. And Evan who stay out in the woods all night sleeping with the raccoons and snakes and shit. I guess money and the white devils don't solve everythang, do they? Tell me, Treeny. What that white-lady boss of yours got to say about this fucked-up family of yours?"

Everyone got very quiet and shifted uncomfortably. Mama's mouth hung open, hurt that Cozy would speak to her that way in front of people and on her own back porch. She was embarrassed that she hadn't been prepared for someone to rebel against her good fortune. She was furious at Cozy, but more angry at me. After all, in her mind, I had caused the initial fall from grace. In her mind, my existence left her vulnerable to constant attack. All someone had to do was mention my name or my "eccentricities" and a great pall was cast on her.

But Cozy Pitts needed to be put in her place. Mama stood and walked over to her chair. Cozy rolled her eyes and looked indifferent, which made Mama angrier.

"You look me in the eye, you ungrateful witch!"

Cozy laughed at her. "Ungrateful!" she shouted. "What you done for me that I can be ungrateful. Gimme some Kool-Aid? Huh!"

The next thing I knew, Daddy had run across the porch, grabbed Cozy's blouse in both fists and dragged her across the floor while she held on to her wig. He deposited her on her butt by the screen door.

"Why don't you take your nasty mouth on home to your loving husband. See if he can't knock some of that sense he knocked out of your head back into it."

Cozy struggled to her feet and went out the

terribly f

her sobs

the screen door slamming. She yelled at Cozy.

"Cozy Pitts! You a cruel, cruel woman!"

A voice replied from the darkness of our driveway. "Well, I reckon the truth hurt sometimes, don't it?"

"Maybe so," Daddy yelled back. "But from now on, you can do your reckoning on somebody else's porch and out of our sight."

"Well, I *reckon* that be just fine with me," she yelled.

I was torn. I couldn't stand the shame I created for my parents, but at the same time, I felt it was about time they did a little of the suffering around the house. I went to my bedroom, got my clothes for the next day, and went to the woods to spend the night. I didn't want to be in the same house with Daddy, who I knew would need to blow off his anger.

Later that night, I found myself in my woodland sanctuary lying on top of Bojack's sleeping bag trying to imagine what must be going through my parents' heads. I imagined them on their bed, silently and angrily staring at the ceiling. And I imagined that they were both thinking the same thing. Wondering what had gone wrong with us. Wondering what I was doing in the woods, and why Mark had turned against them.

In truth, Mark had turned against the whole world. In the four years since my trip to the hospital, his life fell apart. His confusion over how he should live his life eventually got the best of him. It left him with no direction, and when he finally saw that he needed a path to follow, there was no one around that he trusted to help show him the way. So he floundered. He no longer possessed the self-confidence to strike out on his own and become the man he should have been.

He was now nineteen and worked on the loading dock at the meatpacking plant. His immediate supervisor was Daddy. Whenever I pictured Daddy standing over Mark as he sweated, lifting box after monotonous box, I thought of the night that started this whole mess. I thought of Bojack lecturing about parents who didn't want their children to do better than they themselves had, and I hated Daddy. I thought about how Mark had said that same night in the quiet of our bedroom that he had decided he couldn't live like many of the black folk in Canaan. Now I mourned his lost dreams.

I remembered him trying to learn how to pimp. He never quite got it down. I used to turn away when he came by trying to walk like that; it was too tragic a sight. He also had a huge afro and a pick that was stuck in it. Not that there was anything wrong with an afro—I had one myself—but I knew that Mark didn't want one. He wanted to please the cool guys he was trying to hang out with—the ones who could shoot hoops and get any girl but needed their coaches to coerce their teachers into giving them a passing grade. But Mark was not an athlete. He was not cool. He had no coaches to back him up, and the girls found him awkward. But he kept trying to hang in this group rather than be seen in the same light as his little brother. I watched him struggle and lose himself. I watched one of the smartest people I ever knew graduate number 100 out of a graduating class of 110. I watched him grow more and more somber. I watched him go to work at the meatpacking plant and come home in tears.

Mark didn't want to hear anything from anybody. He didn't want to hear "I told you so" from me, and he didn't want to hear "You doing alright" from those who shared the same boat. Those people didn't want to see him moping around making them think that their lives weren't sufficient. So Mark shut down. He worked, watched television, and slept. If he was watching TV and anyone came in to watch with him, he would leave.

When people spoke to him on the street, he ignored them. Once, I left a clipping about ~~~ f~~~~~~~~~~

~~~ ~~~ ~~~~~~ ~~~ ~~~

tractor out of the shed since being forced to lease the farm. I saw him there from a distance. But over that distance, I felt his pain. I could see it in the way he sat, the set of his shoulders as he leaned forward, his arms draped across the steering wheel of his old Massey Ferguson. I didn't know what had hurt him, but instinctively I knew that something wasn't right. And though we were barely on speaking terms, he was still my father. I felt for him and all that we had once meant to each other. Yet, at the same time, I was afraid for what this scene might mean for me. I wondered if I'd done something wrong, or if someone had perceived that I'd done something wrong.

So I decided to leave him be. I didn't need to know about it until I could no longer avoid it.

I decided to go into the house, drop off my stuff, and go out to the woods until everyone was asleep. But when I walked into the kitchen, Mama was standing over the sink quietly crying and looking through the window at her husband. She barely noticed me as I walked in. She didn't bother to do that thing with her face that she usually did. She only blinked as the door closed behind me. On the kitchen table there was a note from Mark.

DON'T WORRY ABOUT ME!
DON'T THINK ABOUT ME! FORGET ME!
I'M GONE!!!

I went to what had been our bedroom and stared at the encyclopedias over his bed. The first step in our family's disintegration had taken place, and though I felt it for a second, I refused to accept the guilt. Mark had known what he needed to do, but he let them fool him into thinking that they had something to offer him. I dropped my head. My brother was gone. His despair would linger over us and sadden us, but at the same time, it stoked my desire to escape the dreadful destiny of Canaan.

I kept fighting the only way I knew how to. I continued to study and learn. I dreamed that someday I would send off applications to colleges. When they saw how hard I worked, they would all accept me, and I would leave Canaan for good. If I didn't keep up the work, I would become a clone of Mark, tossing boxes under Daddy's watchful eye. He would laugh at me, knowing that I was as beholden to him as an adult as I was as a child, and also knowing that I had stolen none of his thunder.

• • •

Aside from my schoolwork and football, you could say that I had no other life. I guess a lot of it was my fault. I probably had an opportunity to try to break back into black society in Canaan, but I never took advantage of the relaxed atmosphere that surrounded me. The community guilt, that is. I used the cease-fire in the war against Evan Walls to retreat, to withdraw into my own world. I circled the wagons and pulled out my Winchester. I was my sole protector, and that scared me because I was wounded. To be alone, wounded, and under the stress of anticipated aggression wasn't easy.

I walked through my life as if I were a spy walking through a crowd, knowing all along that the police had my picture and were on the hunt. I constantly looked over my shoulder. I realized that the people of Canaan had a tremendous hold on my psyche. As much as I hated to admit it, they had me under their control. They could disrupt my life at any moment. All it would take was a word.

Snowball. Tom. Oreo. At any moment someone could be planning a mission against me. If I caught two people whispering nearby, I thought they were talking about me. I thought the conspiracy of the moment was underway, and that I would be ...

... game of the season.

• • •

For three years after my stay in the hospital, Bojack and I spent a lot of time together. He dusted off his old weights that he'd found in a junkyard and taught me how to pump iron, helping me sculpt my body for football. We spent every Sunday studying and refining the game. Lessons that I began put to good use during my one year of junior varsity football at Canaan High School. Lessons that proved valuable, bringing my talents to the fore and into the good graces of my coaches and local sports media. I felt the heat from my old buddies, T. Wall and Flak, who were also on the team. They felt I was shucking and jiving, trying to be the coach's pet. So we stayed away from each other outside of practice and game play.

Bojack and I spent every Friday night together following our varsity team, dreaming of the day when I would be playing with the big boys.

Those boys' nights out always ended with us in Bojack's truck, parked out in front of his house, discussing what was good and bad about the way the teams played. We stayed in the truck because Aunt Mary had long ago declared their home off limits to me.

On this particular night, I hadn't noticed that Bojack was unusually quiet. I was still spinning from the exciting ending of the game. We had lost, and I was talking about how the Canaan players who made the crucial mistake would carry that mistake all their lives.

"I guess that's the risk you take when you go out there and put it all on the line, huh?" I asked Bojack as we came to a stop in front of his house.

I noticed that he hadn't heard me.

"Something wrong?" I asked.

"Huh?" he replied, after snapping to.

"I asked if there was something wrong."

He nodded as he turned off the truck and pulled the keys out of the ignition. "Yeah, I reckon."

"Is it me?"

"Yeah. It's about you."

I sat back and looked straight ahead as he told me how Aunt Mary had declared that night's game as the last football game we'd see together. He said that she had forbidden him from seeing me for any reason. He said that he had put up a fight until she threatened to divorce him again.

I sat there in shock.

"I know how you feels," Bojack said. "Hell, I was shocked, too, when she tossed it my way. I reckon she just wants to hurt you."

"She has."

"Yeah, well I ain't feeling too swift, neither," he said.

"Why didn't you tell her that you were going to do what you wanted to?"

"I told you she said she was gone divorce me. We done done that once already."

"I can't believe she would divorce you because of me. I just can't see that."

"She would. Believe me. I wouldn't lie to you of all people. I thank what it come down to is you and them white folks you be hanging out with. And Mary will go to all kinds of extremes where white folks is concerned."

"What does she care? They're not after her!"

"She figures they might be. See, she feel like you be bringing 'em around into our circles, and then they be forcing their ways on us. And I ain't got to tell you what Mary be thanking about their ways."

"No," I said, shaking my head. "You

Mary and both of us thinking of things gone by and things that were supposed to be. I couldn't believe I was losing Bojack. He was my best friend, not to mention my only black male friend. He was also the last shoulder I had to lean on.

"So, it's over. Just like that?" I asked.

He slowly nodded. "I reckon so, Evan. I reckon so. Worse part is that I can't come to none of your football games next year when you be varsity."

"I'll remember what you taught me," I said, trying to make him feel better.

"Thanks," he said. "I reckon you better go now."

"Okay. Yeah, I guess so."

"I'm sorry, Evan. You know I loves you. It's just that I don't want to be alone no more. I'm too old for that shit, and me and Mary did have something special. Maybe we can get it back again. I don't know. But we do has some history together, and it ain't that easy to just throw away."

"I understand. I'm glad I'm playing varsity next year, though, because without you to buy tickets for me, I wouldn't see any football. I want to thank you for all the games. I mean, it really meant a lot to me."

"Thank you," he said, and he wiped his eyes and gave me a hopeful smile. "Let me work on her, see what I can do."

"Okay," I replied, smiling back. "I'll see you around?"

"Yeah, you'll see me."

So I left Bojack and went to the woods, where I promptly picked up a bottle, called it "Aunt Mary," and then smashed it against my rock.

When I was finished releasing as much of that anger as I could, I rested against a tree, catching my breath and wondering who I would turn to when things went wrong. I had just lost Bojack, which made me think back to nine months after the beating I took at school and a history class that moved me to tears but also signaled the departure of Eliza Blizzard from Canaan and my life.

. . .

I hadn't seen Eliza since she visited me in the hospital. By the time I returned to school, she'd moved to Washington, DC. She had a new job with a big title at the national office of the NAACP. But she was on her way back to take me on this mysterious trip she'd promised. I was anxious to see her and to hear about her new adventures. Bojack drove me to the airport to pick her up, and I couldn't control my joy as we watched her deplane and cross the tarmac into our waiting arms.

It felt like she and Bojack were brother and sister. They talked and laughed across me as I sat in the middle of his pickup's seat. I imagined for a moment that they were Mama and Daddy and we were a happy family.

Within an hour, I was surprised to find us rolling to a stop in a parking lot on the campus of Hampton Institute.

"Is this where we're going?" I asked

"It is," Eliza said. "Do you know much about it?"

I shook my head. "I don't know anything about it."

She looked perturbed.

"It's a beautiful place, Evan. It's an institution of higher education just for black folks. It has a rich history, and it truly pains me that you know nothing about it. It's in your state, for God's sake. Not even an hour and a half away from your home. But you're here now, and soon you'll understand why I brought you. I have a friend who has a friend in the administration here. She made a call for me and helped set this up for us. First, let's take a walk around campus to just get a feel for the place. Then we are going

nap. wake me up for the food," he said as we walked away.

I walked along the waterfront with Eliza past the president's house and deeper into the campus. She took me to the football field, and I sprinted around a bit, pretending to catch a few touchdown passes, imagining what it would be like to play college football.

As we walked to meet my student guide, I did so slowly because I got caught up in everything that was happening around me, just as Eliza knew I would. She smiled at me and kept an arm around my shoulders to keep me moving in the right direction. I kept getting distracted as I walked, glancing here and there at the students all around me, rushing to class and talking a mile a minute. Black students with books, smiling, chatty. We passed intense discussions about classwork between students in leather jackets and huge afros, tight jeans, short skirts, and platform shoes. There was an argument about something math related. But Eliza said that they weren't arguing. It was something different—a passionate intellectual discourse. Something I was not used to. I kept waiting for someone to call someone an Uncle Tom, but it never happened.

There was a fierceness in the faces of these students. They looked anything but timid. They strode full of confidence, purpose, power, and self-respect. Stupefied by the contrast between my world and this new world, I was already getting emotional when Eliza gently stopped me from wandering.

"We're here," she said. "I think this young lady walking toward us might be your guide."

"Look at that building," I said, pointing toward a massive structure behind the student approaching.

She was smiling when she stopped in front of us. "I see you like my dorm," she said.

"That's where you sleep?" I asked. "It's like a castle."

Eliza and the young woman laughed.

"I'm Eliza Blizzard, and this is Evan Walls."

"Good morning to you both. My name is Nomi Washington, and I'm going to take Evan to my American history class. I think you'll like it. We're starting Reconstruction today."

Eliza and Nomi shook hands and planned to meet in an hour by the tree.

"What tree?" I asked.

"That's for later," Eliza said. "You go to class and learn something, young man."

"Yes, ma'am," I replied.

"You might need to keep a hand on him so he doesn't wander away," she called to Nomi as we walked away. "I think all of this knowledge has disoriented him a little."

"I've got him," Nomi said, laughing, as we continued. She began to tell me about her dorm. "Virginia-Cleveland Hall. It's the oldest women's residence hall on campus. The guy who designed it, the architect, also designed the base of the Statue of Liberty. That's cool, right?"

All I could do was nod.

Nomi put me in the seat beside her in the classroom. Within moments, I was in awe of the way the professor ran the class. Back at Canaan High, you were lectured to, took notes, and took tests. That morning at Hampton Institute, I watched a very thoughtful and educational discourse. Sure, there were facts and dates, but he wanted to hear about political strategies. He wanted to know about the motivation for things. He wanted the students' interpretations of events, and he treated each opinion with great respect. It was stunning to me, and I quickly understood why Eliza brought me here. I imagined myself having ~~somo~~

~~followed~~

Nomi all day to soak up everything, but there was a plan. She took me to the tree to meet Eliza, who could tell that I was rattled.

"I think I understand," Nomi said when we stood next to Eliza. "I was tipped off a little about why you're here today."

She gave me a long hug and then taught me a handshake that they did on campus.

"Good luck, Evan," she said. "I hope you come to Hampton when you graduate."

She left after a squeeze of my shoulder and a smile. Bojack joined us as we watched her disappear in the crowd.

"You okay, little brother?" he asked.

I just stared back at the two of them. "Where?" I asked, tears welling. "Where do black people like this live?"

"All over, baby," Eliza said. "All over. And in time, you will find your way to them, but you got to be strong and hold on to what you want. Let's go sit down."

We sat in the shade of an oak tree. Its circumference was simply immense. It had a massive trunk with gnarled limbs that were so long and heavy that they grazed the ground. You could feel its age and the history that it had absorbed.

"This is a very, very special tree," Eliza said.

"You ain't gotta say it," Bojack said. "You can feel that in the air."

She smiled. "It's called the Emancipation Oak. Evan, just after the Civil War, freed slaves began collecting around these parts. They were called *contrabands* by the Union soldiers. After a while, even though it was against the law in Virginia, they decided to start a school for—now, hear me good—all of the newly freed men and women who displayed, and I quote, 'a great thirst for knowledge.' So, in the shade of this tree, a sister by the name of Mary Smith Peake starting teaching. They sat right where you are sitting, hungering for knowledge. So you see, Evan, your dream isn't a new thing. But for many black folk, it's a thing long lost in the weeds of racism and self-hatred. Also delivered under this tree was the South's first reading of the Emancipation Proclamation. So right here they proclaimed the right to be free and to be educated. This is your legacy, Evan. You gotta fight for it."

"Amen," Bojack said. "Amen."

"You know," she said, "my father used to teach me in parables. And one day he taught about the idea of self-reliance. He said, 'One morning you wake up and you need this particular thing and you know your neighbor has some of it. So you go next door and knock and ask for some. Your neighbor says no and you go home but you can't believe it because that neighbor has always been a friend. So you try again because you really need this thing, but your neighbor says no again. A few days later, you try again, but this time the neighbor slams the door in your face, and you go back home and sulk. Eliza, I ask you, how many times will you go and beg before it dawns on you that you're not going to get any help? If you are going to get this thing that you need, you had better figure out a way to get it by yourself.'

"I think that's how it is for you, Evan. You just aren't going to get a lot of help in Canaan. I didn't, either, but we got some things done. You will, too; you just got to stick on the path that you've chosen. It is the right one. I promise you that, young soldier of the cause."

Bojack and I put Eliza on a plane later that afternoon. I wouldn't see her again until I graduated from college, but she always remained in my heart. As did Mama Jennie, who, six months after that trip, did as the old folks used to say and "made her way to Glory" from the same hospital that I had been in.

_____ beeping of the hospital equipment that destroyed my feeling of reverence for the moment.

I sat next to her, suffering from a feeling of inconsolable loss. Her face was sallow, and even as she slept, it was lined with pain. The night before, she had suffered a stroke, and now everything about her was uneven. Especially her mouth, which was pulled down to one side, making obvious the constant tension within her body. I reached out to hold her hand, which was cold and strangely stiff, the suppleness and the warmth of life almost gone.

I closed my eyes and thought about how two weeks earlier, on a Sunday night, she sat in her favorite chair, surrounded by her descendants. She looked bored. At one point, when there was a lull in the conversation, she said loudly, "I'm tired of living. I'm gone be dead before the month is out." Then she got out of her chair, went into her bedroom, and left everybody to wonder what brought on all of that.

When I opened my eyes, she was still there, not resting, her body pulling against itself like a rubber band. A nurse came in and said that I could talk to Mama Jennie, warning that her speech would be slurred.

After the nurse left, I leaned over and whispered her name next to her ear. She opened her eyes and tried to smile. I recognized the effort and kissed her hand.

She said something that I didn't understand. I asked her to repeat herself and she moved her mouth around in a funny way, as if she were trying to gain the proper control of it.

"Hello, my baby," she struggled, her voice higher and coarser than usual. A raspy wheezing enveloped her words.

"Hi, Mama Jennie."

"Didn't thank I was gonna see you again."

"Me, either. They wouldn't let me come in alone. And when I came in with them, they crowded around you so I couldn't get near you."

She made a face like she was disgusted. "What they doing out yonder?"

"The truth?"

She gave an awkward nod.

"They were talking about who was going to get what from your house."

She made that face again. "Well at least they waited until I gots one foot in the grave."

"Don't talk like that. You'll be alright. I need you to be alright."

She sighed heavily and gave me a very tired look. She had no more to give. I felt lumped in with my parents and the relatives out in the waiting room.

"I'm sorry," I said. "I didn't mean to be selfish."

She nodded. "That be alright."

"I just wanted to let you know how important you are to me. What you have meant to me."

"Thank you, son. I know you worried that you gone be all alone. I know that be scary. But ole Evan Walls, shoot, he gone do just fine. Mind what I say now. Hear me?"

"But who's gonna teach me about life?"

"You will, by living it. You just do one thang. Remember this. Life goes on mostly with a small circle of trusted people. Life goes on all around you, but you gone move in and out of it with your special friends and loved ones at your side. Might just be a couple of friends.

Might just be your wife and children. And you will find out, honey baby, that they is all you really need. They'll get you through. When you get out on your own and figures this out, you be able to get rid of the need for all them other folk that h—

[text obscured]

[text obscured], either. You always gone need them, but you ain't got to have them. Catch my meaning?"

"Yes, ma'am. I do," I said, smiling. "Do you know I think about you like I do the Bible. Like you always have the right answer for questions about how to live life."

"Oh, you giving me way too much credit now. I ain't hardly got nothing on Jesus. See, I ain't never done no work where I had to use my noggin. Just field work and laundry. So I guess I thought a lot while I worked. And, chile, I'm near about as old as Methuselah, so I done had a lot of time to be thanking. If I was this wise all my life, I'da had the white folks licked," she said, smiling. "Naw, chile. Ain't nothing special in this old head. Just the years talking."

"I read where it says experience is the father of wisdom."

"Well, I reckon that sums it up then."

"Yes, ma'am."

She smiled and yawned. "Why don't you let the old lady get some sleep now."

I said okay and got up to leave, but she called me back.

"Give me a kiss, honey baby. I might not see you again."

"Don't say that."

"But it's true, Evan. And I wouldn't stop thangs if I could. Death ain't scary to me like it once was. I can taste it already, and it sho' is sweet."

I looked deeply into her eyes. I took a snapshot for my mind and heart. Even today, I can see her exactly as she was right before I kissed her for the last time.

I sat at the end of our pathway, alongside Bullet, and thought about how much I had come to hate riding bus number 58, about Mama Jennie, about Hampton Institute, Bojack and how I wanted to escape the misery of another school year in Canaan. No one dared sit next to me, no matter how crowded the bus might be. I knew it would be the same my sophomore year. I'd lose myself in thought, staring out the window, only to be shocked into reality by being beaned in the head by a book or ball, or anything else someone thought was funny to throw at me. As I stood waiting, my stomach burned again, and I worried that my ulcer would be bleeding freely before the first week of school was over.

However, I was saved. At least as far as the ride to school was concerned. A horn blew in the distance, and I was pleasantly surprised to see that the car contained two of the three teenagers in my life that I could call "friend."

"My saviors!" I shouted.

"Thought you might like a ride," Dee said. "Tex here got this piece-of-junk car a couple of weeks ago. We'll pick you up every morning if you like."

"You must be kidding. Of course I like!" I said as I jumped into the car.

"We couldn't let a fellow jock down," Tex said.

I settled into the back of Tex's convertible Chevy Impala. I noticed Dee's shoulders. He was wearing a tank top and looked so much bigger than when school had let out.

"Dee, you've really been lifting."

"Yeah, man," he replied. "Trying to get a body like yours."

I laughed. The changes had made Dee seem somewhat a stranger to me when I saw him two weeks before at football practice. At that point it had been two months since we'd seen each other. I wondered if he'd noticed any changes in me. I still hadn't seen or spoken to Eddie. Although we could mix during the school year, blacks and whites separated during the summer.

Two years earlier, Eddie tried to break that rule. He'd invited me to a church picnic. I went, without my family's knowledge, of course. People were stunned, and one of the women running it took Eddie aside for a short lecture. Then she asked me if I would do her a favor and leave, and not return to any subsequent functions at her church.

"One of you might be fine," she said. "But it never stops there, does it?"

Richard Baker, or, as we called him, "Tex," had shown up three years before. From Texas, he was a junior, and the best receiver on our football team. One day, he'd go on to win a Super Bowl ring.

"Like my ride, E?" he asked.

"Yeah, it's nice."

"Dad got a new one, so he shifted this one my way. Says if I catch six hundred yards this year, he'll get me a new one for senior year."

"That's great."

"Yeah," Tex continued. "And I'll be able to get all the best girls."

"Lucky bastard," Dee said. "Wish I had my own car. How about you, E?"

"Wouldn't help me any," I replied.

"But you could get—"

"Nothing!" I shouted, quickly ending that piece of conversation.

Girls were definitely poor topics. It was more than taboo to date a white girl, and no black girl

"Practice has been really tough the last couple of weeks, right?" Tex asked.

"Yeah," Dee said. "Coach really wants us to take state this year."

"We could have done it last year, but our defense was weak."

"Well, that's where Evan and I come in," Dee continued.

"You'll be the best middle linebacker in the state this year," I told Dee.

"I think you'll make an average-at-best free safety," he replied, and we laughed.

"There's only one thing that can hamper you," Tex added.

"What's that?" I asked.

"Taliferro Pitts. That's what. He's been waiting on you. That mountain hates your guts. And he's got a lot of people on his side."

"Well, not many people like me," I replied, trying to show no emotion. I recalled seeing T. Wall and Flak on the first day of practice hanging out with Taliferro, their hatred for me on display.

"But most of them ain't like Taliferro Pitts. He hates you to the core. He says football is a legit way to bust your ass, and that the moment is at hand since you'll be a lowly sophomore in your first year of varsity. Dee and I heard him talking to some of the other black guys. They're gonna be laying for you. Said they were going to teach you a lesson."

"Ha!" Dee said. "I wonder what lesson he thinks he can teach you."

"How to be sufficiently black," I replied.

• • •

I found my homeroom and took a seat in a back corner. The teacher was a tall, skinny white woman who walked in, announced herself as Mrs. Childers, and promptly started calling the class roll. I hated this. All the white kids responded to their names with "Here" or "Yep." From the black kids came assorted replies like "Yo!" or "Solid." I wanted to have something clever to answer, but I couldn't. If I had come up with something and used it, the response would have been, "The little wannabe white boy is trying to act black." If I just said "Here," I would be acting like whitey.

So I did my usual and raised my hand, forcing the teacher to look up from her notes and ask me if there was something wrong with my voice. But that was okay, because I'd rather have Mrs. Childers a little miffed at me than give the kids another reason to taunt me. You'd think that calling the roll would be an easy thing to get through. Everything that I was a part of, no matter how small, carried some political fallout.

When the teacher got to the Cs, I had my head down, wanting to separate myself from the goings-on as much as possible. But I raised it and turned around when I heard a new voice respond to Mrs. Childers. This "here" was different. Her voice tore at my insides. It was deep and husky like that singer Mama Jennie had liked, Bobbie Gentry. When this new girl spoke, I could just hear Bobbie Gentry singing her "Ode to Billie Joe."

"You are new in Canaan, correct?" Mrs. Childers asked.

"Yes, I am," responded Patty Cunningham. "I'm from Philadelphia."

"Well, I guess you're welcome even though you're a Yankee," Mrs. Childers said, laughing.

Patty Cunningham didn't react, her face stoic. Then she looked in my direction, but I wasn't sure why. I smiled back at her, hoping to let her know that it didn't bother me that she was from Philadelphia.

She smiled back at me. Right away, I thought of a poem by Thomas Campion I'd stumbled across one day while reading in the Canaan library.

back at her the entire time we sat in homeroom. Her hair was black and fluffy, and it fell well below her shoulders. Looking into her blue eyes was pleasantly unsettling. At one point, she got up and walked over to the trash can. On her way back to her seat, she smiled at me again, and I was lost for a second in that beautiful face. Lost until a little voice inside my head yelled at me, *Hey, she's white!* I dropped my head again and began scolding myself for losing my perspective. As quickly as all those emotions had come, they had gone, banished by Patty Cunningham's skin.

At lunch, I found myself alone. I saw Dee, Eddie, and Tex down in the parking lot trying to get some of the cheerleaders into Tex's car. Other students strolled around me at a distance, and that was just fine with me. Over the past few years, I had become the ultimate wallflower. Only when I was alone did I feel truly comfortable. I had pulled out my journal and begun to write when I heard that voice again.

"Homework already?"

I looked up, dumbfounded that Patty was standing over me. A white girl and a black boy talking anywhere in Canaan was unheard of. If anyone took notice, I would be right back in the thick of gossip and a prime target for retribution by angry whites—and, of course, blacks. Even still, I didn't want her to leave.

"I'm Patty—"

"Cunningham," I interrupted.

"Yes, I'm surprised you remembered."

"I'm not."

She smiled. "Mind if I join you?"

"No, not at all," I said, trying to figure out why she had come to visit.

"I hope you don't mind my intruding, but you seemed so friendly this morning, and you looked so peaceful over here. Peace is great when you feel out of place."

"Yeah, I know all about that."

"So I hear."

"What do you mean?"

"You're Evan Walls, right?"

"Yes, and I'm really surprised that you remembered my name."

"Why? You're the only one who tried to make me feel comfortable. It was so cute the way you kept stealing glances at me."

I cringed. "I'm sorry. I guess I couldn't help myself."

"No need to be sorry. Really."

While she talked on about getting settled at a school with a bunch of people who were not fond of Yankees, I looked her over. She was just so beautiful. After all the trouble I'd had with girls, I couldn't believe she was sitting beside me.

"Yeah," I said, agreeing with her. "Most of these people make me uncomfortable, too."

"I guess I'll have to get used to it."

I didn't know how to respond to that, not knowing why she was in Canaan. So I just nodded.

"So, you play football," she said, changing the subject.

"Yeah. Who told you that?"

"Some guy with the good-old-boy name of Tex who was trying to get me to take a ride in his car."

I laughed.

"Anyway," she continued, "I asked him about you."

"Why?"

"Because you were so nice and I saw you talking to him before lunch."

"Well, I play free safety."

"Oh, you do?"

"You're not very popular. I asked one black girl about you. Before she told me to mind my business, she called you a 'whitey wannabe.' A white girl told me that not too many blacks like you much."

"Well, you certainly picked up a lot in one morning."

"I'm afraid it's not hard where you're concerned. You inspire some pretty intense feelings."

"Yeah."

For a few seconds, the conversation died. We both stared out at the other kids hanging out. I thought she had pulled back because she felt she had come on too strong, but I was wrong. She was mulling my situation, feeling bad for me, and trying to find some way to bring me a little of the comfort I'd brought her in homeroom.

"It was a shadowy region, a no man's land, the ground that separated the white world from the black that he stood upon," she said, breaking the silence.

"Wow!" I replied, thinking about how she'd put everything in place with one sentence. "Did you just make that up on the spot?"

"No. It's from *Native Son*. Don't you know it? It's a novel by a famous black author, Richard Wright."

"No, I don't know it," I said, embarrassed. I wondered if the Cozy Pittses of the world knew about black people like this writer. If they did, they might understand that what I wanted was not foreign to us as a people. But all that aside, I was happy to have met Patty Cunningham for reasons other than her looks. I knew that I could learn from her.

"I know that this will make me seem stupid," I said. "I mean, I love books. I read all the time, but I really didn't know that there were any famous black authors. The library here doesn't have books by black people. I'm embarrassed."

"Oh, don't be. There are a lot of great black writers. I'll bring you some books."

"Thank you."

She smiled. "Maybe we could talk sometime about that shadowy region you live in."

"I'd like that," I replied, as the bell ending lunch period sounded. "Would you show me to my next class?"

"I'd like that even better."

"Football," Bojack once said to me, "is a game of strategy, see. It's a whole lot more than one man's strength against another. It's all about using your opponent's weakness to your advantage. It's about making him thank you has a certain weakness that you really ain't got. When he builds up his game plan around your fake weakness, you surprise him. And you nail his butt."

In the days before Aunt Mary's ban on our friendship, lectures of this sort would come on crisp fall and winter mornings. Bojack didn't go to church much after what happened with me and Eliza Blizzard. So while everyone else was in church, we met in the field next to my house, and Bojack taught me football. We read from a coach's manual, and he recalled lessons from his favorite ex-football players who acted as analysts during NFL games. We practiced blocking, punting, and the proper way to hold a football when throwing. We practiced running receiver routes, catching punts, how to take a handoff, and tackling, which I enjoyed the most. I lived for Sundays during football season. On this particular Tuesday, I was very happy I had paid strict attention, because I was now standing face-to-face with Taliferro Pitts.

"All right, Walls," Head Coach Kendel yelled. "Here's the drill. You're a lineman. The man behind you with the ball is the running back. The man in front of you is your defensive adversary."

I saw pain in Taliferro Pitts' smile.

"Now," the coach continued, "you cannot go outside of the two blocking dummies on either side of you. But you have to clear the defensive player out of the space between them so that the back has a clear path. Understand?"

"Yes, sir!" I shouted.

The pain in Taliferro's smile grew.

"Good," the coach said. "'Cause the back will run straight up your asshole if you don't get Pitts and yourself clear of the hole. When I blow the whistle, let's get at it."

Pain now glowed in Taliferro's smile.

Quickly, I recalled one of Bojack's lessons. He'd said, "There's a trick to blocking a man bigger than you is. He can't get down as low as you. Big men likes to make contact on they way to standing up. So what the little man gotta do in this kinda blocking situation is this here. The ball snapped, right? The big man, he steps forward and starts to standing up. The little man, he comes forward, too, but he stays really low. When they hit, the big man gone be at a loss, see? The little man got what Pat Summerall call a lower center of gravity. He just hit the big man at his waist or thigh level, and move the big man whichever way he wants to. Heavy shit, huh?"

I crouched in a three-point stance. There were no more than two feet between me and Taliferro. Dee and Tex stood behind him, cringing. They knew how much he was looking forward to this. And just to emphasize that point, Taliferro mouthed to me, "Your ass is mine."

When the coach blew his whistle, we charged. Taliferro began to rise, and I stayed low and got in an incredible shot to his midsection. It sent him crashing to the ground, and I stood above him victoriously for just a second. "A wise man knows how far to push thangs," Mama

Jennie had told me once.

"Good hit! Way to block, Walls," the coach yelled. "Take notes, gentlemen."

I looked at Dee and Tax's

embarrassed. That would give him and his crew ammunition. But I guess I didn't minimize things enough. As the coach repeated his orders to the next three players, Taliferro walked by me, fuming.

"You made a play and you thank you something special, huh? A show-off. Oh, but you ain't seen real showing off yet. I'm gone put your Uncle Tom ass back in place with a little extra since you got my mama kicked out the session. Your daddy laid hands on her. See what we gone do to you. Yeah, this ain't just about football, baby."

I turned to walk away, and that pissed him off more. He forgot himself and yelled, "I'm gone fuck you up, punk! Gonna fuck you up, baaaaad!"

Everyone turned to look at us. Coach Kendel pointed at Taliferro and screamed, "It's not Walls' fault you don't know how to do your job."

That, of course, did me no favors. There was only silence, so much that, as I turned to walk away from the situation, I could hear my shoulder pads rubbing against my jersey.

Quietly, I lingered around the action until we moved on to running some plays. It was very difficult to concentrate the rest of practice. The fact that I knew my position well carried me through. In between huddles and tackles, I wondered how I'd make it through the season. It was hard enough not to get cut from a team with that much talent. It took a lot of mental toughness. I would have to do it while wasting a lot of precious energy on fending off Taliferro, T. Wall, and their boys. The thought left me tired. I just wanted to play football.

• • •

I spent a lot of time, on and off the practice field, wondering why Taliferro Pitts chose to up the ante where I was concerned. I didn't lay hands on his mother. And it would have been so easy to just let me linger in the world of cold shoulders. I saw no reason for him to actively seek to bury me, both literally and figuratively.

I concluded that he needed me as a form of stress relief and a referendum on his control. I recalled Taliferro saying his father had beaten his mother in order to feel like he controlled something. Now Arthur Pitts was dead at the hands of a white deputy who had beaten him to death with a billy club. It happened right outside the ABC store. The store manager called the police, saying that Arthur had stolen some liquor, but he was so drunk he couldn't move very well and he was ranting and raving.

When the police got there, they confronted Arthur and they found the stolen liquor on him. When Arthur put up a fight, the deputy beat him to death right on the sidewalk in front of the store. There was no official investigation into the beating. It was deemed justified, and even a huge protest led by Eliza Blizzard couldn't change the right minds.

As you can imagine, Taliferro's hatred of whites had grown. Yet, like his father before him, he still felt impotent in the face of whites. He needed revenge, but he couldn't seek it against whites, so he sought it against the next best thing—a black kid who embodied their ideals.

Starting with the football team, he set out to avenge the life and death of his hated father and his mother's banishment by doing me in. Others, like T. Wall and company, were willing partners. Dee, Tex and I discussed it one morning on the way to school.

"Oh, for crying out loud. It's this simple," Dee said. "They follow him around because they're afraid of him. He's crazy. He's a maniac. Everybody's afraid he might go off and kill someone. I am. Aren't you?"

"Well, he doesn't have to threaten anyone in this town to take shots at me," I replied.

Pitts."

"Well, I agree with Dee," I said. "That's stretching it quite a bit, but I get the point. You must be on the World War II chapter in history."

Taliferro wasted no time in emphasizing that point. During the first week of classes, I passed him in a stairwell and he proceeded to trip me. I was just about to take my first step off the landing when he stuck his foot between my feet. I tumbled headfirst down the staircase, causing an avalanche of students. A girl named Tawanda Jeter broke a leg in the pileup. I was blamed for the incident. Tawanda's parents demanded that I be suspended, but after some consideration, the principal decided that I wasn't to blame. Others were anxious to follow Taliferro's lead. From all quarters, the verbal abuse intensified. The nickname "Snowball" was revived, along with the other old standards. It seemed no one could stand to pass me without slinging a verbal arrow.

But these days things were different. Often I was able to parry their insults and then scoff at their intentions. I could do this because Patty Cunningham had introduced me to black writers who had endured experiences like mine. Not exactly like mine, but enough to make me feel that I wasn't a freak of nature. That I was not alone. Enough to convince me that I was right to live my dreams, and that, despite what anybody in Canaan thought, I had not lost my blackness.

I will never forget the warm Saturday afternoon that I sat in my circle in the woods reading *Black Boy* by Richard Wright. On page 125, I came upon this.

I walked home slowly, asking myself what on earth was the matter with me, why it was I never seemed to do things as people expected them to be done. Every word and gesture I made seemed to provoke hostility. I had never been able to talk to others and I had to guess at their meanings and motives.

Then:

The routine of the house flowed on as usual; for me there was sleep, mush, greens, school, study, loneliness, yearning and then sleep again.

Later, I came upon this:

I knew that I lived in a country in which the aspirations of black people were limited, marked-off. Yet I felt that I had to go somewhere and do something to redeem my being alive. I was building up in me a dream which the entire educational system of the south had been rigged to stifle.

Then:

My classmates felt that I was doing something that was vaguely wrong, but they did not know how to express it. As the outside world grew more meaningful, I became more concerned, tense; and my classmates and my teachers would say: "Why do you ask so many questions?" Or: "Keep quiet."

I felt relief and then strength. I gained more strength from the words of people like James Baldwin and Zora Neale Hurston.

It wasn't as if Mama Jennie and Bojack hadn't helped me. I could never explain the depth of my feelings for them. But they were on the outside helping, like a doctor to a patient. What gives the patient the special, indescribable comf...

...and a child of society. She'd followed her well-known wealthy parents to all sorts of posh Philadelphia events. She'd worn modernized pinafore dresses, smiled when she was supposed to, and of course, she was her daddy's little girl. At least in his eyes.

Patty loved the life she'd led in Philadelphia. She loved those events and the celebrities who attended. When she got older, she bought books, the plays of Eugene O'Neill and Tennessee Williams. She saw all the latest films with her mother. When report cards came out and she had earned straight As, her mother always took her to New York for a weekend visit. They would spend the time running from theater to theater, catching plays from matinee to evening performances. Sundays were set aside for museums.

Patty liked rock music, but she could take it or leave it. Folk music was her favorite—Joan Baez, Joni Mitchell, Bob Dylan, Neil Young, James Taylor. These artists taught her about feelings that her parents never talked about, and they made her question her life. The result was that Patty could never accept anything superficially.

"There's a deep meaning to every aspect of life," she liked to say.

I came to know all of these things about Patty in the first weeks of school, as we had been sharing our peacefulness together. Every day during lunch we met behind the cafeteria, out of sight of the playgrounds, discussing the deeper meanings of life.

"My daddy doesn't really appreciate the deeper meanings," she told me one day. "I drive him crazy, and he blames my mom for trying to make me grow up too fast."

"In what way?"

"He doesn't want me to think about anything of substance. He just wants me to be his little girl and sit around with an empty head, adoring him. The other night they got into an argument over me. I'd complained to Mom about moving here. I don't mean to hurt your feelings, but it's pretty damned boring."

I laughed. "You're not hurting my feelings."

"Anyway, he told Mom that I questioned too much. That I take everything so damned seriously and that I'm always arguing about the way things should be. Mom told him that I was a thinker and that he'd be proud of that fact if I were a boy."

"I bet he didn't like that."

"He told her to spare him the feminist shit. That I'm angry about too much, and I have to analyze everything. What do I care? I'm sixteen years old. Why can't I be a cheerleader like normal girls and enjoy something . . . superficial."

We both laughed.

"He told her, 'She's growing up too fast and it's going to come back to haunt you.'"

Patty ended up in Canaan because of her father's obsessions. His company had purchased one of the local meatpacking plants, and instead of sending one of his vice presidents, Alex Cunningham, president and CEO, brought his family there so he could reorganize the plant's operation. He thought if he could get Patty away from the city and its theaters, huge libraries, and artsy-fartsy films, she might not grow up so fast.

"Country girls are slower to mature," he told Patty before they moved. "Maybe you can join the Girl Scouts or something."

"You brought me here to deprive me of stimulation so I could be your daddy's girl again, and to put Mom in her place."

"Like your mother, you can be cruel."

"Dad, look in the mirror."

Talking about her dad made her sad, so we didn't. But we did talk about everything else in our lives on those very special lunch breaks. I loved learning from her and

FOURTEEN

I was sitting on the dining room floor, drinking some cherry Kool-Aid. It was a warm September night, and the windows I was sitting beside were open to allow for the light breeze. The fresh air felt great to me as I sat there proudly in the blue-and-gold football jersey that I would wear to school the next day and in my first varsity game the next night. On my chest, back, and sleeves was the number 5, which was Bojack's lucky number.

Drawn in with the breeze were the voices of the session members, complaining as usual while Mama and Daddy continued their role of the sympathizers. Chauncey Mae, Aunt Mary, Ethel and Jim Brown had their sad stories cranked up to a fever pitch, and when things were on a roll like that, the session, like a Reverend Walker sermon, usually ended up going long. I got up to leave, figuring this was the perfect chance to talk to Bojack about my conflicting feelings.

As I crossed the field beside my house, I was smiling but confused. I could handle the bad thoughts, but this calmness that made me smile out of nowhere was foreign. I thought that Bojack might be able to shed some light on my state of mind.

On the way up the dirt path to Bojack's, I thought about Dee's declaration of fear regarding Taliferro.

"The word has been passed around on the team," he had told me.

"What word?" I asked, even though I k

As I walked up the steps to Bojack's house, I saw him through the kitchen window. He was sitting at the table, his chin resting on his hands. Beside him was a bottle of whiskey. In front of him was a checkerboard with both sides set up. Once in a while, he would move a checker and jump it with a checker from the other side. Then he'd stare at the situation, his head bobbing as he nodded in and out of sleep.

I knocked on the door. Finally he answered. He screamed.

"Boy, what in the goddamn hell! You ain't supposed to be here!"

I had to laugh. "I just came for a visit."

"Well, is you crazy or what? Mary will bust both our butts."

"I don't think so. The way they were carrying on, she'll be on the porch for a while. I got a good feeling that we'll be okay."

"Well, just in case you a little rusty on applying yo' intuitions, I thank we ought to go out back of the shed just in case she gets a mind to come home early. Let me get my elixir of life."

After he'd gone back in and gotten his whiskey, we went out behind his shed, leaned against its rotting wood and stared up at the sky.

"So, tell me something. How you been doing?" he asked. "I must say, I do miss you," he continued while slowly nodding. "Yeah, I reckon I do."

"Likewise," I replied. "I'm okay. You know, ups and downs."

He turned to me with a look of amused disbelief. "Shit, did I hear there was an *up* in there?"

I laughed. "Yeah, that's different for a change, huh?"

"Well, tell me about the down first. I'm in a proper groove where the blues is concerned."

I told the story of the Canaan Hogs and Taliferro Pitts and Bojack didn't seem surprised.

"I've heard tell about his attitude, and I seen him play, of course."

"And?"

"I thank he average at best. You way better than he is."

"That's the other part of the problem. Not only am I an Uncle Tom, but I'm a good Uncle Tom athlete. I don't know what to do."

"You stand up to him. What else? He ain't gone leave you alone if you don't, so you might as well."

"You do remember how big he is, right?"

"You ain't so small. You right at six feet and solid. You pretty powerful. I bet you can punch just as hard as you tackle. Here, hit this."

He held up an open palm and I adjusted my position, drew back a fist, and thrust it into his hand.

"Ooooh, baby!" Bojack said. "You hear that shit?"

I dropped my head, covering a modest smile while he shook his hand.

"Yeah, it was a good pop, huh?"

"For real, baby. Sweet! Now you tell me if you don't thank that peach Pitts' old face won't feel that."

"I guess he would."

"Damn straight. So you go on doing what you been doing. If he bothers you again, pop the sucker one. Them damn bullies. You pop 'em one, and they soon enough leave you alone."

"I sort of figured that's what you'd say."

"And I knew you knew what needed to be done."

"Mama Jennie used to say that when we came upon a problem,

we knew what we should do. We just needed someone to confirm what we felt."

"There you has it, then."

"Thanks, Bojack," I said

Johnson at attention, right?" he laughed.

"Don't be so crude."

"Oh, excuse me! I reckon this is some serious shit, then. I'm sorry and surprised, too. What sister girl up there got enough nerve to be out with you?"

"She's not black."

"Well then she must be Puerto Rican."

"There are no Puerto Ricans in Canaan. You know that."

"Then she must be Indian."

"Nope."

"Chinese?"

"No Chinese here, either."

"Mulatto?"

"Close."

"Lord help me, Jesus. I just know you ain't gone tell me she's a white girl, is you?"

"What else can she be? You named everything else."

"What is you thanking, Evan?" Now, he was angry. "What color satin do you want in your coffin, boy?"

"Be serious."

"Oh, my ass is serious, alright. What can you be thanking 'bout? Ain't you had enough shit to deal with? Your daddy gone kick you out for sure if he finds out you dating a white girl. You ain't gone get no sympathy from nobody around here, 'cause they all consider that a mortal sin."

"I can't recall when I got support around here for anything anyway. What do you think?"

"Well, I don't know nothing about sin, seeing that I don't go to church no more. But it's hard to stand behind you on this one."

"Then don't. All I know is that she makes me happy, and I'm going to keep talking to her. And talking is all we've been doing. I'm not dating anybody."

"But you'd like to be dating her?"

"Yes."

"My Lord, Jesus, Joseph, Mary, and the Holy Ghost!"

I felt my friendship with Bojack unraveling. He looked truly disappointed.

"All I said was that you should want to be a success in life. Success ain't measured in being with a white girl. That don't get you nothing. It just makes everything harder."

I got up to leave. If he didn't want to support me, it didn't matter much. It wasn't like we'd seen much of each other lately, and I had been doing all right. Patty made me happy, and I wasn't about to give up that feeling. I hadn't had it since the night he talked me into being somebody.

"Okay, okay," he called to me as I rounded the corner of the shed. "I know you ain't been happy for a long, long time. And I know a lot of that is my fault. All I hope is that the extra pain you gone get is worth sitting around talking to a white girl."

"You don't know her."

"Well, go on, tell me about her, then."

I hesitated.

"No, I mean it. Come on back, and sit your butt down here beside me."

So I did. I told him all about Patty Cunningham. After which I admitted that I was falling in love.

"But that's one-sided," I continued. "I thought about asking for more, but I don't want to come on too fast and ruin things. We can really talk to each other. And I learn so much from her."

"Smart lady, huh?"

and I got embarrassed."

"What happened?"

"She asked what my favorite museum was."

"And what you say?"

"The Pro Football Hall of Fame."

"Umph, umph, umph," he said, shaking his head. "And you ain't even been to it."

"Yeah."

We laughed, and Bojack put his arm around me. It was a touch of love, and I shivered a little beneath it, hoping that he didn't notice. But even if he had, I'm sure he didn't care, because I think he was feeling the same thing.

"Well, now that we have talked about me, what about you?" I asked.

"What you mean?"

"I saw you inside. With the checkers and the booze. It didn't look healthy. In fact, it seemed pretty sad, Bojack."

"Yeah, well, I been playing that same game of checkers for a while now. I sit here every night feeling sorry for my ass. Mary's gone tonight, but when she home, we don't talk much."

"What happened?"

"Human beings ain't meant to be dictated to, especially in they own homes."

"Is that what she's trying to do?"

"Hell, she done it, ain't she? You and me is just one example. Love can't survive under no dictatorship. I just spend a lot of time sitting around talking to myself."

"I'm sorry."

"Well, don't be. While I'm sitting, I'm thanking, too. I'll get thangs straight. Don't you worry none. We both gone get thangs straight."

"Works for me."

"Here, drink some of this before you go."

"But that's whiskey."

"Yeah, and as far as I can see, you needs a taste."

I took a sip and winced as it burned my throat.

"Good. Take it like a man, and get up and gets your behind on home. Get some rest, and I mean in bed for a change. If I was your coach, I'd beat your butt for being out this late the night before a game."

There were no movie theaters in Canaan. No bowling alleys, no skating rinks, and no place to sit and drink while listening to live music. There wasn't even a McDonald's. Save for visiting the local watering holes, there just wasn't much entertainment to be had. So in Canaan, like similar rural towns, high school football reigned supreme.

The night after Bojack and I sat behind his shed, our football stadium was filled to capacity. You could feel the excitement. People felt good about the season's prospects. The year before, the Canaan Hogs had made it to the regionals. It was the last game that I watched in the stands with Bojack. We had driven all the way to Richmond to see it.

Canaan led by three points. The Thomas Jefferson High Cougars from Richmond, winners of the last eight state championships, were on their twenty-five-yard line and there was only a minute left in the game.

"If them Jefferson coaches know they football, they gone take advantage of the weak deep coverage," Bojack yelled in my ear. "I wouldn't waste my time like they normally do with moving the ball ten yards here and there, trying to get out of bounds to stop the clock. No, I'd play action, fake that run, and go deep."

"Isn't that what everyone would expect them to do?"

"Not at all. See, they got a whole minute. That's forever in a football game. Especially in a two-minute drill when you got all your timeouts. No, our coaches ain't thanking they gone try for it all in one pop. But I bet they is. If you was back there, I wouldn't worry, though."

"Not even with Bill Jackson as a receiver?" I yelled back.

Bill Jackson was Jefferson's deep threat. He had the most career yardage receiving in the history of high school football in Virginia. He was also already Olympic material in the 100-yard dash.

"He might be a little faster than you, but you could outthank him and that quarterback. You got to remember that brains and physical strength makes you a winner. Just strength can only beat just strength. And that's all most kids your age do. That's all that boy out there do. He just rely on how fast he is. But if you been listening to me—"

"I have," I interrupted.

"Then I know you could handle the situation."

I had smiled because on the very next play, the Jefferson quarterback dropped back in the pocket. Our pass rush was fierce, but it got distracted because Jefferson had faked a reverse, which sent our defenders in the wrong direction. The quarterback took advantage and found Jackson had beaten the cornerback and the free safety by ten yards. The game was over. Thomas Jefferson was on its way to its ninth state championship.

"Damn," Bojack shouted. "See how I read that call? I ought to be coaching somebody's damn team somewhere, instead of stuck in that damn plant."

A year later, a similar crowd gathered to watch the Hogs embark on a new season. The press had dubbed Canaan the number one contender for Jefferson's throne, since we had been the only team to lead them during a game. I was smiling all day because the morning of the game, a special edition of our weekly paper, the *Canaan Courier*, came out. It had been proclaimed that I was the best addition to the varsity team. "*Walls' skill and ... ...*

"I don't guess they be saying how strange you is now at the plant," he said. "I'm proud of you."

I was stunned. My face must have shown it, but he chose to overlook that. After the years of barely speaking to me, now he was telling me that he was proud of me. But then I remembered that image was everything to my parents. My athletic ability was something that no one could say anything negative about. And begrudgingly, they had to respect it. After all this time, I had finally done something that was within the realm of social acceptance. And I was happy. If I played well, then maybe—just maybe—I could turn things around.

After I showered and dressed, I found a warm breakfast waiting for me on the table and money for lunch. Before, I had always eaten cereal, and I had to beg for lunch money.

The first team to test the Canaan Hogs was the Rebels of Merchant's Hope. Every year, we opened against them. They were the arch rivals from the next county, and though they weren't considered a good team, Canaan always had problems beating them. That's the way it was with intense rivalries, Bojack had said. In the past, during halftime of this game, the principal of the school leading at the half had the privilege of being pushed up and down the field in a wheelbarrow by the trailing principal. The tradition was ended the previous year because Merchant's Hope principal fell out of the wheelbarrow after celebrating a little too early.

I was smiling about that very fact as I stared down the Rebels, who were loosening up on the other side of the field. I'd spent most of my free time that week reading up on their projected strengths, and our team had watched a lot of film with our coaches. I felt I knew their offense pretty well.

The captains of the teams met at midfield for the coin toss. Merchant's Hope won and elected to receive the ball. I put my helmet on and psyched myself up as the band started into the national anthem. I saw Mama and Daddy in the stands smiling like I hadn't seen since Daddy started earning enough money to stop renting our land to the white farmer. Aunt Mary sat beside them. I was surprised to see her. I knew she didn't like football, but it was a social event, and I guessed she didn't want to be at home with Bojack since things were not going well.

A few rows up from them, I saw Patty. She was obviously frowning at the cheerleaders. I smiled. "Some of them have such wastelands for minds," she'd said to me one day as we walked past one of their practices. "All they talk about are boys. They actually get a thrill from riding in a jock's car. They're disgusting."

"It's their right to be," I'd said, laughing.

When she saw me staring at her, she threw her hands over her face in embarrassment. I'd caught her red-handed. She shrugged and smiled. I tipped my helmet to her, and I proudly walked onto the field to play my first varsity game.

After the kickoff, Merchant's Hope found itself on its thirty-yard line, first down and ten yards to go. Out onto the field ran their number one addition, Rudy Rainey. He was a transfer fullback who was just as big as Taliferro Pitts and equally intimidating.

When our two teams faced off at the scrimmage line, the big fullback stood over everyone. The ball was snapped, and the quarterback tossed the ball to his right.

"Sweep left!" Dee, at middle linebacker, yelled. Taliferro Pitts had broken through the offensive line and met Rudy Rainey head on.

The Canaan crowd stood in disbelief as the Rebel fullback casually knocked Taliferro over, stepped on his face mask, broke it, and kept on running. It took five of us to get him down, but not before he had gained twenty yards. Taliferro ～～～～～

～～～～～ the Rebels had called a draw play, a delayed run. On his way back, the quarterback handed the ball off to Rainey, who burst up the middle, leaving Hogs all over the ground. By the time I caught up to him and dived on the crowd already tackling him, he'd made it to our thirty-yard line. The Merchant's Hope crowd was going wild.

When we lined up again, everyone knew where the ball was going. Quickly, I thought back to my Sundays with Bojack. "You can't tackle a big running back with superior upper body strength by hitting him up high. And you is a fool to meet him head-on unless you bigger than he is."

"What do you do then?" I'd asked.

"You take his legs out from underneath him. From a angle. If you hits him head on, you most probably catch a knee in the gut or something. Hit that sucker hard in the legs from a angle, and it'll kill him every time."

So I watched the quarterback and the big fullback carefully. I thought that they could pull a switch and throw a pass, so if I charged into the backfield, I might get burned. But I decided to gamble.

On the snap, Dee again yelled, "Sweep!" and Rudy Rainey came barreling around my side. He knocked over Taliferro and several other Hogs. When he broke into the clear, everyone in the stands rose to their feet. The Merchant's Hope crowd screamed, feeling a touchdown was unfolding in front of them. The Canaan crowd was rows of open mouths and drooping chins. Rainey was at full speed when he saw me and tried to clash head-on. But I was too quick and dipped below his stiff-arm and into his legs at an angle, just like Bojack said.

The Canaan crowd roared when I sent the big fullback airborne. I jarred him so badly that he lost the ball. I landed on my stomach and saw the fumbled ball bouncing toward the sideline. Quickly I got up, grabbed it, and took off toward the goal line. As I passed the Canaan bench, I heard the coaches urging me on. Seconds later, with the crowd screaming, I crossed the goal line. When I reached the back of the end zone, a cheer came from the woods beyond the stadium fence. I saw Bojack bouncing up and down.

"For you!" I yelled. "For you!"

When I turned to face the field, I was met by Dee and Tex. They jumped all over me in excitement and almost knocked me down. On the way back to the bench, I received congratulatory pats from much of the team. Aggressive warrior-like growls of appreciation, head butts, hugs from my coaches, and some of the cheerleaders led a chant with my name in it.

"Who do we want? Evan! Who do we need? Evan!"

Mama and Daddy were waving and yelling. I hopefully returned the gesture. Above them, Patty smiled, and I was warmed over inside. It didn't matter that Aunt Mary was sitting and looking in the other direction, attempting to show me that she couldn't care less. Nothing really mattered except the fact that Patty Cunningham seemed proud.

I was all over the field the rest of the night. I was in that zone where you feel warm and loose all the way down to your bones. And that heat leads you into a rhythm that you can't understand; you just go with it. When it was over, I had two interceptions and eleven unassisted tackles. After I told Dee how I tackled Rainey and he passed it on, our defense managed to hold him to two touchdowns. We won big, 34 to 14.

Still, all was not well. Inside the field house, Taliferro stormed over to my locker.

"You gone pay for showing off," he said.

During the game, I had not been afraid. ~~~~~

~~~~~ Most of

~~~ were enemies, so I thought it perfectly all right to dwell on my physical prowess. From Saturday morning on, I read the headlines over and over again.

"WALLS SPARKS THE CANAAN DEFENSE," said *The Daily Pilot*.

"WALLS LIVES UP TO PREDICTIONS," from *The Canaan Courier*.

"A STAR IN THE MAKING," proclaimed *The Virginian Press*.

At lunch hour on Monday, I sat in Patty's and my usual spot, my head lost in that morning's paper, which anticipated what I would do on the upcoming Friday. As I read, I relived the past Friday night and pondered my future. With continued good play and the kind of publicity I was receiving, I was sure to be chosen by a Division I college. *The pros!* I could just see myself intercepting a Terry Bradshaw pass and dodging tacklers all the way to the goal line.

Patty caught me in the act. I know she must have guessed that I was chasing some more glory because my body was rocking as if I were eluding blockers.

"Are you getting to the quarterback?" she asked.

I laughed and dropped the paper quickly, trying to look at least a little modest.

"Reading and dreaming about yourself, huh?"

"Well—"

"Oh, it's okay."

"Why, thank you," I said. "I appreciate your allowing me to indulge."

Patty laughed. "Why, any time."

"So," I continued as I dropped my head to cover my embarrassment. "Did you like what you saw?"

"I did."

"Really?"

"Yes." She smiled. "I was very proud."

I tried hard not to smile, but I couldn't help myself.

"I was proud of you and worried for you."

"Why?"

"Because of something my father noticed," she said, pulling a sandwich out of her lunch bag.

"What was that?"

"You want a bite?"

"No, thanks."

"Well, he thought that some of your teammates weren't too excited about you."

"Was it that obvious?"

"Only to those who know that after the play is over, you don't spear your own teammate in the back with your helmet."

"Damn."

I was hurt and embarrassed that everything I did had to be tainted somehow. There was nothing I could do to get away from being controversial. I imagined Ethel Brown or Chauncey Mae showing up at my house and saying something like, "Well, you might thank you got something special on your hands and all 'cause he can play a little football, but his teammates can still see the real him. Ain't you seen how they can't stand Evan?" That would likely ruin the excitement my parents were feeling for me. The new feeling I had at home was built on shaky ground, but it felt good to be treated like a son again. It felt good not to have to go to the woods for fear of being beaten up. It felt good to be talked to without being yelled at.

"Dad wanted to know if you were a prima donna because you were so good," Patty continued.

"What did you tell him?'

_____ Finally,

, ___ said, Dad, what's wrong with you?' And he told me to watch myself. He told me that all Southern black boys want to get in the pants of white girls. He said it was one of the great goals of their lives. He said he didn't mind my being friends with you, but that I should be cautious. He acted strangely the rest of the night. And all I said was that you were my friend."

"I'm not surprised," I said. "I'm not surprised at all."

"Well, I am. You don't know my dad . . . Well, I guess I don't either, huh?" She laughed uncomfortably. "I mean, he always talked the good liberal talk and walked the good liberal walk. Both my parents did. And I believed them when they laid out the people-are-people routine. I'd always believed him until Friday night."

I was scared listening to her talk. I really liked Patty. And truth be told, I needed her. Her liking me gave me back some of my self-esteem. But now I saw the handwriting on the wall. Her father had warned her off, and she was preparing to let me down easily, because we both knew that we were well on our way to being more than just friends.

I guess Patty could see it in my eyes. She looked at me and smiled. She shook her head. "Don't worry, Evan. I'm not going to run from you. No one has been as wonderful to me here as you have been. You were the first to be nice to me, and your friendship is very special. Don't let my dad's hang-ups worry you. His hang-ups are not mine."

She took my hand and squeezed it. Then she took my chin and pulled me to her. And we had our first kiss, which I could not savor because as we pulled apart with smiles on our faces, we saw Eugenia Pitts standing in front of us shaking her head. I froze. Eugenia frowned and walked away.

Immediately, I recalled a conversation from the previous school year. I'd been sitting on the short brick wall that bordered the walkway into the main school building. Not far from me, a group of black girls, including Eugenia, were sitting and talking about dating boys. I just happened to glance in their general direction when one of them attacked.

"What you looking at, wannabe white nigger?"

"Nothing. I'm just sitting here minding my own damned business."

"You was listening to us. I could tell. Probably trying to figure out how to get one of us to like you. Well, you can forget that shit."

Eugenia said, "Snowball don't want no sister girl. He don't like nothing but them honkies anyway. I bet you think you gone marry a white girl."

"So what if I do?" I shouted back at her. It still hurt me badly that she and Rosetta Jones treated me poorly, because we had once been close friends. Not as close as the guys, but they were on my damn porch every Thursday evening for all of those early summers, and we'd had a lot of fun.

"You're a traitor to black women," Eugenia had continued.

Even though at the time I had no thoughts of interracial marriage, this was a point that I tried to be sympathetic toward. Especially after hearing about Aunt Mary's rape. But the black girls I knew always made me feel defensive. They tore at my pride.

"If I don't date or marry someone white, would you go out with me or ever consider marrying me?" I asked her.

"Shit no!" she replied. "You ain't man enough or black enough for me."

"Then what the fuck do you care who I go out with?"

"You're a damn disgrace to black people!" she shouted. "Poor little white boy locked up in his black skin. You musta done something terrible in your life before this...

"I think you're right."

"Yeah," I continued. "She hates me too much to ignore a kiss from a white girl."

Throughout the rest of that afternoon, I constantly looked over my shoulders. I searched hard for Eugenia's imminent attack. I wanted to be prepared. But she never even acknowledged me, which was normal. Nevertheless, she made me sweat. I played mind games with myself. She knew that playing it cool was driving me crazy. I thought she would get me all worked up and then lower the boom. I couldn't stand the tension.

Patty would glance at me from across the room and catch me nervously twitching. She'd catch my eye and move her lips, saying, "Be cool." And although I would nod, I couldn't.

By the time I reached football practice, my left eyelid was twitching uncontrollably, I'd entered a new realm of paranoia. Luckily, the coaches hadn't planned a serious practice. Just a lot of running, stretching, talking about the game. The first thing on the agenda was the game film. Over and over again, Head Coach Kendel pointed out my "excellent" play. I wasn't the only one that he pointed out, but I was the only one Taliferro and gang didn't want to hear about.

Out on the field, Taliferro strode past me and shouted, "Fucking showboat." I tried to ignore him, but I could not. My defenses had been at war since lunch, and they were weak. Like an animal, he sensed the fear. He put the word out, and I began getting elbows and knees shoved into various parts of my body.

"We're supposed to be walking through this play!" I shouted at one guy.

"Fuck you, punk," the guy replied. My eyelid began to twitch more and more.

"Oh, you gonna pay," Taliferro said just before practice ended.

By the time the final meeting in the field house ended, I was shivering. I took deep breaths at my locker to try to calm down.

Coach Kendel helped a little when he patted me on the shoulder as he walked out the door. When I turned to follow him, because I didn't want to be left in there alone, I found Taliferro in the middle of my path.

I opened my mouth to shout for coach, but Taliferro drew back a fist and was ready to hit me when a player named Harrison called his name. Taliferro dropped his fist and turned to find several white players confronting him. Then T. Wall, Flak and the rest of Taliferro's guys lined up behind him. I couldn't believe this. White guys were going to fight black guys on my behalf? But it turned out they didn't really care about me. They just wanted to win.

"He's the best player on our defense," Harrison said.

"I'm the best player on defense," Taliferro countered.

"Well, whatever. But I know this. We need Evan if we are going to win this year. So, lay off him."

Taliferro was beside himself with anger, but he backed down. That had to really hurt because now, like his father, he had knuckled under to the white man. And in front of the whole team.

As he walked away, Harrison said to me, "Don't get me wrong. I ain't in love with you. You start fucking up, and he can have you."

I skipped the shower and quickly changed. As I walked out of the field house, I saw Patty at a distance. She curled her finger and nodded in the direction of the bleachers. I followed and found her sitting on the ground between two of the cement supports.

"Why are you still at school? And why are we here?" I asked.

"I hung around because I needed to talk to you. And we are here in this lovely spot because I figured we blew our cover at our other meeting place. I saw some kids playing basketball...

"That sounds good," Patty replied. "But I think a little vacation might help even more."

I laughed. "Yeah, right."

"I'm serious. Three weeks from now, I want you to ask Dee if you can tell your parents that you are spending the weekend with him."

"Patty, I'm just getting my parents back. I can't ask them to spend the night at a white boy's house. Not to mention that, while Dee's parents have been great to me, that might be too much to ask of them. And why would—"

"No, you wouldn't stay there. You'd just say you'd be there. You'd be with me."

"Okay, but where are we going to be?"

"That's my secret. You just see if you can make it work. Tell them about the white boys who stood up for you today. Maybe they'll find a white boy soft spot."

I looked at her and chuckled. "You know you're crazy, and I can't believe I'm even considering this."

"Do it! Just let me do something nice for you. You need a break from Canaan and especially this school."

I was really touched by her wanting to take care of me, and I couldn't bear to disappoint her.

"You're incredible, Patty."

"I'm your best friend, Evan Walls."

"I believe that. I really do."

Patty smiled and placed her hand on my cheek. I could see how much she cared. "Come on," she said. "You scrunch down in the back seat, and I'll drive you home."

By the time three weeks rolled around, I was extremely excited. We were undefeated, it was game day, and all of us players were once again in our jerseys. I loved walking through the halls and seeing all of that blue and gold dispersed throughout the student body. Just after lunch, we had our weekly pep rally, and as usual, I was really pumped after it was over. But this week there was more to be charged up about. All day I thought about spending the weekend with Patty Cunningham.

As darkness fell, I stood loosening up my legs. The band had just finished playing the national anthem, and across the field stood that night's enemy, the Hawks of Burnt Mills High School. They came to town boasting of their superb passing attack. "Unbelievable for a high school team," their coach said in a newspaper article. But he didn't know about Bojack, and he didn't take my reputation seriously. That night, I stole three passes from their quarterback and his receivers. The interceptions set a Canaan record. In the locker room, I was surprised by a college scout.

"Good game, Walls. Jack Davis," he said, holding out his hand. "University of Maryland."

"Thank you," I replied. "And nice to meet you."

"Likewise. You put on quite a show out there."

I glanced around the locker room, and Dee and Tex were giving me the *well aren't you special* look along with a couple of very big smiles. I returned the favor later with Tex because he ended up with a couple of college coaches standing around his locker as well.

"Just doing my job," I said.

"Maybe we could talk sometime?"

"Yes, sir. You say when."

"I guess that means you're interested in playing college ball?"

"And maybe professional."

Davis laughed. "One step at a time, my man. I'll get in touch with Coach Kendel and set up a meeting with you and your parents."

"Sounds great."

"Keep in shape," he said and punched me on the shoulder as he made his way out.

"Fuckhead," Taliferro yelled from across the field house.

"On the floor!" my defensive coach yelled at Taliferro. "Give me fifty."

Taliferro got into position and began doing pushups, and I could feel the heat of his anger. Then Coach Kendel came in and cleared the room except for the players. He gave us the usual post-game talk about staying focused. One game at a time. No need to get ahead of ourselves. During his speech, I felt Taliferro looking at me.

I dressed nicely and found Patty's car in the parking lot. I snuck over to it, knocked on the back door, and curled up on the back seat with enough clothes for the weekend.

"You look pissed off," Patty said when she saw me.

"A little."

"Don't worry," she said. "Tonight, I'm going to take you away from all this nonsense. I'm going to take you to a place where people won't care if we kiss. If they do, they don't bother to waste their time telling you about it."

"There's a place like that?"

"Yes. It's not perfect, but it's better than Canaan by a long shot."

We drove about an hour and a half and I was shocked when we got to the Norfolk airport.

...ow can you afford this?"

"My parents. They think I'm alone, though."

"But how did you pay for my ticket?"

Patty held up a credit card and smiled. "I've got it covered."

Since I had never flown before, Patty gave me the window seat. I watched the lights of Tidewater twinkle and fade as we broke through the clouds. Patty then told me how this trip came to be.

"I got this idea a while back, and I've been working on Mom for quite some time. I just kept telling her that I was bored all the time. After a while, she asked me to tone it down because I was really getting on Daddy's nerves. So, I struck a deal. You let me go to New York to see a play once in a while, and I'll shut up about boring old Canaan. I convinced her that I was old enough. And we have an apartment in the hotel, so it would be sort of like being at home. She came through with the credit card and some cash."

"Excellent strategy," I said, impressed.

"I thought so," she replied. "And speaking of that, you never told me how you got your folks to agree."

"Well, it was easier than I thought. I told them that some of the team was getting together at Dee's place. I suggested I just stay the night, and they wouldn't have to come out late at night to get me. And I knew Daddy didn't want to be driving through a white neighborhood in the dark.

"They were definitely shocked, and for a moment I could see some anger rising in Daddy's eyes. But I think the three of us knew that we had turned a corner in our relationships. For whatever reason, things are looking up. They get to be proud about football, something acceptable by everyone. I get to work on being somebody without them trying to halt the process. We can pretend it's not happening, you know. The football overwhelms it, anyway.

"With Mark gone, I don't think they want to risk losing another son. I just need to not rub it in their faces. Stay under the radar, and I think I'll be okay. I'm in a really good place, Patty. I feel like I'm beginning to get my parents back, I get to play the greatest sport in the world, I get to be me, and I have you."

"Yes, you do," Patty replied.

I smiled. "Despite Taliferro Pitts, it's hard to remember when I had it this good."

"Okay, that's the last time you get to say that name this weekend."

"Yes, ma'am!"

• • •

We got into the city late. I watched Patty operate, giving directions to the cab driver, dealing with the city itself and the Essex House, where they knew her and treated her like royalty. They looked at me curiously, but I was quiet, and Patty offered them no explanation.

We were tired, and we decided to go right to bed. Even though it was what I wanted, I was uncomfortable when we entered her bedroom and I saw that there was only one queen-sized bed. Patty acted as if it were no big deal. She went into the bathroom and came out in an oversized T-shirt. She looked at me as if to say, "Aren't you going to get undressed?" So, I went into the bathroom and came out in gym shorts. We got into bed. Patty said we had a long day ahead, and we smiled and kissed each other goodnight. This time, I could savor her kiss, and I did. I was well aware of every sensation it created in me, and I loved the warm feeling of her body against mine. I turned out the light, and Patty fell asleep in my arms.

The next day we were up early. We ate breakfast at some famous place, and Patty pointed out a movie actor who strolled by reading his paper and sipping on a cup of coffee.

"Anything's got to be more fun than watching Guy Lombardo and listening to grownups talking while they sit around eating black-eyed peas," I recalled, thinking back to the days when we used to spend New Year's Eve at Mama Jennie's house.

Next, it was on to the Empire State Building, and then we hopped a ferry to see the Statue of Liberty.

We finished touring around four and went back to the hotel for a nap, and then we had dinner and Patty took me to a play. An extraordinary day for a country boy.

After the play, I stood by the window of her room, looking out at an empty Central Park bench right under a streetlight. The light seemed to cast a halo over it. Pretty soon, a couple sat there, and she put her head on his shoulder. I was wondering what they might be talking about and admiring the pretty picture they made when Patty called to me.

I turned around and she stood across the room, nude in the dim light of the one lamp we'd left on. To me, her body was perfect. I was deeply moved as well as sexually aroused by the symmetry of her figure. She smiled, and I felt loved.

She came and stood before me. As she began to unbutton my shirt, I placed my hands on her hips, paying particular attention to how her wonderfully curved body moved beneath my touch as she undressed me.

I'd always wondered about the day when I would be naked with a girl. I imagined that I would be embarrassed, wondering if she would find something strange about my body. If I had enough to offer, you know. But I was fine. I was so consumed by the heat of the moment that it never really crossed my mind. I felt heat all the way down to my bones.

I walked with her to the bed. We hadn't said a word up to that point and continued in silence as we lay side by side. We just looked at each other for a while. Patty softly brushed her hand over my face.

"I know," she said, "that you probably never thought your first time would be with a white girl. It must be doing things to you inside."

"Truthfully, Patty, I haven't thought about anything or anybody but you."

"Well, that's what a girl likes to hear," she said, smiling. "It's just that I know you carry around so much extra baggage. You can drop all of that tonight. I will never willingly hurt you by taking advantage of your honesty. So drop all your defensiveness, and try to relax. It's our first time, and we'll always remember it. Let's try to get as close as possible, body and soul, with nothing between us."

"Okay, no extra baggage."

I trusted Patty completely.

"And don't worry. I'm protected. I have a diaphragm."

"Oh, man, I hadn't thought about it. I'm glad you did."

We laughed about it as we began to kiss. Some time went by, and then we looked at each other. She rolled over on her back and pulled me on top of her.

Then, she whispered, "Stop."

"What is it?" I was all of a sudden tense, afraid that I'd done something wrong.

"Nothing bad," she said. "I just want to feel what this is like."

I closed my eyes and lay my head beside hers. I felt like I was a part of her body. I felt whole in a way I never could have imagined.

She pressed on my lower back and I moved inside of her. We kissed. And when we were finished, we wrapped ourselves around each other and looked into each other's eyes. After a while, she got

SEVENTEEN

The chatter coming from inside my house that Sunday morning surprised and momentarily disoriented me. Mama and Daddy never missed church unless they were really ill, and I couldn't remember a time when they were both too sick to go. So, I approached the back door cautiously, growing angry at the fact that my plan had not worked out.

No one was supposed to be home when I got back from New York. I began to wish that my relationship with my parents had not gotten better, because they wouldn't have cared where I'd been. I'd just have to lie.

But when I looked through the window, I saw Mama sitting at the table with her head in her hands. Daddy was nodding at something Aunt Mary was saying, and Ethel Brown was urging Aunt Mary on. *What are they doing here?*

I opened the door, and Aunt Mary turned and walked right up to me and shouted in my face. "If I was your mama, I'd take a hot iron to your Uncle Tom ass!"

She then went over and kissed Daddy and told him to do what he had to do and that Mama Jennie wasn't around anymore to stick her nose in his business. Then she left and slammed the door behind her.

Ethel Brown left next, after kissing Mama. "Take care, girl," she said. Then she walked past me and said, "Boy, you should be

Daddy set out to trap me in the lie by asking how Dee was doing. I felt there was no need for this little parental game.

"You know I wasn't there," I said, and Mama burst into tears.

Over the years, she had tried off and on to protect me by urging me to give up my dream. It hurt her back when Daddy beat me. But now I looked at her and wondered if she felt she'd had enough.

"Yeah, we know you won't there. 'Cause we had police here in this house, like we was criminals or something. You know how embarrassing that was for us. Asking us about the whereabouts of our son. But I reckon you don't care that your mama feel like she can't go out of the house."

"Police?" I asked. My mind was spinning.

"Yeah, that's right. That's what I said. PO-LICE!" He was getting angrier. "And since you don't know nothing about that, I reckon you don't know that your white boy you was supposed to be staying with spent the night in the hospital."

"What!" I thought, *Jesus.* "What happened to Dee?"

"I guess if you knew, you woulda been beat up, too. But no, here you is all nice and clean."

"Where was you?" Mama asked, looking up from her hands.

I just stared at her. "I can't tell you, Mama," I said.

She started crying again and then came to me.

"Look at what you done to us," she said. "All this mess you and that damn Bojack conjuring up. Lost all your friends, and trying to lose ours for us. Causing your daddy trouble on the job and at church. You ain't got an ounce of respect for the woman who bore you and sacrificed so much to raise you. You broke my heart. You hurt me to the core. You run your brother away, and I swear you trying and trying real goddamn hard to put me in my early grave."

"I'm not, Mama."

"The hell you ain't. You ain't never gone get nowhere or have nothing. You know why? 'Cause you don't do what the Bible say. Honor thy mother and father and your days will be long on this earth. You!" she shouted, her finger in my face. "You working a real short life."

Then she picked up a glass of Kool-Aid and threw it into my face and all over my white sweatshirt. She walked away, and from down the hall I heard her saying, "I'll be damned glad when you old enough to get out of my life."

I'd lost my mother for good. Daddy just looked at me and turned away.

• • •

I ran out the door and over to Bojack's house. Luckily, Aunt Mary wasn't at home, and he was working in the yard.

I don't know if he heard my heavy footsteps or my frantic breathing. He looked up at me a while before I got to him, dropped his rake, picked up his beer, and sat on his front steps.

"I been expecting you," he said. "Where's Mary?"

"I don't know. She just left our place a few minutes ago."

"I reckon we better go around yonder then."

"Okay."

We went out to the shed and sat. He told me that Mama and Daddy had known since late Friday night. Taliferro beat Dee badly enough to put him in the hospital. While I slept in Patty's fancy New York City apartment, an ambulance took Dee to Obici Memorial Hospital, and a police cruiser took Taliferro to the town jail.

In a few hours, much of Canaan's black population surrounded the local police station.

"It was just crazy that they did that," Bojack said. "I couldn't

Reverend Walker had been chosen spokesman. But before he could speak, the sheriff came out and told them that Taliferro was inside and wouldn't be released anytime soon.

The reverend spoke up. "You listen here, Sheriff. We have brought bail money for the boy. We want him out. We know what y'all do to us in places like that."

"Well, boy," the sheriff replied, "I believe you must have been hearing some bad rumors or something." He laughed.

"First off," the reverend replied, "I ain't no boy, and second, I don't deal in rumors. We got enough firsthand witnesses in this town. Now, I got enough money here to give to the judge to pay Taliferro's bail, and I suggest you take it."

"You threatening me, boy?"

"If that be what it takes. And I ain't no boy!"

The sheriff and his officers began to laugh, and the crowd got louder.

"Well, I don't like threats," the sheriff said. And he nodded down the row of officers, who started rubbing their nightsticks in hopeful anticipation.

"Well, I reckon the people out here don't much care about what you think about threats. All I know is that you better take this money and let that boy in there loose. If a white man had beat up a black boy, he'd be at home by now watching the game on TV. That's of course if y'all woulda arrested him in the first place. And I'm here to tell you that we gone have it the same way for us tonight."

Reverend Walker threw the envelope of money at the sheriff, who let it rest at his feet for a little while and then he spit on it. The crowd, now more than a thousand and growing, began to get agitated. Then the sheriff stomped on the money and ground it into the cement. Some people rushed the building. Several of the policemen were dragged into the crowd. Other officers fired their pistols into the air, and when the commotion stopped, they aimed them into the crowd.

"Now you niggers get yourselves together!" the sheriff yelled. "Next one of you moves one sloth-footed goddamn inch is shot."

Reverend Walker then stood on the roof of a police car. All around him, people stood shouting at the police.

"Now!" Reverend Walker shouted. "There are no fools here in this street tonight. We all know the deal. But let me say something to you. You can shoot them guns and kill some of us, but those police over there being held, they will be dead too, along with the rest of you. Look down that street, sheriff. There are so many people, you can't even see the end in either direction. And we know you ain't got no reinforcements on the way. So, like I say. You can kill some of us, but God shall have his revenge on this night when these nice churchgoing folks out here show you what a lynching is really like."

The sheriff went inside and came out with Taliferro. He picked up the envelope of money and shoved Taliferro toward the crowd, which had broken out into a chorus of "We Shall Overcome."

"The police," Bojack said. "They come to your house before all that happened at the jail. Rumor mill say Flak been saying that Taliferro actually wanted you. He came after you and Dee 'cause he heard you was staying at Dee's house. He figured that was about the ultimate Uncle Tom thang to do. And he was gone make you pay for it. When Dee wouldn't tell him where you was, Taliferro jacked him up. Then the cops came to your house to see what happened to you. If you was dead or alive or whatnot. And folks figure that make you for sure Uncle Tom, 'cause the police don't usually go nowhere to check on no black folk."

"It must have been the Flea's dad."

He nodded, looking concerned.

"Patty took me to New York for the weekend."

"Damn! That's something. All the way to New York."

I nodded.

"And where you stay at?"

"Patty's folks have an apartment in a hotel. I also saw a play and went sightseeing."

"Where did you sleep?"

"With Patty."

"Well, I'll be goddamned," he said, shaking his head in disbelief. "You never know about teenagers these days."

"You can't tell anyone."

He laughed. "Hell, I ain't crazy. I might get shot just for knowing about such sin."

I laughed with him.

"Well, Mr. Lover," he said. "What you gone do now?"

"I need to go see Dee."

"I reckon that'd be the right thang to do. I would take you, but—"

"I understand. I'll take that old bike you fixed up way back when."

"I think you a little too big for that thang."

"It'll do."

As I rode the bike, I felt my heart pumping hard; partly from the riding, but mostly from the anxiety of awaiting Dee's reaction to me. Even though he didn't know where I was going, he'd kept his mouth shut and taken a beating for me. I felt good about our friendship and wanted to tell him so. I wanted to let him know that I owed him.

When I got to his house, I saw his mother going in their front door, dressed like she'd just gotten home from church. Though I'd always thought she liked me, I could tell she wasn't thrilled to see me at that moment. I mean, there I was, panting, looking half-crazed with my stained clothes. But it had to do with more than that. As I approached her, she asked me to stop at the sidewalk.

I was stunned. I could hear Chauncey Mae in my head saying, *"Boy, didn't I tell your black ass that white folks will cut your behind loose at the drop of a hat? They ain't going through no changes in order to be the friend of no nigger."*

I felt dirty, and yes, inferior. A stereotypical young black man who only knew how to cause trouble in the lives of white folks.

"I think you should leave, Evan," she said.

"I just wanted to see how Dee is."

"Dee will be just fine if you stay away from him."

This hit me like someone had dropped a bale of hay on my head. She was cold and serious, and I got the message. Just as I was about to turn away, Dee hobbled out onto the porch. He convinced his mother that he would be all right, and she went inside.

"It's not that bad," Dee said. "Black eye, two bruised ribs, bruised shin, and assorted other small bruises. I'll miss a couple of games, but I'll be okay, man. Really."

"Dee, I'm so sorry."

"Hey, Evan. Don't feel bad. I don't know what you had going on, but you wouldn't have asked for the favor if it wasn't important. And I know you would have done the same for me. After all, you took a knife for Eddie. Remember?"

"How could I forget?"

"Now I can relate."

We laughed, but it felt uncomfortable and forced.

"What's with your mom?" I asked.

"My parents, they think my friendship with you isn't worth the risk of being attacked again. I guess I should have never talked about all the changes you've been going through with Taliferro and most

"It's just that I'm scared. I hear that they gave Taliferro a long suspension from school, but his henchmen are still there and on the team. I'm tired of being scared of those guys."

"I don't need to hear it," I said, backing away on my bike. I was thinking of the night Bojack told me he could no longer hang out with me. That feeling of loneliness was closing in, and it seemed final with Dee. There would be no clandestine visits when his folks weren't around. Plain and simple; it was over.

"And I probably should tell you that there won't be a car in the morning. Tex's folks feel the same way."

"Well," I said on the verge of breaking down, "there's always Eddie. I mean I did take a knife for him, right?"

Dee simply shook his head, and then he turned around and walked inside. My heart sank. Mama Jennie was dead, Eliza Blizzard was gone, Bojack was pretty much gone, and now it was Dee, Eddie, and Tex.

I got on my bike and rode to the church graveyard. I rode fast, fueled entirely by my anger at the world, the cold wind drying the tears on my cheeks. Once there, I found Mama Jennie's grave and fell on my knees. And then I lay across the slab and held onto it for all I was worth. I cried like I had done years ago on her front porch. I told her how much I needed her. I told her how much I loved and missed her. I fell asleep there, hugging her spirit, remembering the kindness in her face, her iced tea, and most of all, her completely unconditional love for me. There had been no other like it in my life. Just being there a while gave me strength to return home.

After some time in my bedroom, I calmed down a little and decided to call Patty, using a signal we'd decided on. I let the phone ring once, hung up, dialed and let it ring again. Patty answered, sounding out of breath.

"Evan?"

"Yeah, it's me. You heard yet?"

"I heard. So now your folks know you lied to them."

"Yes, but I didn't tell them where I was," I said and then told her that Dee, Eddie and Tex had dropped me.

"Oh, Evan. I am so sorry."

"Me too. New York seems so far away."

There is something very special about the way natural grass looks under the powerful lights of a football stadium. Up close, there is a golden glow that immediately calls to mind great plays, spectacular hits, and roaring crowds. Looking at it would get me excited, revved up to the point of goose bumps. In this magical light, my pads took on the feel of a warrior's armor, and my heart became that of the strongest gladiator, battling enemies before the emperor and citizens of Rome.

Weeks after my weekend in New York, these thoughts filtered through my mind as I stretched my hamstrings on the sidelines before the biggest game of my career. It was the regional championship between the Hogs of Canaan High and the Cougars of Jefferson High. And it was also the first time that a regional game was to be played on our home field.

Across the field was Jefferson's famous deep receiving threat, Bill Jackson. The wide receiver was sitting on his helmet taking his competition as he usually did—lightly.

In the stands were loads of football scouts. They had come to see the war between Jackson and me, and to see Tex, who had come on strong toward the end of our undefeated regular season and seemed to be catching everything that came his way.

The write-ups in the papers hyped the three of us. The experts thought that Jackson would dominate the night. They gave him the edge because he was a senior and a "man playing with boys." I was a lowly sophomore, and Tex was only a junior. But Coach Kendel gave me the upper hand.

"Walls is not only a good athlete, he's smart. He's a student of the game, and that gives him an edge in my book," Coach told *The Canaan Courier.* "Evan has a career all sewn up. The scouts are not coming to this game to see if he is good enough, but just to see if it is possible for him to get any better while still in high school. He's a once-in-a-lifetime athlete. I think he will have a wonderful college career and, barring injury, I believe he will go pro. Look at the stats. They don't lie. But I've got him for two more years!"

I couldn't believe he said that. I'd always dreamed of playing pro ball, but I never knew that anybody besides Bojack thought I had a legitimate shot at it. But my stats were pretty good. We had a strong defensive line and linebacker corps, yet I led the team in tackles. For the regular season, I had eleven interceptions and countless knockdowns of passes that one quarterback or another tried to sneak past me. I ran back four of the interceptions for touchdowns.

Just thinking about the stats got me pumped up. I got up from my stretching position, put on my game face, and stared across the field at Bill Jackson, who was still sitting on his helmet.

The team captains took to the field for the coin toss. We won and elected to receive the kickoff. After that, we lined the sidelines and the band played the national anthem.

I turned my head and glanced up into the stands. Mama and Daddy were in their usual places, and they had on their best fake smiles. For weeks after I'd lied about staying with Dee, they boycotted my games and went back to the cold shoulders at home. That sent me back to the woods, where I broke about thirty glass Taliferros on my rock.

Mama and Daddy missed out on all of that great anger-produced

son. I found her behavior to be sad, and I promised myself not to look at them during the games because they would only distract me.

As the national anthem ended, I looked around for Patty. I was shocked to find her sitting one bleacher down from Bojack, directly in front of him. I couldn't believe he was there; it was the absolute show of friendship as far as I was concerned. At the same time, I knew it meant something unfortunate had happened in his marriage. After all, Aunt Mary had banned him from going to my games.

I waved to Patty, who waved discreetly back. Bojack waved and shouted something like, "You the man!"

Patty turned and looked at him and then back at me. She pointed over her shoulder, and I nodded yes as I took to the field. As I awaited the kickoff, I saw them talking in the stands. As the ball left the foot of the Jefferson kicker, I had a good feeling.

By the time the clock ran out on the first half, I still felt good in that I was playing well. But I felt more winded and bruised from this one half of playing than I did from the regular season. The score was 0 to 0, indicative of the brutal defensive battle taking place. Along with the rest of the Hogs, I hobbled into the field house and found a place to lie down on the floor. No one said a word. It was as if we were conserving every ounce of energy for the second half.

The coaches came in clapping their hands and patting players on their heads. They were being positive, reinforcing the play of the first half. Their eyes glowed with the possibility of knocking off the perennial champions, and they shouted those typical coaching clichés in order to keep us fired up. We didn't need it, though. Everyone knew the importance of this game, including Taliferro Pitts, who had recently rejoined the team after his suspension.

"We know you want it!" Coach Kendel shouted. "So I'm not going to say anything more. Each of you has played a brilliant game so far. Take this time to think about that and how you can take it a step higher in the second half."

I glanced at Dee and Tex, who were sitting in an opposite corner discussing the game. They hadn't come near me, and at one point during the game when I shared a tackle with Dee, he refused my attempt at a high five.

I changed my focus. I scolded myself for thinking of anything other than the game. I replayed the first half in my mind. I saw myself winded but sticking with Bill Jackson stride for stride. Jackson had not caught a pass, and he was frustrated. He'd tossed more than a few obscenities and illegal elbows my way and complained to the referee that I had been holding him. But there was no holding, just the orders of Coach Bojack being carried out to a tee.

• • •

When we returned to the field, police cars were leaving the end zone near the entrance. A couple of cheerleaders told us that some of the Jefferson people had gotten so wound up by the game that they booed the Canaan band. When Jefferson's band took the field, some Canaan people attacked them. Then the visitors' bleachers emptied and parents and high-strung fans ran out to protect their own. Somewhere in the ruckus, a Canaan man had been stabbed. The police were taking the attacker away as we took our places on the field for the kickoff. Somebody yelled, "Don't get hurt now. The only ambulance is gone!"

I was uncomfortable about people who could get so caught up in a game. I wondered what would happen when it was over. *Who's going to get stabbed on the way to the locker room?*

We lined up to kick off to Jefferson. Their return man fumbled the ball, and we recovered. The Canaan crowd came to life. The beating both teams had taken in the first half left everybody stiff, and

The Canaan crowd was crazy. The band played our awful school fight song, the cheerleaders danced, and the Hogs moved to the sidelines still slapping fives all around. I told myself to remember what Bojack had said to me one day in the field while we were practicing. "Keep your shoulders strong and smooth. Strong to meet and withstand the pressures, and smooth enough to let 'em roll right on off without doing much damage."

Our kickoff was delayed because Jefferson fans had thrown trash onto the field. While this was cleaned up, I had to listen to threats from the players on the Jefferson bench. It pissed me off. When the kickoff was finally allowed, I blew past the guy who was supposed to block me and punished the Jefferson runner.

We lined up for the first play of the series. Some of the Jefferson players yelled to me, "We got your number, punk!" Then they ran the ball down our throats and scored a touchdown.

"Told you we had your number," Bill Jackson said after the touchdown.

"You got my number?" I replied in my best trash-talking voice. "You didn't run over me to score."

"But we scored, jerk."

"It's not tied yet."

"It will be!" the kicker shouted as he took the field.

The referees broke up the shouting match and managed to get the two teams apart and set up for the extra-point kick. As they organized, I thought back to a Sunday afternoon in the field when Bojack had said to me, "Now, as far as I can tell, the key to blocking a field goal or extra point is raw speed and timing. You line up with the ball about five yards behind the nose guard. When the kicker goes into his motion, you go into your motion. At the end of the run, you crouch and fly across their center. You gotta be in the air when the kicker plants his support leg."

I was, and I blocked the kick. The Canaan crowd began to rock the bleachers. The ball was covered by a Jefferson player and blown dead by the referee. I ran by the kicker on my way off the field and said, "My number is 5, and we're still in the lead!"

We retained our one-point lead throughout the rest of the third quarter, throughout several fights and several players being thrown out of the game, and most of the fourth quarter. It looked as if we had the game wrapped up with one minute and fifty-two seconds left. Our fans had already begun celebrating. Then our quarterback mishandled a simple snap from center, and the Jefferson nose guard recovered the ball. The Canaan defense took to the field feeling the pressure to keep the Cougars out of the end zone. I kept looking at the game clock. There was a minute and forty-seven seconds left, and they had two timeouts.

Our fumble had occurred on their forty-five-yard line, which meant they only needed to go thirty yards to get into comfortable field-goal range. Bill Jackson was their go-to guy, which meant the play was coming at me.

I looked up in the stands at Bojack, who was looking right at me. We were both thinking about the year before, when the Hogs lost on a long pass to Jackson in the final seconds. The only difference was that on this day, I was specifically assigned by our coach to cover Jackson no matter where he lined up, no matter where he went.

Later, Patty would tell me about Bojack's argument in the stands. Five football scouts sat a few bleachers up from him. One said to another, "You know what's going to happen, right?"

"Yeah," the other replied. "History is about to repeat itself. Jefferson is going to prove again that Jackson can't be stopped when the game is on the line."

during the game. I figured I could make the last minute and a half with no problem just doing what I had been doing the entire game— covering him closely, as they said in Canaan, "like some stink on shit." And for the first plays of the series, I did just that. Jackson got mad and hysterically complained to the side judge about me holding him as he came off the line. The Canaan crowd booed him and heaved bottles and cups onto the field. Once again, play was delayed while the field was cleared. Both teams' fans were warned that any more such outbursts could carry with them penalties for their team.

Only fifteen seconds were left on the clock as Jefferson lined up for what would be their final play if they failed to score or at least gain the necessary yardage to stop the clock with their final timeout and kick a field goal. Bill Jackson and I lined up face-to-face. I glanced at the referee, who was looking directly at the two of us.

I realized that Jackson had finally used his head and that this kind of thing was what the papers meant when they wrote about his senior experience. He was a star, and the officials knew it. They hated it when the stars got pissed off. Bad press and everything else. In a tight squeeze, the biggest star always got the call in his favor. In other words, Jackson knew exactly when to have his temper tantrum and to pull all the side judge's attention to him. The slightest touch from me would be considered interference, and a penalty could cost us the game. So it was time for me to use my head. I stared at Jackson and then backed off five yards, still looking him in the eye.

He smiled because in his mind, he had me. He thought I was afraid.

I heard my defensive coach yelling at me from the sideline. "No, Evan. Don't back off! Bump and run! Bump and run!"

I glanced at him and then up at Bojack, who was smiling.

"What are you doing, Walls?" Coach Kendel yelled.

Just before the ball snapped, I turned my back to Jackson and ran to the middle, deep, as if I thought the pass was going inside to another receiver. When the ball was snapped, Jackson headed straight up the field. I was fifteen yards deeper and more toward the center of the field.

I hoped that the Jefferson quarterback would have an "I just can't believe my eyes" moment and not realize that this was a trick. Knowing no defense would be foolish enough to leave Jackson intentionally uncovered, it had to come down to a blown coverage, in which case an easy pass to Jackson was money in the bank.

The quarterback took the bait and lofted a bomb to Jackson. I was waiting for it.

When I'd turned my back before the snap, Jackson was tricked into thinking that I had misjudged the play. So he made it easier on me. Instead of his normal blazing speed, which I was prepared for, he was moving at three-quarters pace. When the pass was thrown, I was coming back toward it as Jackson ran to get under it. Because he was looking back at the oncoming ball, he didn't see me. According to Bojack, the quarterback threw his hands up in disgust when he realized he'd made a terrible mistake.

Jackson was coasting as the ball fell toward his hands. Then a blur passed him, and he grabbed air. I'm sure he finally located the ball, but unfortunately for him it was tucked into my left arm as I strolled down the sideline for the biggest touchdown of my short career. The stadium was, as one of my favorite TV announcers used to say, "bedlam." The Canaan bleachers bounced under the crowd. Bojack and Patty were standing side by side, jumping up and down cheering. We had beaten the great Cougars of Jefferson High. We had ended their nine-year reign.

On the field, I was mobbed. In the midst of our joy, guys on the team forgot they hated me or that they should stay away from me.

Many college coaches and scouts squeezed their way into the field house. They shook our hands and congratulated us. We drank Pepsi instead of champagne. Coach Kendel was like a limp dishrag of joy. It was his greatest triumph as a coach. He couldn't stop shouting, "Boys, we did it! Boys, we did it!"

In two weeks we would play for the right to call ourselves the best high school football team in the Commonwealth of Virginia.

NINETEEN

By Thursday of the following week, I was feeling let down. There was no game. Nothing to get hyped about. I missed it both mentally and physically.

At home, things moved rapidly in reverse. All the gains that I'd made faded when I got caught lying about New York City. Mama told me for the millionth time how I embarrassed her and how she couldn't go outside. Daddy wished out loud that he could get away with kicking me out of the house. I, in turn, spent a lot of time in the woods, sleeping, eating and breaking more bottles by the light of a fire.

I headed out there to meet Patty. I'd introduced her to my circle in the woods, and we'd already made love there twice since New York. Before I crossed the road, Bojack called my name. As he walked toward me, I was thinking that I'd finally get to know why Aunt Mary had allowed him to go to the game. He must have done some pretty smooth talking. Either that or something had gone terribly wrong.

"What's happening, big man?" he asked.

"The usual," I replied.

"For you, I guess that's right."

We both had to laugh at that one.

"I can't tell you," I said as we began to walk into the woods, "how ⸺ ⸺ ⸺ ⸺ in those stands. It just lifted my spirits. I've

twice to the same woman and divorced twice from the same woman. If I was gone go through all of that, you thank I woulda tried a different woman the second time around. Makes me feel like I kinda wasted some years, you know?"

I nodded. As we found my place and sat down on the ground, he spoke about how good it felt to him to return to Canaan stadium and that the almost-fistfight he had suffered through with Aunt Mary was well worth it. He spoke in a voice tired of being muzzled.

"It ain't that a football game is more important than marriage, but it's the freedom thang, you know. To do what makes you happy."

"Oh boy, do I know."

"Anyway, there was lots of thangs she wanted and didn't want. And they was always the opposite of me. One day we just looked at each other, and we knew. So I helped her move out."

"I'm sorry, Bojack," I said. "Looks like I ruined your life, too."

"Oh, no. I see thangs the other way around. I turned on your mind and led you into something you couldn't know about. I set you up, and yeah, they has been some blowback, but I'm good with that. I got to own it. I earned what come my way all by myself." He patted me on the shoulder, and there was a noise in the distant underbrush.

"We got company?" he asked.

I nodded and smiled. "Patty."

"Nice girl," Bojack said. "I liked her. Ain't never said that 'bout no white girl, but it's so. She got it bad for you too, you know."

"Hi, guys," she said as she broke into the clearing, holding a large pizza. "Nice to see you again, Bojack. You like pizza?"

"If it's got sausage on it. I'll eat a shoe that a dog pissed on if it's got sausage on it."

We all had a good laugh at that one. Patty brought dinner that night because Mama didn't want to cook for me and yelled at me every time she caught me in the kitchen.

"So what's up?" I asked. "You look frazzled."

"I had a major blowup with the folks."

"I'm sorry," I said, and Bojack picked up on things.

"You don't mean," he interrupted, "that your folks be knowing about Evan?"

"Not completely. They suspect that I'm seeing him, but they're afraid to come out and ask. And they are afraid that I'm serious about this because I stopped talking about what I was missing in Philadelphia and how Canaan was so boring."

"I reckon it is boring for you," Bojack said before biting into a slice of pizza. "I like a slow pace in life, and this is even boring to me."

Patty laughed. "They figure the only thing that could make me forget what I had before is a boy here. Since Dad saw my reaction to Evan at the last game, they've been acting funny."

"Do you think they ever found out about New York?" I asked.

"I'm not positive, but it's a good bet. All the people at the hotel know us pretty well, and Dad's been back there since we visited."

"Well, they your parents. Why don't they just come on out and ask?" Bojack asked.

"Because they have always raised me to believe that race shouldn't be considered in any way in dealing with people. If they confronted me, they'd be admitting that they didn't really mean it. I guess they don't want me to think that they're two-faced racists."

"Race, race, race," I said. "Man, I get so sick of it."

"Well, if it got you sick, it'll probably kill you, then. It ain't a disease that can be cured, you know," Bojack added.

"I know what you mean, though, Evan," Patty said. "Everything in this town seems to be tainted by bad race relations."

"............ this town," Bojack quickly said. "It's the whole damn

Patty looked concerned. "You don't think it will ever be solved?"

"Of course not. It can't be."

"That's a terrible thought."

Bojack nodded. "It's damn for real, though. I mean, let's face up to it. You can't build a house on a crooked foundation and expect it to settle right."

"I never thought of it that way," I said.

"Well, I talked about this very thang with Eliza Blizzard," he said. "You got to remember the Declaration of Independence. Even while ole Thomas Jefferson was writing all that bullshit about all men being created equal, a ole black nigger was probably bringing him his tea and cake."

"I don't like that word," Patty said.

"You join a long list of folks tired of hearing it. I just need you to feel what I'm saying, so I'm speaking the real deal here. You see, there was also a strong, black buck slavin' in Tom's fields when Tom raped his wife. Eliza say they was a slave name Sally that was his mistress. But I call her *raped*. What I'm saying is that piece of paper he was writing was supposed to be the foundation of this country, but it was built wrong."

"I get it," Patty said. "Hypocrisy makes for poor mortar."

"There you go," he said, pointing at her. "A sad, sad truth. So the country is a house slipping and sliding on top of hypocrisy. And I'm sorry, but it ain't never gone settle right."

"So what do we do?" I asked. "Just give up?"

"I reckon I have. I ain't doing nothing positive. You two are, though, just by being friends. But if I was gone answer the question with some kinda moral answer, I guess I say you treat it like you treat crime. You fight it to try to keep it down, under some kinda control, even though you know it ain't going nowhere. Just try to keep the hard heads on a low profile so most people can walk the streets."

"Do you hate white people, Bojack?" Patty asked.

"I don't hate you," he replied. "But I do hate a fair amount of them. I ain't gone lie to you now."

"Why don't you hate me? Because of Evan?"

"That's got a lot to do with it, but I don't hate nobody no more just 'cause they white. I'm willing to give even white folks a chance these days."

"How come?" I asked.

"I reckon I learned a little bit watching how people be treating you. Every white person ain't out to kill you, and I guess I'm just getting tired of hating. It just eat you up inside, and you end up dead from it and them devils still living and laughing. Hell, I ain't gone kill myself for nobody. So I don't waste my time hating no more. I just stay within myself and do the thangs I like to do. The rest I just let roll off me."

"You keep your shoulders strong and smooth," Patty said with a smile.

Bojack looked at me and laughed. "You been passing out the wisdom, huh?"

"Every chance I get," I said.

We, the very proud Canaan Hogs, won our first state championship 41 to 7. We couldn't figure out why the other team was even on the field. We all agreed that the real championship had been the game against Jefferson. But we weren't giving it back, and it was just the first of two championships we would win during my varsity years at Canaan High. We rolled into the new year on an incredible high, which, for me, soon collapsed like Wall Street on Black Tuesday.

Until Eliza Blizzard came to Canaan, February had always been thought of as simply a very cold month. Since Eliza, who forced the acknowledgment of Black History Month, February was hotter than July.

For starters, *The Canaan Courier* refused to print any "provocative" editorials written by blacks proclaiming the month theirs. Of course, anything promoting blacks was incendiary, so no editorials or letters to the editor were published. It refused requests by blacks to run small ads honoring the great blacks of history, even when blacks offered to pay double the advertising price.

"That's a unique hatred there," Ethel Brown said to Mama one day. "White folks usually don't mind swallowing they pride when a dollar be involved." So the local blacks, led by their ministers, picketed the paper.

All over town, blacks put up posters of people like Booker T. Washington and Harriet Tubman. White people tore them down. Fights broke out, and all blacks involved were promptly jailed. Then more blacks marched on the jail to get them freed.

In the schools, tempers flared daily. Especially in history classes. While the other kids battled over their racial pride, Patty and I remained quiet, glancing at each other once in a while for support.

Rosetta Jones and Eugenia Pitts loved history this time of year. They turned every discussion toward race, and in most cases, they were right. They had studied up on the few great blacks mentioned in our history books, and when a situation arose where a white man was getting the credit for something a black had done, the two girls let it be known. This the white teacher and a few of the white kids could understand, since history has always been unfair to black accomplishments. But none of the whites could stand it when Eugenia and Rosetta chopped up the pedestals on which white heroes stood.

"George Washington ain't shit," Eugenia shouted.

"Do not swear in my classroom!" the teacher shouted back.

"What you mean by that?" one white boy named Willie asked Eugenia.

"I mean he ain't shit," she replied.

"Eugenia!" the teacher shouted again, but no teacher could control her.

"He was an honorable man," Willie said. "How about the cherry tree?"

"That ain't true," Rosetta yelled. "Every year you white kids bring that up. It's like you got a brain freeze about that. Got your heads in the sand."

"It's true!" shouted a chorus of white students.

"I'm sorry," the teacher said. "There's no evidence to prove that. It's just a nice story as far as anyone can tell."

"Just 'cause you white, you thank you

George . . .

Tammy said.

Rosetta looked at the teacher. "Give it up, teach!"

The teacher curled her mouth in disgust at Rosetta calling her "teach," but she answered. "He was a slave owner."

"That ain't in our history book," Willie said, feeling that he now had the edge.

"So what does that tell you about the history books?" Patty asked. The white kids looked shocked.

"Thanks," Rosetta said. "But I don't need no help from you."

"You don't understand, Rosetta," Eugenia said. "Patty likes dark meat, so she sticks up for 'em."

"What you talking about, girl?"

All the students in the class perked up, becoming one giant ear. The teacher also seemed interested, and what I had felt blowing in the wind on the day Eugenia saw us kiss finally landed in my lap.

"Tell 'em, Patty. Tell 'em about the day I caught you and Snowball kissing behind the cafeteria," Eugenia said.

People looked around the room, their mouths open, their eyes glowing with the acquisition of such juicy knowledge. The secret was out, and Patty and I looked at each other helplessly.

"You freaking witch!" I shouted at Eugenia. "Go fly your broom somewhere else."

Eugenia, never one to turn from a challenge, jumped up from her desk and ran over to me. I stood to meet her. She hauled off and smacked me twice before the teacher was able to move between us. I pushed the teacher aside and punched Eugenia right in the mouth. There was a pop, like when I hit Bojack's hand. Then, there was blood and the bell ending class. Patty grabbed my hand and yanked me out of the room as the teacher tried to help Eugenia.

By the time Patty and I got to my locker, rumor had it that she was pregnant with my black baby. And fact had it that the principal wanted to see me and that Taliferro was out to do me in once and for all.

Patty and I were holding hands, as there was no more need to hide. We were standing by the door of Patty's next class, talking about how I should go to the principal's office and get things over with. In mid-sentence, my head was forced into the doorframe in front of me. It split the skin of my forehead, and blood ran down my face.

I turned around to find that I was encircled by students, and Taliferro Pitts was standing angrily in the middle of them.

Patty was pulled away from me. When I went after her, the crowd threw me back in front of Taliferro. Eugenia, still in a frenzy, took out her revenge on Patty, slapping her several times in the face. Patty was thrown to the floor. I ran for her again, but Taliferro jumped into my path.

"This is it, muthafucka," he said. "Now you best believe I'm gonna kick your natural-born ass. Nobody hits my sister."

As I looked around him to Patty on the floor, I conjured up all the hatred I'd felt toward those who'd stood against me. And I just did not care anymore. I knew that Patty and I were history. She was as good as on the plane to Philadelphia. And that being the case, there was nothing left for me. Though Mama Jennie had told me not to think it, I hated my life. Patty was all that had kept me going. If she was going to be taken, then I really didn't care if I died. I suddenly felt free.

So, like Bojack had taught me many years ago, I dipped my shoulder and surprised Taliferro, who, because he could see the unabridged rage on my face, seemed suddenly too afraid to make the first move. I drove him into the lockers behind him and tried to free Patty at the same time. She was just sitting there, crying, held ~~~~~~~~~~~~~~~~~~~~~~~~. The sight simply ripped at my heart.

~~~~~~~~~~

and we parted a moment to recover. As we faced off again, the look in his eyes told me that he was definitely seeing a very different Evan Walls, that he had gotten himself into something that he didn't want but that he couldn't back down from, and this gave me more confidence and released more of the power of my anger. I figured he could tell that I knew it was all over for me and that I no longer cared what happened. Carefree, careless, and crazed. Those are the only kind of people who frighten the likes of Taliferro Pitts.

I got off the next punch, which dazed him, but he managed to punch me back. Then there was another flurry of fists. I couldn't even feel it when he hit me, yet I could feel the solid connection of my fists against his body and head. I felt like I moved him when I hit him, and finally I dropped him to his knees with a hard right hand. To this day, I can feel it connect.

He stayed on his knees for a few seconds, and we both tried to catch our breath. The kids were yelling for him to get up. There were saying things like, "You can't let a Tom beat you, man!"

I turned and wiped the blood from my face. I saw Patty sitting still now, unbothered because the boys were too caught up in the fight. She seemed to be in a trance. Tears were rolling down her cheeks, and my body shuddered with hatred and as I turned back to finish him off, which I knew was the only way to free Patty. Taliferro was standing up with a knife in his hands.

Someone yelled, "Taliferro's got a blade!"

A teacher screamed, "That's enough, goddamn it! The police are on the way!"

But I couldn't have cared less. I was too wrapped up in my vengeance. "I'm not afraid of that knife," I said because I truly wasn't. "Come on. Kill me!"

He lunged at me but missed by a lot. He lunged a second time, but he was too tired, and he was slow. I let the knife pass by me and nailed him with another right, which dropped him to his knees again.

There was a locker behind him that had come open during the fight. I kicked Taliferro in the face, and he dropped the knife as he fell flat onto the floor. I grabbed him and yanked him up, and then I rammed his head into the locker, and the sharp, steel edges cut his ears as his head went in. I closed the door around his neck and with all the strength I had left, I punched the locker door. Taliferro went limp, and blood ran down the side of his head and neck.

I stepped back to get out of the way. When I turned, the hall was clearing. Everything was now happening in slow motion. Students disgusted by the gross ending to the fight were screaming and running. Their mouths barely moved when they spoke. The words all came out like yawns. When they ran, it seemed like they were trying to run up the steepest hill. As I continued to back away, a teacher pointed at me and in an awfully slow drawl yelled, "You're in a lot of trouble, young man!" He crouched in a linebacker-ready position as if to keep me from escaping. Other teachers ran to Taliferro. I turned a little more, and I saw Patty, sitting on the floor where they'd left her. She was still crying.

I turned my back on the teacher and helped Patty to her feet. We stood there staring into each other's eyes. Then we hugged, and though I knew that I loved her, it was only then that I knew what 100-proof love was really like. It became tangible, and as I held her, I held it. I fully realized the depth of my feelings for Patty Cunningham, and it was incredibly intense. More intense than the knowledge that, after that day, there was no chance my family would ever accept me again. Nothing meant anything to me except the fact that her eyes told me I was loved. And for the first time since Mama _____ _____ _____ conditions.

she screamed my name as I was slammed to the floor and my hands were yanked behind me to be cuffed. He cuffed my ankles too. Then he grabbed me by the feet and dragged me through the halls to the principal's office. I had to hold my head up the entire time so that my face wouldn't become one gigantic floor burn. Patty ran behind me yelling at them to stop. They didn't, and one of the cops turned to her and told her to shut her "nigger-loving mouth."

At the office, I lay like a bug on the floor. My neck was killing me. They just left me there as people came and went doing business. One policeman kept a foot in my back while they called our parents. They reached Patty's mother first, and she said she was on her way. When they reached Daddy, he told them to do what they had to do. He'd come by the jail in the morning if he had time.

The policeman who stood with his foot in my back uncuffed my feet, picked me up and walked me outside to put me in a waiting police wagon. But when we were out in the pouring rain, he said he'd forgotten something, and he took me over to the flagpole in front of the main building and cuffed my hands behind my back and around the pole. I fell to my knees as he left me in a freezing February rain. Before long, I was shivering badly.

Patty came running out because she had seen me through the main office window. She ran to me and hugged me tightly, trying yet again to keep me from falling off the edge of my dignity.

"Evan," she whispered into my ear. "Oh, Evan."

I looked up and saw the faces in windows of the surrounding buildings looking down at us. I hated them all and wished I could do to them what I had done to Taliferro.

"I'm so sorry, Evan," Patty continued.

"No, I'm so sorry. I grew up here. I knew what this could do to us, and I didn't think clearly. It's just that you liked me, and I didn't—no, I mean, I *couldn't* let it go."

"You didn't do anything wrong."

"I did something wrong because I'm going to lose you, right?"

She didn't answer. She just hugged me tighter, and I closed my eyes to concentrate on what I was feeling. I was trying hard to imprint upon my memory the feeling of her cheek against mine, her body against my body, and the soft way she now cradled the back of my neck. I tried hard to smell her hair, but it was different because of the rain, and it upset me that I'd missed the chance to place this into my memory. I had loved the smell of Patty's hair.

We just stayed like that for I don't know how long. It was obvious that the policeman hadn't left anything. He was simply having fun punishing the uppity nigger. Patty, I knew, realized this and she tried to cover me entirely to protect me from belittling eyes and to protect my quickly deteriorating pride. I loved her for trying, but she could not help me. You see, the thing about shame is that it grows from within, and only the person feeling it can put it to rest.

Patty's mother arrived before the police returned. "She's here," I told Patty as I gazed over her shoulder. She hugged me tighter, but her effort was in vain. I already felt her drifting away, and I began to feel all numb inside.

"I love you so much, Patty."

She smiled. "I love you, too, Evan Walls. Moving to this horrible place was worth the chance to have you in my life. I will never, ever forget you."

Patty still hadn't looked at her mother, who stopped just a few feet from her car. She was just standing there in the rain, taking in

the moment and, I think, feeling for her daughter. I was sure I saw a
mother's pain in her eyes. Though she didn't agree with what Patty

_____ _____ __ _____fere in this final moment.

And no extra _____ ___

I nodded, and Patty backed away. She walked backward until her
mother came and turned her toward the car. It was the last time I
saw Patty Cunningham face-to-face. And as they drove away, fading
into the rain, I remembered being over at Bojack's sitting in his
pickup and listening to him sing the blues. "The sky is crying," he
would sing. "Just look at the tears roll down the street."

I lifted my head to the sky and saw the flag looking back down
at me. I was thinking, *God bless America, land of the free and home
of the brave.* And I was laughing when I was caught by surprise by
the policeman who, along with his partner, unhooked me from the
flagpole. He cuffed my hands behind my back again and pulled me
to the police wagon. They shoved me inside, and I sat up on a bench.
Across from me was Lost Boy.

Here is what my life had come to.

I had sympathy for Lost Boy and tried hard not to think of myself
as a better human being than he was, but I couldn't help feeling a
huge measure of disgrace for ending up at the same level as this poor
soul, who was in the process of lecturing the ceiling of the wagon. I
wondered how long it would be before I was talking to the statues and
squirrels and eating black snakes. I fell on my knees and screamed
as the wagon began to move. I kicked the walls and the floor. I rolled
from front to back, with him yelling at the ceiling and laughing.

I was still on the floor, but calm by the time we reached the jail.
The policemen were smiling when they opened the doors. One of

them said, "Damn, I thought you niggers had done killed each other back here. And it wouldn't have been no skin offa my back, just so you know."

Minutes later they opened a cell door, took off my cuffs, pushed me inside and slammed me into the brick wall face-first. I barely felt a thing. I only noticed blood on my sweater, which dripped from the scrape on my cheek I got as I slid down the wall.

I rested there with my arms wrapped around my knees, cradling them against my chest. My chin rested on my knees and I stared down the hallway to the front of the jail waiting for I don't know what. A few minutes later, they brought Lost Boy in, put him in the cell next to mine, and told him to dry out. I lay my head back and closed my eyes as he began talking to something in his cell. That's when the situation caught up to me, and I began mumbling to myself.

"You're in jail, damn it. You are in jail!"

There would be no crowd outside screaming for my release. Reverend Walker was probably sitting at home laughing, if he knew. Hell, my own parents weren't even there to get me, and I wondered how long they would let me sit.

Then I thought of Patty and how I had watched her get into her mother's car and leave my life. Later, I fell asleep as I tried to recall the feeling of Patty holding me for the last time.

• • •

When I awoke, Lost Boy was gone. I looked out of the little window at the top of the cell and saw that it was dark out. I got up and used the toilet and thought about what it would be like to be in a room like this for any number of years. Then bolts slipped and clanked. Doors opened, and shoes echoed off the tiled floor. I smiled when I saw Bojack walking behind the deputy.

He took off his sunglasses, looked at me, and shook his head. He rubbed his hand over my head and cheek where the blood had dried.

"Least y'all coulda cleaned him up a bit," he said to the officer.

"I ain't nobody's nurse," the officer replied. "If he didn't go around

 ~~ ᵏⁱˡˡ neonle, he wouldn't be in here all busted up."

                                    ᵇⁱⁿᵈⁱⁿᵍ, although I

have a criminal record, I thought.

walked out of the police station without a word to anyone. They hadn't taken a mugshot or fingerprints. When Bojack returned I asked why.

"My brother, you is one lucky cat. The wheels of justice just drove right on by you. First of all, you know they ain't thanking about wasting their time when two colored bucks get to fighting. Throw some cold water on you like a couple of wild dogs and kick yo' ass to the curb. You ain't worth the paperwork. On top of that, it's like you did this po-lice station a favor. They been hating on Taliferro Pitts ever since the church mob rescued him. Hell, you might even be a hero to them. Naw, you ain't got nothing to worry about."

I let my head fall back on the seat. "I'm not sure I should care, but I want to know. What happened to Taliferro?"

"They took him to the hospital, but he won't there but for a couple of hours. Lot of blood from his head and cut up his ear real bad. They stitched his ass up and sent him home. But I can double-dee guarantee you one thang."

"What's that?"

"He ain't gone be bothering you no more. From what I hear, you scared everybody, which mean ain't nobody gone be giving you no more trouble. You just lay low and you be living in high cotton."

"I can do that," I replied. "That's exactly what I've been trying to do all along."

When he pulled away from the jail, he said he was sorry I had to sit in that place for so long. He said he came as soon as he heard about it and found out that Mama and Daddy had left me there. He went to see Daddy and they got into a fistfight; he said he'd given Daddy a taste of his own damn medicine. I couldn't say that I felt sorry for Daddy, but I did start to have second thoughts about going home. Jail began to look pretty good.

I nodded off to sleep again even though my house was only a ten-minute ride from downtown Canaan. I woke up when the truck stopped and we were sitting in front of Bojack's house.

"You're not taking me home?"

He looked back at me and took off his sunglasses again. "From now on, this is your home."

Turns out that Mama and Daddy had all they could take, and they'd finally thrown me out. That's why Bojack had fought with Daddy. Because he was abandoning his child.

"Yeah," he said. "When I got to your house, thanking I was gone check on you, I find all your clothes and shit throwed out in the path. And when I went into the house and said, 'What's up with this?' Augustus tells me that you won't there, and you won't coming back. That you could rot in jail far as they was concerned. He said they didn't want to see you again. Ever. So I told his ass what I thought of that and then I introduced him to this." He held up his fist.

My head was spinning. I just sat there listening and thinking, *I can't believe that this is all happening. I just can't.*

"I'm going to leave," I said. "I can't stay here. I've got to run away. Maybe I'll try to find Mark."

"How you gone even start to do that?"

"I don't quite know. I can't think properly yet."

"Well, I guess I can thank for you. You ain't going nowhere. You gone stay right here with me."

"I can't do that to you. Look what happened with the people who made me. The people who were supposed to love me no matter what. Look what having me around brought to them."

"Well, I ain't them. I am gone stand by you," he said. "You look at me now."

not let thangs come at you like your folks better than I did. I thought that in the end, they would see the light and do right by both you and Mark. Now he gone, and you want to give up on your life, too. No, I don't thank so. You gone live with me, and I'm gonna be your mama and your daddy. I am gone make sure you stay on track, getting them good grades, and working your way out of Canaan. You are gone study, play football, and graduate if I have to break both your legs, and take you to class in a wheelchair, and beat the shit outta anybody that got anythang nasty they want to say.

"No sir, Evan Walls. Not every black face in this messed-up town is gone let you down. They ain't gone be no more Lost Boys in Canaan if I can help it. I love you, and I'm gone show you that."

I smiled and nodded. "What do you think Aunt Mary will say when she finds out that I'm going to be in the house?"

"Mary who?" he asked.

That night, his guest room became my room, and now, when I think back to a comfortable place in Canaan, it's not the cornfield. It's not my circle in the woods, because there was just too much pain in the air there. It's not my parents' home. It's that room in the back of Bojack's place.

• • •

After everything went down, Mama rarely left the house. Daddy only went to work and back. They stopped going to church, which was really something, because Daddy loved being on the deacon board. And during the upcoming spring and summer, the porch sessions never got started and faded away for good.

After Patty, my parents were never a part of my life. I saw them from time to time, Mama in the grocery store, or Daddy in his car as we passed each other on the road. But nothing resembling love ever passed between us. I know they never forgave me.

I played two more seasons at Canaan High, without having to worry about Taliferro Pitts. He never returned to school. After he recovered from the fight, he went to work at the packing plant.

I spent lunch hours out behind the bleachers, where I remembered Patty. I stayed away from the rest of the students, especially the black kids, as much as I could. I barely spoke. In the end, I graduated first in my class and received a full athletic scholarship to the College of William and Mary up the road in Williamsburg, the second-oldest institution of higher learning in the country and one founded by slave owners.

I kept my head in the books and on the field. In the off-season, I worked at a gas station. After four challenging years, I was set to graduate with honors, and as Coach Kendel predicted, I was expected to be drafted into the National Football League.

Yet, if it hadn't been for Bojack, I wouldn't have played one down in the NFL. The morning of the draft, I woke up and took a long walk through campus, settling in the Sunken Gardens, awash in its beautiful spring foliage. It made me think of Mama Jennie's hillside. A few fellow students stopped to congratulate me on becoming an NFL prospect. I thanked them kindly and wondered, as they walked away, what they would think of me when I opted out of the draft later in the day. At W&M, I had fallen headlong into the rigorous academics and loved every minute of it. My classroom experiences opened my eyes in ways I never could have imagined; a bit like exposure to the books at the Canaan library had done many years before; a bit like the experience I had with Nomi Washington at Hampton Institute. I had become a student of the world and considered myself solidly on the road to becoming *somebody*.

~~With each step I took in college,~~

find a way to help your peop~~le~~

In my junior year I had an idea and spoke to a trusted professor about it. He suggested that I double major in business and economics as a way to bring my idea to fruition. I followed his advice and he helped me create a framework for a nonprofit organization dedicated to providing help and guidance to all of the little snowballs and oreos out there who loved to read. I began to feel like this was my mission. If, as people say, things happen for a reason, what happened on my porch was an introduction to destiny. It just took all of the ensuing years for me to see it. This was what I was meant to do. I didn't want to play football anymore. My life's work was clear.

That afternoon, I met Bojack in the parking lot by my dorm. I joined him in his pickup truck and smiled. Whenever something important happened in either of our lives, we always seemed to end up talking about it in that truck.

Bojack was stunned when I told him that I would not be playing in the NFL.

"How long you been thanking like this?" he asked.

"A couple of years. I would have stopped playing football, but I needed the scholarship money."

"Why didn't you tell me?"

"I didn't tell anyone other than my professor. And especially you. I didn't want to break your heart." Bojack nodded as I told him that I needed to help children like me. It was a calling. He said he couldn't argue with that, and we sat quietly for some time.

"Well," he said. "I ain't no college professor, but I still thank you should play football, but for a different reason than I woke up thanking about this fine day. I won't even try to stand in the way of what's on your heart. Hell, it's like what I was preaching at you on the porch lo those many years ago. But I'm sittin' here thanking, how you gone do it?"

"What do you mean?" I asked.

"Where you gone get the money to get started with your plan to help kids like you?"

"My professor's been trying to get me in the door with some investors."

"But he having a problem, right?"

"A little."

"Yeah! See, you still black, and them kids you want to help, they still black. People ain't in no hurry to throw down them greenbacks for our children. Am I hittin' on it?"

Sadly, I nodded. My professor, who was white, had been somewhat embarrassed by the responses he'd received while trying to help me find funding. Black children were not near the top of anyone's list.

"Well, there you have it, then. This is why you need to play football. Now, hear me out. You already a star. Ain't but a handful of pro players come from schools this small. You already in them sports magazines. I saw you on the cover of one in the Colonial Store just the other week. And I imagined some people who won't in your corner back in the day had to see that too. I hope it grated 'em to the bone. But damn," he said, laughing. "I done got myself off topic.

"Here's what I'm saying. Use the fame, little brother. When you a star in the NFL, and you will be, doors to the money gone fly open by theyselves. You ain't gone need no professor. People gone want to help you, just to be near you. I know where yo' heart is and I loves that. I am so proud of you for it. But you need to use every God-given talent you got to get you there. Remember back in the old days, I told you how you got to use yo' brain and yo' athletic ability to win?"

Who could have ever predicted

down Eliza Dillard

"Yes, I had been thinking along those lines myself."

I looked at the big grin on my lifelong friend and decided that I would play football to help me help the kids like me. "Thank you for your wisdom," I said.

"Hey, I'm the game with you. Trust in old Bojack," he said, before slumping in his seat. "Whew! Now, I'm 'bout wore out. I done used up all my thanking for the next couple of weeks."

I laughed so hard my stomach hurt. Bojack was everything.

Later that day, April 28, 1981, I was drafted into the NFL. The commissioner said, "With the second pick, in the second round, the New York Giants select Evan Walls, safety, from the College of William and Mary."

1993

LURAY, VIRGINIA

I finished my saga five days before the opening of what would be my final training camp. It took me an entire month to tell Izzy the whole story. I opened up a little at a time, breaking off when the memories became too much, and resting until I felt restored enough to continue. Izzy took it as it came and either had a hug for me or gave me Jennie to hold onto when things got rough.

When I uttered the last words, the three of us were rafting on the Shenandoah River. We were in a little cove, and our two rafts were secured by ropes tied to cinderblocks on the riverbed. Izzy drank a soda while I sipped beer. Jennie lay asleep on Izzy's chest. It was a warm, sunny day. We waved now and then to people in canoes or other rafters drifting by. I closed my eyes to feel the rhythm of the water.

A great part of my burden had been the tension from hiding my childhood from Izzy. Now it had been lifted, and strangely enough I felt sad. It had been bottled up inside me for so long. It had been a part of what made me whole, even if it kept me unsettled. Now that I had freed the dragon, I didn't know if I'd miss it or not.

"I just love this place," Izzy said. "We should have bought the other A-frame up the road, you know."

I laughed. Izzy said that every year. Our good friends, the Wilsons, always loaned us their place the week before training camp started so Izzy and I could enjoy intense one-on-one company before the long, grueling season began. I was always against buying the house just down the road from Glen and Ava because I was afraid I'd get traded across country, and one house was trouble enough to sell in a hurry. Izzy would wave her hand at me and tell me that I was a household name in New York, a sure bet for the Hall of Fame, and that I would be a Giant until the day I quit. She was right. I was thirty-three, still a Giant, and I was going into my final season.

But this had nothing to do with anything. I think the silence was killing Izzy. She could see the confusion on my face. She didn't know how to approach a conversation about my life until my emotions had leveled out somewhat. A house on the Shenandoah was safe conversational ground.

Later, when a tear or two had dried on my cheeks, she spoke.

"I'm so sorry, Evan."

"Oh, I don't want you to feel sympathy for me. It's not what I need. I'm decades past when it could have helped," I said, thinking back to times when I had come home from school longing to be consoled by my parents. I thought back to the days when Mark's sympathetic gaze would turn away from me, fearing the sting of our parents' displeasure.

"What can I do for you, then?" she asked. Her sincerity touched me.

"Nothing that you haven't been doing for years. You are absolutely wonderful, Izzy," I said. I meant it, which is why I sat in my raft feeling tremendously selfish. It should have been obvious to me over the years what I was doing to her with my silence.

"I thought I was protecting you as well as myself," I continued.

"Excuse me," she replied. "I don't follow."

"Until now, I never really understood what my silence was doing to you."

"I just worry for you."

you if it had. I really never thought of it as a negative."

"What about the other?"

She smiled shyly. "You tend to fall in love before you know every little thing about a person. I did that with you. I mean, I found it weird that you kept your past from me, but at the same time I had a feeling that you weren't an axe murderer. You were too gentle. You had too big a heart. I was afraid, though, that you hadn't been loved, and you didn't want me to know about whoever'd shut you out. Bits and pieces clued me in. I remember the look of sadness in your eyes when I first asked you what your parents would think of us. You said, 'What they think will never be a problem for us.'

"I have heard you talk in your sleep and then cry. The vibe I was getting was not that of a crazy man but of a man with a wound of the heart. I didn't marry you to heal you. I did it because I loved you. And Bojack also assured me that you were a good person."

"Oh, he did, did he? He never told me he talked to you about this. What did he say?"

"He came back to see me in the church right before our wedding. He said, 'They didn't say I couldn't see the bride beforehand.' I laughed. You know I adore him. He said that if I were worried, I shouldn't be. He said that you were the best person he had ever known, but that there was a part of your life that you no longer wanted to think about. He told me that even though he lived in Canaan, he rarely spoke about it to you."

I nodded.

"Don't worry about my love," she said. "It will always be here for you."

"Thank you," I said as I reached into the water and pulled out another beer, which was in a bucket off the side of my raft, cooling in the river.

"I have wondered, though, why Bojack is the only black person really in your life. I have wondered why Glen is the only good friend besides Bojack, why you shun all black gatherings held by some of your teammates when they sense some kind of discrimination on the part of the team, why you know no black women, why you won't go to black colleges that ask you to speak, why your life, in a sense, is that of a white person's."

She paused and looked at me for a reaction, but I was blank.

"Are these questions fair?"

"Yes."

"Do you hate black people?"

"No."

"Are you afraid of them?"

"Yes."

I was embarrassed to admit it out loud. Even to Izzy. Most of my life I'd struggled with this question. I guess I felt that as long as the fight went on internally—if I never let the words slip out of my mouth—there would be no definitive answer. Admitting it, as I had finally done, would and did mean that I had really lost touch with black society. It was a hard reality to swallow.

"Why?" she asked gently.

An ill-at-ease chuckle escaped without warning. "Every time I'm in a situation where I am introduced to someone black, I just know that they're sizing me up and that they can instinctively tell there is something wrong with me. I start to feel as if I'm being psychologically attacked. I pull an emotional cloak around me, but they always see through it. As they shake my hand and tell me how

great I am, and what a role model I am to their children, I look
through their smiles and know that in their heads, they are saying

and get away as quickly as possible, because

"Isn't that me? You just asked me why I lived a white person's
life."

Izzy was getting angry. "What's it called when a culture turns its
back on one of its own?"

"I'm just one person," I responded. "I guess you're expendable if
you don't toe the line."

"Well, you tell me. Who's Tomming who?"

"If I knew that, I guess, I wouldn't have this struggle. For the most
part, I'm just me, and I believe in what I'm doing and how I live my
life. But there are times when I'm around black people that I lose
faith. I find myself trying to show that I know what's going on, and
that I'm still a part of the group. Just like I did when I was a little kid.
For instance, sometimes I'll be driving along with the windows down,
and I'll stop at a light. I'll see black people standing on the curb, and
I'll turn to an all-black radio station, just in case they can hear.

"There are other things, too. Sometimes I feel the need to try
and change the way I walk if I'm in front of black people. It's like
they can tell I'm a Tom by my stride. But even as I try to walk the
walk, I'm moving quickly, trying to escape them because I know that
they have seen through to the real me. I don't want to hear them talk
about how I have let my people down.

"And then there are the times when I'm approached by a group
of black folk to sign autographs. I find myself trying to grasp for
the right language and handshakes to show them that I'm hip to

whatever I'm supposed to be hip about. It's ridiculous, I know. I tell myself not to let these things happen, but I'm ruled by the moment at hand and some deeper problem that I'd rather leave buried in my subconscious."

"Sweetheart, it sounds like you are still trying to get Canaan to accept you."

"Maybe so."

"Do you not want anything more to do with black people?"

"No, it's not that. Deep inside, I still want to be accepted. I just can't get past believing that no one will have me. I turned down Hampton Institute to go to William and Mary for that reason."

"Does that make you angry?" Izzy probed.

"Only when I'm in the situations I just told you about. Then I get angry at them for making me feel I need to change in order to be accepted."

"What do you feel about them the rest of the time?"

"Indifference."

"What about black women in particular?"

"I'm afraid of them most of all. I've never dated a black woman, and I've never had a black female friend since I was a kid. Not only do I feel black women think I'm a Tom, but I'm also a wimpy Tom. They threaten my ego, and also I feel I'm hated because I'm married to you. I feel like there's no way I can win with them, so I don't even try."

"Do you feel like you've betrayed them? You know. So few black men and all."

"No, I haven't betrayed anyone. I just got tired of trying to convince people. Like I said, I went where I was wanted. It wasn't that I was looking for a white girl when I met Patty Cunningham, or you. It's just that when I met both of you, I was accepted without conditions. I didn't have to have whatever it is that a real brother is supposed to have. I got tired of being told I wasn't black enough or cool enough, and then at the same time being told I'm a traitor if I'm not with a black woman. Like I said, I don't even try."

"What do you think the black guys on the team think about you?"

"I don't really know. Over the years, a couple of white guys told

people. You have taken care of more black people than any one of your teammates. When you're giving away houses to needy black families, why don't you, for a change, show up at the door and hand them the keys? When you are helping to provide access for young African Americans to universities and corporate America, why aren't you on television and in the papers standing by them after you've opened up the world to them? You have Eliza out front, and she's getting all the credit. I love her, but you should step forward. Then people would know your heart. You are still a soldier of the cause."

"Izzy, I've just been away too long. I have no frame of reference to draw on if I ventured into these situations."

The conversation stopped because Jennie began to move around and we didn't want to disturb her nap. Izzy stared out at the water, slowly peeling the label off her soda bottle.

"Being black in America carries more than just the obvious burdens, huh?" she asked.

I nodded. "And these things make me worry about Jennie. I dread the day when she is confronted with the knowledge of her heritage."

"She'll be fine."

"No, she won't. It's impossible to be fine when someone—check that, a whole society—is telling you that you're less because of what you look like. Do you remember how much you cried when we visited that Civil War battlefield and they called you 'nigger lover' and chased us away? Remember how scared we were? Do you remember how much that hurt?"

"Yes, and you tried to run out on our relationship."

"I didn't want to put you through any more of that crap. Like I shouldn't have wanted to bring Jennie into this world. When I think of her future, I wonder if we should have had her. You were an adult and in our relationship of your own free will. Jennie had no choice. She didn't ask for the trouble she will face. I'm afraid that she will come to me one day and say just that."

"All of this is true, but if people didn't have babies for fear of the trouble they would face, there would be no mixed-race and, for certain, no black children."

I nodded. "I guess that's true."

"And Jennie is lucky. She will have you. She is a child born of both races. You were a child forced in between the races. How the two of you got there may not matter. What does matter is that Jennie has your experience to live by, and maybe she will be better able to deal with life because of that. You should write down what you've told me. Jennie could use it. It might keep her from being all those things you fear. The snowball, the misfit. Maybe you should write a book."

"And we'd have to go in a cave to live."

"So? We'll be in it together. And that's what counts, right? Us together. Isn't that the most important thing you will teach Jennie?"

"You mean what Mama Jennie said. 'They don't put no food on my table.'"

"Yeah. That."

"Yes, I'll tell her that. After all, it keeps me sane knowing that Bojack and you are always there for me. No matter how uncomfortable I am elsewhere, I'm always comfortable with you two, and now Jennie. And it also answers your question of why I only hang around with Glen. He's a great friend, and that's enough for me. I've gotten used to being alone otherwise, and I'm happy with that. I don't need anything more. I don't want anything more."

We smiled at each other. Then she changed the direction of our talk. I guess for her there were still pieces of the puzzle missing.

"Do you think about it often? That other life, I mean?"

I thought of him, and during my interview from the locker room, I thought about asking him to contact me through the team."

"Why didn't you?"

"I didn't want to deal with the question of why I didn't know where my brother was."

"What do you think has happened to him?"

"I think he's dead. And if he's not really dead, he's probably the living dead. He's the second Lost Boy from Canaan. When I think about him that way, my heart breaks. It wasn't his fault, what went on with us. They came between us with their demands, and he didn't have the support I had in Mama Jennie and Bojack. I feel sorry for him, and unlike my parents, I do miss him."

"What about your folks? Are they still in Canaan?"

"Yes."

"What do they do now?"

"According to Bojack, they live just as they did when they threw me out. They're reclusive."

"Does he know how they've dealt with your fame?"

"Bojack says they won't discuss me. The word around is that you don't ask Treeny and Augustus Walls about their boys. I guess Daddy beat some guy half to death at the packing plant for teasing him about throwing out the bank."

"Of course, I know Tex plays in LA, but what about Eddie and Dee?"

"I've never heard from them. Bojack has bumped into them over the years. They still live in Canaan, and they're married with kids."

"Why haven't they contacted you, do you think?"

"They're embarrassed. I'm embarrassed. It would never be the same for us, but I don't have any bad feelings toward them. I think nothing but the best thoughts when I think of them."

"And you know I've been waiting to ask you about this since she popped up in the story."

I laughed. "I cannot believe you waited this long to ask!"

"Well, I didn't feel like she was the first thing I ought to ask you about."

"And now?" I asked, still laughing.

"Is it *the* Patty Cunningham?"

"The one and only."

"Oh, my God," she said and broke out laughing. "You actually slept with *the* Patty Cunningham?"

"She wasn't a famous actress then."

"But you were her first?"

"I was."

"Can I tell my friends?"

"Izzy!"

"Okay, okay. How about just Ava?"

"I give up."

"And what about her? Have you heard from her?"

"Yes. After the first Super Bowl, she called. She asked me if I was happy. I told her that at times I was still troubled by my past, but that I was extremely happy with my life overall."

"Did she ask if you were married?"

"She read that I was. In *Sports Illustrated*. I told her you were the best part of my life."

"Well, that must have made her feel great."

"It actually did. You don't know Patty. She's a realist. She was happy that I'd found someone I could love and who loved me without conditions."

"Is she happy?"

"She says so. She's married to a sculptor. She said he's a genuine

pretty fast."

"I guess. At any rate, we said we'd be around if one of us needed the other. Do you mind that I said that?"

"Oh, of course not," she replied. "Just one more question."

"Shoot."

"Do you have any pleasant memories from Canaan?"

"Sometimes I dream about playing in that old sandbox that Daddy made out of a used tractor tire. And at other times, I think about how when it snowed in Canaan, people didn't drive cars. They drove tractors. I can remember going to the grocery store once during a really bad snowstorm. There wasn't one car or truck in the entire parking lot. It was a sea of tractors. I like that picture. It still makes me smile. And I guess the only other times I think about are the moments before the session began that night. I think about how happy I was helping Mama make Kool-Aid, and how content I was pulling the wings off a fly to feed Mantis. Everything after that makes my skin turn cold."

Izzy paddled her raft around next to mine. She hugged me as best we could, and we shared a long kiss. Jennie yawned beneath us, and we laughed. Now, I was beginning to feel good.

"Do you still like Evan Walls?" I asked her. "The man I am. With all the extra baggage?"

"Absolutely," she replied. "You're my heart."

Jennie woke up, and we gathered ourselves and walked back

to the house. We played with her the rest of the afternoon, giving her our undivided attention. Later, after she was in bed, Izzy and I cooked dinner. Izzy put on a dress that I'd bought for her in New York, and I wore her favorite suit. We put the table in front of the big window and looked out at the night as we ate. We spoke about our future—no more about the past.

Later, I was in bed in the loft, lying on my side, staring out of the same window. I watched what seemed like a sea of fireflies lighting up the night. Izzy climbed in behind me and snuggled her body next to mine. She kissed me softly on the back of the neck. She whispered sweetly in my ear. "Goodnight, Mr. Somebody. I love you."

ACKNOWLEDGMENTS

I did have a great-grandmother named Mama Jennie. I passed her name to my character to honor her and the place of respect she held in my life. However, we did not have the relationship dramatized in this book. I give thanks to my mother, Doris Delk Blount, for providing the heart, soul and love that is this character.

There was no Bojack in my life. I give thanks to my father, R. Edward Blount, for providing the heart, soul and love that is this character.

To my family, my wife, Jeanne Meserve, my son, Jake, my daughter, Julia, and son-in-law, Jeffrey Kenny—I thank you for agreeing to take this journey with me. It means the world to me. You are my heart.

I want to thank my amazingly caring and dedicated agent, Marly Rusoff, who ushered my work and me through the publishing maze. I can't begin to explain . . .

Many, many thanks to Koehler Books. To publisher, John Koehler, executive editor, Joe Coccaro and editor Hannah Woodlan. I so appreciate you all for your clear, reasoned and thoughtful guidance from manuscript to novel.

To Leslie Wells for helping me find the story within.

To Wiley Saichek for helping me bring it to the world.

I want to thank my friends who have suffered the pain of listening to me talk about this project for years and those who have influenced

Madures, Brandford Sonny Stanley, Nikki Madures, Julia McIver, Marty Meserve, Susie Meserve, Ben Davis, Jenet Lynn Dechary, Kimberly Golden Malmgren, Lindsay Nielsen, Jeffrey Hunsberger, Albert Oetgen, and Susan Wandmacher.

And finally, thank you to the gentleman at the copying shop on Wisconsin Avenue across from the post office. Back in the day, before email, I handed him a 400-page manuscript in a box. He opened the box to check out the contents. He looked at the title page, looked up with a big smile on his face and said, "Is this you? You wrote this?" I told him that it was definitely me. He closed the box, patted the top and said, "We will take great care with this." He reached out and took my hand. Thank you, sir. I hope my story finds its way to you.

CPSIA information can be obtained
at www.ICGtesting.com
Printed in the USA
LVHW052351160919
631220LV00005BA/966/P